"You must read *Exposed*. Not only will you see the lives of a porn star and a porn addict's wife, you will also see the face of God. The raw pain and reality in this book will twist your heart, but the hope will move you."
—Shelley Lubben, ex-porn star
  founder of The Pink Cross Foundation

"Honest, raw, redemptive, surprising, fearless—*Exposed* is storytelling at its finest. Ashley Weis has woven two compelling stories into one, highlighting the devastation of both sides of the porn screen."
—Mary DeMuth, author
  Thin Places and *Life in Defiance*

"Ashley Weis takes us where few in fiction dare to tread. She addresses every woman's nightmare with devastating frankness. Her style is clean and efficient, her story line, powerful. Weis shows that hope can shine just as brilliantly among the neon of the sex industry as it does through a stained glass church window. Anyone who claims that Christian fiction is pat and irrelevant hasn't read *Exposed*."
—Gina Holmes, best selling author
  Crossing Oceans and founder of Novel Journey

"*Exposed* is a "must read" novel for all married Christians. Ashley Weis cleverly intertwines the lives of two very different women, both suffering from the devastating effects of porn. She dives into each of their hearts and exposes the raw pain that is true to real life. It is also a story of hope as God works in mysterious ways. I found this book very hard to put down. Being a wife of a porn addicted husband, I identify very close with Ally. It brings great promise and joy to a wife that finds herself overcome with pain from a porn damaged relationship."
—Jenna, wife of an ex porn-addict

"Wow. This story . . . there are no words. Read Taylor's story. It may be dramatic for some, but it is my experience as a stripper and prostitute. Ashley has broken my heart with this book—in a good way."
—Anonymous, ex-stripper and prostitute

"*Exposed* took my heart from my chest and sprawled it out on the page, only to show me the beauty of hope and redemption. I can't stop thinking about it."

—Anonymous, wife of a porn addict

"As a wife of a porn-addict, this book gave me hope. It's intense, but realistic. Few fiction is as real as this. Ashley, you are brave for writing this. Thank you. Thank you for being willing to go where few are willing to go."

—Anonymous, wife of a porn addict

EXPOSED

A Novel

Ashley Weis

WINSLET PRESS

WINSLET PRESS

Exposed: A Novel
Copyright © 2010 by Ashley Weis

To learn more about Ashley Weis, visit her Web sites:
www.ashleyweis.com
www.exposedanovel.com
www.morethandesire.com

Library of Congress Control Number: 2010927835

ISBN-10: 0615370993
ISBN-13: 978-0615370996

This novel is a work of fiction. Names, characters, places, and incidents either are the product of the author's imagination or are used fictitiously. Any resemblance to actual events, locales, organizations, or persons living or dead is entirely coincidental and beyond the intent of either the author or the publisher.

All scripture used is from the NIV Bible.

Cover & Interior Design by George Weis of Tekeme Studios

Printed in the United States of America

First Edition: September 2010
10   9   8   7   6   5   4   3   2   1

To my husband:
for showing me the true colors of love.
To Jesus Christ:
for making all things new.
And to everyone affected by the porn industry:
you are loved.

NOTE TO READERS:

Throughout these pages you will see the aching truths hidden behind the porn industry's mask. This is not reality for every porn star, but it is for many. I have chosen to omit language and details to protect the minds of my readers, but the porn industry can be much, much worse than it is portrayed in these pages. Also, the wife's story may seem melodramatic to some, but it is loosely based off of my story and the story of many women who write to me. No story is the same and some may be better or worse than the lives I've chosen to show in these pages, but for many of us ... these stories are painfully real.

Chapter 1 *Ally*

The sound of my cell phone buzzing across the dining room table, the scent of Pine-Sol from the kitchen sink, the strange feeling that my life might change forever—I remember that Friday as though it were yesterday.

I picked up my cell phone before it slid off the edge of the dining room table.

"Ally, are you home yet?" Jessie's voice forced its way through bad reception.

"Yeah, I left work early."

"Oh." He paused. "So, you're home? What time is it?"

"4:30 or so. About to start dinner." I paused. "Is that okay?"

Silence.

"You're not planning something romantic, are you?" I smiled. "Did I ruin it?"

"Maybe," he said. "I'll be home soon. Love you."

We hung up. I sat down at the dining room table, tapping my foot, daydreaming about a growing belly. We'd been trying to get pregnant for two years. No luck. My hand moved to touch my stomach, but I accidentally jostled the mouse of Jessie's shiny Macbook Pro. The screensaver displaying our wedding pictures disappeared, then an image of a naked woman starred at me from the screen.

My foot stopped tapping.

Unable to blink or move, I trembled from my hands to my lips. Unclothed women drove their teeth into my heart, shook it around, and slobbered on me. I scrolled down the page as the slender arms on the screen reached out to choke my dreams. I checked Jessie's browsing history, the

Google search bar, every centimeter of his computer I possibly could.

Each site I found showed the same thing. A blonde woman posed in ways I never imagined, wearing things I never knew existed. Her silky hair cascading down her shoulders and chest, highlighting features my own body lacked.

My chest tightened. Memories flashed in my mind, like the first time I discovered pornographic magazines in Dad's dresser, tucked under a pyramid of t-shirts.

"What's this?" I said to Mom.

She never said a word, but her eyes glazed over and I knew something wasn't right.

I blinked away tears. My thoughts centered on Dad and the pain he caused Mom and me. I didn't want to end up like them.

Jessie should have told me his secret. We could have worked through our problems together. As partners. Now the one person who wrapped his arms around me during every storm in life created a typhoon. Head in my hands, lips hugging tight to each other, I screamed inside. Tears streamed down my neck and my shirt collar caught their fall.

Who would catch me?

His computer screen went black, but I still saw them—the women he admired.

He lied. He told me he never struggled with porn in his life.

Until this moment our marriage seemed to be so alive, so healthy, so honest.

I replayed his words in my head. The sound of his lying tongue jarred me. The steady deliverance of his words, the serious eyes I thought were faithful—all of it made me want to throw the computer at him and leave without a word.

I awakened the computer and clicked on a link he visited a few hours earlier at 4:24am. The page loaded. Images of women loaded. There's no mistake with that word. Loaded. I swear it felt like a rifle blowing my life to pieces.

I closed the browser window, disgusted at myself for viewing something so raunchy. So hard to imagine my husband, the man beside me every morning, immersed in pornography—the one addiction I swore I'd never tolerate in marriage.

Sweat-inducing fury took a roller-coaster ride through my body, heating my face and tightening my lips. I clenched my teeth and closed my eyes, trying to erase the images from my memory. But every pose and body part of every woman grafted themselves into my brain.

I wanted to run away but my feet stayed planted, and I hated that my roots were so strong.

The door opened.

THE FLOOR CREAKED. JESSIE'S BLACK DRESS SHOES, LOOSELY tied, stood before me.

I refused to look at his face, but I imagined it. Red cheeks, balloon eyes, pure shock lining his every feature.

One step. He stopped. Another. His heel scraped the floor. He stopped again.

I saw a picture of us ten years from now. Lines on my face like Mom's. A strained marriage if any at all. No kids. No passion. No love. Life peeling like toxic paint chips onto the floor.

He reached for my hand. "I'm sorry."

My shoulders dropped.

His untied left shoe stepped toward me as I wilted in my chair. Reminiscent of the night he proposed, Jessie bent his knee and knelt before me. His hand hovered above my hands, folded in my lap. I crossed my arms and tugged at my sleeve.

"How could you do this to me?" I said to his shoe.

He sat in the chair beside me, close enough for me to hear him breathe but far enough that I could take a breath. "I wanted to tell you."

I wiped my nose with the back of my hand and sniffed. "Jessie, you lied to me."

I looked up. He looked down. Reminded me of the day we met.

I moaned and looked at his eyelids. "Say something."

He stood. My eyes traveled up. His arms hung alongside his cream shirt, un-buttoned and un-tucked. His eyes. I saw tears.

He licked his lips. They shimmered in the beams of May's setting sun.

3

Along with his glistening eyes. No sound. No words. Nothing could fill the emptiness in the room. Nothing seemed to matter anymore.

I looked at Jessie and saw naked women. People can say that Internet pornography is simply a form of betrayal, but right then, those images told the truth. My husband cheated. He lied. He hid.

"Ally, I was going—"

"Please stop," I whispered, but my chest burned. I rubbed my palms on my favorite work pants and stared at Jessie's shoes. But those shoes wouldn't budge. I combed my hair clip through my hair, swept it back up and re-clipped, then stood and walked away from him—to get away.

I stopped at the counter to search for my keys, but I couldn't see them. Jessie walked over to me. Part of me wanted to work through things, but most of me didn't. So I hunted my keys in the dining room.

Jessie approached me from behind. "Ally, let's talk about it."

"There's nothing to talk about. I need some time to myself, to think through this." I raised my hand to my face and pinched the bridge of my nose.

Don't cry, Ally. Don't cry over him. But I loved him. And I hated that I loved him.

Jessie lifted his left hand—complete with meaningless wedding ring—and swiped his hair from his forehead.

"Why did you do this to us?" I said.

He warmed my back with his arms and pulled me into his chest. I pushed away, hoping he'd pull me back in, but hoping he wouldn't at the same time. I didn't know what I wanted. The past. I wanted the past back. *Oh, God, please. My Jessie. . . .*

He pulled me back into his chest and cradled me. I let him.

We slumped down to the dining room floor, two feet away from the computer, and held each other. I wondered if the naked women watched us, mocked us.

"I wanted to tell you," he said. "I didn't know how. I didn't want to hurt you."

The lie cuts deeper than the act, I thought.

Unwilling to move, unable to speak, I reclined on the floor and analyzed the IKEA lights strung across our dining room ceiling, trying not to remember the day we bought them. Trying just as hard to restrain my tears. Jessie joined me on the floor.

"How long?" I said, not looking at him.

Silence answered back. I pretended I was at work and turned on the marriage counselor in me. "When did you start?"

He cleared his throat and swallowed. "It started when I was thirteen."

My bottom lip dropped. Of all the couples I've counseled, you'd think I wouldn't have been shocked.

"My neighbor took me into his attic."

I barely heard him.

"He showed me magazines. I knew it was wrong. I tried to leave, but he told me a real man likes to look at naked women. So, I stayed."

"So you wanted to say no?"

"Part of me did, yes. I felt guilty, but I was curious."

"Okay, so what happened?"

"He told me to sit on the floor, so I did. Then he pulled a box from a closet shelf." His eyes twitched while he looked at everything in the room but me. "The rest is history."

"What did the women look like?" My eyes stung with tears I wouldn't cry. "Did you masturbate?"

"Ally." He pinched his tongue between his lips and shook his head. "I don't remember what those women looked like."

I watched his lips, wondering how many women he imagined kissing. "Did you masturbate?"

"Not at his house. I did later that night."

"Was that the first time?"

"It was the first time I knew what I was doing. Only because he told me."

Memories of our wedding day danced in my mind. A single tear fell to my neck. I wondered if he looked at other women on our honeymoon. "So when did the Internet come into play?"

"When my parents got a computer. Kids at school talked about porn all the time. Wasn't hard to figure out."

I sat up and shook my head, trying to shake the nightmare away.

"Sometimes I felt awful, sometimes I didn't. I've tried changing my

5

computer password to Jesus so that I'd think of Him every time I logged on. Didn't work. I just dismissed the thought and made excuses. No matter what I did to punish myself, nothing made me want to stop."

"Not even me." My words lingered.

He reached his hand toward my face. I moved away. "Actually you were the first reason I wanted to stop," he said.

"Did you ever do it while we were dating?"

"No."

"But you did when we were married? That doesn't make sense."

He rubbed the hair on his chin.

"Are you sure you didn't when we were dating?" At least part of our relationship wasn't a lie. Just everything after the wedding vows.

"I'm sure."

"Promise me." Jessie never made false promises, or so I believed.

"I promise," he said.

I sighed. "You watched porn while I slept upstairs alone? And you didn't care enough about me to stop?"

He covered his eyes with his hands. "I don't think of it like that."

I wanted to cry again, but the tears hid behind closed lids.

"I tried to stop. I don't want this in my life. It sneaks up on me when I least expect it."

I veiled my eyes with my arm.

"Sometimes I'm in the car and an image randomly flashes in my head."

"Right. And next thing you know, you're staying up late, in our house while your wife cries upstairs because she can't get pregnant, and there you are, sitting downstairs with a cup of tea as you fantasize about other women. These aren't just airbrushed magazine models you're talking about, they're real women! And they're not me!"

His mouth froze.

"Why do they titillate you, and I don't?" I used the word on purpose.

He inhaled, expanding his entire chest.

"What do they have that I don't?"

"You're everything I ever wanted."

"How have you shown me that? I mean, after all this, how?"

"I can't explain it."

I stood. "Try."

"It's just, I don't know. A man can have all he's ever wanted in a wife, but sexually, in his flesh, I don't know, it's like I want everything."

Ouch.

I looked at the man I married, for better or worse, wishing I never had to experience the latter. "I can't believe I'm hearing this from you."

He stood. "I guess you shouldn't have expected Mr. Perfect in the first place."

"No, Jess, I just wanted someone perfect for me, and I wanted to be perfect for him."

The clock chimed. Six o'clock. No dinner. No romantic surprise. Oh, God, take me back to the beginning. Take this day away. I looked at the clock, wishing for a fast-forward button, a rewind button, anything to take the pain away. The second hand traveled around the clock. I wondered what our future looked like. I looked at Jessie and back to the clock. Part of me didn't care about the future. Part of me wanted to leave him and find someone else. Part of me believed I'd never heal.

Jessie's eyes searched my face. I looked away.

Somewhere inside, somewhere beneath the shadows, I knew I loved him. Life without him wouldn't be life at all. But who is he? I wondered. He's not the man I thought I married.

Chapter 2 *Taylor*

I didn't know I'd become what some people dub a porn star two months after my eighteenth birthday, but I did.

Mom told me to find a job, get out there in the real world and be independent. I didn't know how to wash my clothes, much less find a job. But the last thing I wanted was another bruised cheek for my "attitude," as she would say. So, I went to Walgreens and bought a newspaper, sat down on the curb outside, and scanned the job listings as the sun heated my face.

Models 18+ needed, $500 a day, stopped my searching eyes. I never thought much of myself in the looks department, but Daddy always told me I was pretty. And maybe I'd feel better about myself if I told people what I did for a living.

I pulled my cell phone from my purse and dialed the local number. One, two, three, four rings, then silence.

A man's voice said something, but I couldn't hear.

"Hello?" I said.

"Yes, yes," he said as though a huge smile were on his face. "Andy Cross, how can I help you?"

"I'm sorry, I must have the wrong number."

"Are you calling about the modeling ad?"

Don't kid yourself, Taylor, I thought.

"Are you interested in the modeling job? I bet you are. I can tell you're beautiful just by the sound of your voice."

Whoa, his words felt like Chapstick to sun-scorched lips. "Um, yes, could you tell me more about it?"

"Sure, would you like to meet for an in-person interview?"

I looked at the gravel by my feet, unsure of what to say.

"What's your name?" he said.

"Taylor."

"Taylor, I will make sure you get the attention you've always dreamed of. You want to feel good about yourself? I'll help you. And to top it all off, you'll make $500 just for a two-hour photo shoot." He paused. "I'll tell you what, you can try it out for a day, if you don't like it you can stop—no contract until you're ready."

I straightened my back and looked at the shopping center across Joppa Road. "But you don't even know what I look like."

"You must be pretty if you dialed this number. How old are you?"

"I turned eighteen two months ago."

"Perfect. When do you want to set up an appointment to learn more?"

$500 for two hours sounded nice to me. Within one week I'd be in my own apartment, on my own, free from Mom's emotional disasters.

"Taylor, I take care of all of my models. If you're shy, I promise you'll feel confident after one photo shoot with me."

I cleared my throat and stood, balancing myself on the edge of the curb. "I'm just not sure if I have what—"

"You will." Such a sugary attitude?his enthusiasm oozed like syrup through the phone. "What time can you meet with me?"

He seemed so encouraging, more than most people I knew. Most people shunned me, bruised me, ignored me for being introverted, different, too quiet—this guy cared and he didn't even know me!

"How about tomorrow at noon?"

I hopped off the curb and walked toward my leaking Camry. "Sure. Where am I meeting you?"

He explained directions as I drew them on a receipt I found in my purse, then we hung up. Before I got in my car I looked at my phone and wondered what I'd gotten myself into. A model? Me?

Unsure but hopeful about my new future, I couldn't help but laugh. The girl voted "Least Likely to Succeed" in middle school, go figure. And Mom, this'd really blow her away. All those times she told me I'd fail at everything. Maybe I'd finally prove her wrong.

I got into my car and looked in the rear-view mirror. Taylor Jane Adams. A model. I smiled at myself. Yeah, maybe life would go uphill for once. Twisting my keys in the ignition, I kept looking at my reflection.

I saw Daddy's eyes in my own and couldn't help but wonder how proud he'd be if he were still alive.

I turned the music up as loud as it could go and drove out of the parking lot singing with Steven Tyler.

Life, finally, might be worth living.

ANDY CROSS LOOKED NOTHING LIKE I IMAGINED. SHORT hair, adventurous eyes, well-toned arms—gorgeous.

He opened the front door and greeted me with a smile as wide as his face. "Taylor, you look stunning!"

"You too. I mean, um—"

He laughed.

I smiled, sponging the attention from his charming eyes.

He ushered me inside, looked me up and down, spun me around, then stared me dead in the eyes and said, "Wow, you're perfect."

Not sure how to respond, I scanned the house. "I didn't realize you worked from home."

"How about we go sit down in the living room?"

Something drew me to Andy Cross. I followed him down a narrow hallway, through the biggest, cleanest kitchen I've ever seen, and into a living room with an enormous television mounted on the wall. He sat down on the coffee table and motioned to the leather couch across from him. I sat and placed my purse beside me.

He pulled his leg toward him, and rested his foot on his knee. "Are there any questions I can answer for you?"

Looking down, I searched for a question. Clueless, I peered up at him through my bangs. "Um, I'm not sure."

"Well, how about we get started?"

My shoulders lifted. "Now . . . you . . . what?"

His laugh soothed my thumping chest. "I'll get my camera and we'll take a few pictures for practice, how does that sound?"

"But don't I need a wardrobe or something?"

"You look perfect." He stood and disappeared around the corner.

Elbows on my knees, I analyzed the carpet and shook my foot so fast I thought I'd fling my shoe across the room.

Andy walked in the room with a digital camera no bigger than my shoe. "Ready?"

"You don't have a professional camera?"

Laughing, he held out the camera. "Oh, you'll be surprised at the beauty this thing captures."

I smiled.

"Ah, do that again." He held the camera in front of him.

With my hands on the couch, I leaned forward and smiled up at him. A few flashes and *You're beautifuls* later my foot stopped freaking out.

I could get used to this.

Andy sat down beside me and showed me the pictures he took. Seeing myself through his eyes made me smile. Someone thought I was pretty. Someone believed in me.

"Now," he said, touching my shoulder. "How about we try something else?" Slow and steady, he touched my shoulder and glided my sleeve down my arm.

His gentleness reassured me. And three hours later I left his house with $500 in my purse feeling like someone finally accepted me, wanted me, and believed in me. The PG-13 pictures he took of me? Eh, I didn't think about them. I ignored the voice in my head that kept saying, "What are you doing? What if someone you know finds out?"

But then I realized that no one cared about me anyway.

No one except Andy Cross.

Chapter 3 *Ally*

Two days of brief conversations passed until I finally opened up to Jessie. He came to bed, late as usual, and I couldn't help but wonder if he'd been looking at those women again. I rolled over to ignore him, but I wanted to probe his brain for details my heart didn't want to hear.

"How many times did you do it?" I finally said, still not facing him.

"About three or so. I can't remember."

"You can't remember?"

"Ally, it's not like I try to remember every detail when it happens. It just happens."

"Promise me it was only three times since we were married."

"I don't know. It was about that."

"Did you ever rent videos or buy magazines?"

"No."

I believed him, but had to be sure. "Promise."

"I promise."

Then I tried to forgive him, but only nodded when he asked if I could forgive and work through everything.

Honestly, fear birthed my forgiveness. Fear of what people would think of me, what kind of Christian wife would I be if I didn't forgive, and better yet, what kind of marriage counselor I'd be if I didn't give my husband another chance.

"Do you really forgive me?" Jessie said as I turned away from him.

"I don't feel it. But maybe one day I will."

He reached for me.

I turned back around. "I need time, Jess. I still need time."

"But I'm your husband."

"That didn't stop you from doing your thing."

He sighed. "Take all the time you need."

I closed my eyes and thought of the time I counseled Shane and Gina on my second day of work at MacPhail Christian Counseling. Similar situation. I remembered Shane's face like a day hadn't passed since he left my office, all twisted over his marriage. He wanted it to work.

An image of Gina's body flying off a 190-foot rock outcrop fogged my mind. Chills ran down my arms. I could almost hear her body cracking tree limbs and thumping on the ground. Suicide. Over her emotions. I often wondered if I could have prevented it, but I'll never know. She died after thrusting her body off King and Queen's Seat in Rocks State Park. Crazy.

Sounds ridiculous, but it's not hard to see why.

Jessie's light snore brought me back to reality. My reality.

Okay, so I forgave, but that didn't mean I wanted to be married to him. I mean, part of me did, part of me didn't. A big part of me didn't. I tried clinging to the beginning, to all of our memories, but the more I thought of them the more I realized they were fake. Years of betrayal masked by unauthentic faithfulness.

I closed my eyes. Naked women posed on the backs of my eyelids. I opened my eyes, hoping to peel back the shade of women over my eyes, but they stayed, posing in the moonlight across the room.

And they posed until I fell asleep an hour later.

MONDAY ROLLED AROUND, BUT I DIDN'T THINK I COULD handle work. So I planned to reschedule my appointments, which I'd never done before.

On my way out the door, to sit and read and think at Barnes & Noble, my cell phone rang.

"Hey, Ver," I said.

"You okay?" she said.

"Yeah, why?"

"You sound different."

"I do?"

"Oh, stop. I've known you since the good 'ole days when you'd spit out your gum and I'd pick it up and eat it, dirt covered and all, remember those days?"

Ah, I almost forgot what it felt like to laugh. Only Verity, my best friend since we were in first grade, could make me laugh like that. "Speaking of gum, it sounds like you've got about ten pieces in your mouth. Why aren't you at work?"

"Two weeks off. We had vacation planned but there was an emergency and Tim had to fill in." She chewed in my ear. "That's life. Why aren't you on your way to work?"

"Can you stop chewing so loud?"

"You got your period or something?"

"If only you knew."

She laughed and sloshed her gum around. I pictured her sitting there amused at her own joke, twirling one of her braided pigtails. "So, really, what's wrong with you?"

"Nothing."

"Yeah, right."

Verity doesn't let things go. But I couldn't tell her. Especially after years of making it sound like I had the most perfect husband in the world. She'd just say, "I told you so," and that's the last thing I wanted to hear. She didn't believe any marriage could be truly good. Everything was a mask to her, covered up to make the world think we're strong when we're not.

"We'll talk later," I said. "Love ya. Bye."

Bits of rising sun peeked through our Autumn Cherry tree whose white flowers would bloom in Fall as most trees leaned toward nakedness.

A blonde woman slipped into my thoughts.

I picked my cell phone back up and speed dialed MacPhail Christian Counseling. Lauren answered in her typical joyful way.

"Hi Lauren. It's Allyson. I'm not going to be able to make it—"

"Is everything okay?"

"Just a family emergency. If you could reschedule the Porter's for next Thursday afternoon that'll work."

"Okay, I'll keep you in my prayers."

Thanks, but they won't work, I wanted to tell her. "I should be in tomorrow. Could you let Mr. Almond know I'm sorry?"

"Oh, sure. But you know what kind of boss he is. Family first." The word family lingered. "I hope you feel better soon. Thanks for calling. Don't worry, I'll handle everything."

I hung up and wondered how to counsel couples when I had a dying marriage of my own. My dreams of helping couples stay in love seemed impossible. Another blonde interrupted my thoughts. So different from me. So blonde, so curvy, so not me. So my husband's secret type.

Jessie turned on the shower upstairs.

I walked to the garage door and grabbed my purse from our coat rack, tossed my keys and phone inside, and opened the door.

Cold cement.

Shoes, I needed my shoes.

I tip-toed up the stairs and to our bedroom. Trying not to be heard, I slipped on a pair of flip-flops and headed for the stairs.

"Ally?" Jessie called from the shower.

Flip-flopping through the house, I ignored him and left.

Everything in my life gleamed with romance. My dreams all came true, except for not having a baby. But as for my marriage, I couldn't have asked for more. Jessie gave me a beautiful life. More beautiful than I imagined it could ever be. Fairy-tale like.

Perfect.

Until now.

I DROVE AROUND ALL DAY WITH NO DESTINATION AS I replayed those stupid images and wasted ten dollars and nineteen cents worth of gasoline.

I turned right onto Route 24 in Bel Air and speed dialed Mom, returning her call.

"Everything okay?" she asked.

"Yeah, Mom." My voice trembled. I gulped, stopped at the red light, and tried speaking again. "What's the news you needed to tell me?"

"You're not at work?"

I stared at Barnes & Noble in my rearview mirror and accelerated the car. Memories. So many memories. The lines on the road blurred. My ears rang so loud I thought blood would trickle out. I blinked my eyes and pictured another woman. My husband fantasized about her. I inhaled. My chest hurt. Life hurt.

I'm not good enough, I thought.

I did everything right, everything I told my clients. I kept the house clean. I never doubted his decisions, even when I worried he might be wrong. Not one day passed when I didn't try to look pretty for him, making sure to wear clothes I knew he loved. Breakfast, lunch, and dinner waited for him every day, even when I wasn't home. And sex, we had great sex at least twice a week since the day we married. Okay, partly to have a baby, but still.

Anything I'd ever known to do as a wife, I did. I checked off my wifely duty list with zeal. I worked so hard to please him. Gave him everything. All of me. All I had.

And he lied.

"Ally, you still there?"

"Sorry. I'm here."

"Everything okay?"

"Fine, Mom. No worries. So what did you need to tell me?"

"It can wait. Can you come over on Thursday? I get off work early. I'll tell you then. You sure you're alright?"

"Stop worrying, Mom."

"You've said that since you were five. You should know by now that it's my job to worry."

She took pride in her worry. Thought it made her a good mother. I wanted to tell her to give her life to God, to give her children to God. To not worry so much about everything. But I couldn't say that. My Bible collected dust, deserted in the same spot I left it three months ago. God drifted as far away from my thoughts as she wanted Him to be from her.

I hung up with Mom and parked my car with a front row view of Panera Bread. Not that I wanted to eat, I needed to think, cry, or something.

A couple walked into view. Fingers locked. Eyes fixed on each other. Obviously well inebriated with love. A car screeched to a halt to avoid hitting them. With hearts in their eyes, they had no idea. The frustrated driver beeped her horn and threw her hands in the air. Still oblivious to the world around them, the man opened the door to Panera for his love without letting go of her hand. She kissed him on the cheek and entered. He followed. So did my heart.

I missed my old Jessie. The Jessie who didn't betray me. The Jessie who held my hand the first night we met and gave me five beautiful reasons why he wouldn't kiss me. That brisk April night floated through my mind with such clarity I could almost taste his kiss.

JESSIE AND I MET IN THE CAFÉ AT BARNES & NOBLE WHEN I was twenty and he was twenty-two. After he fake proposed to me on that chilly April night, he walked me to my car. You wouldn't believe me, but I parked only two cars away from his black Honda Del Sol. I took that as a sign from God that I'd met my soul-mate.

With his elbow on the roof of my car and his head leaning against his hand, he said, "Can I tell you why I won't kiss you?"

Not quite what I wanted to hear. "I guess so."

"Five reasons. One, I respect you. Two, I respect my future wife. Three, I respect myself. Four, I respect God. And five, I need to give you a reason to go on another date."

I smiled. "So, you're a Christian?"

"Yes."

I respected him and accepted his offer to wait for our first kiss.

We said our parting words. I sat down in my car, closed the door, wound the window down, scribbled my phone number on the back of a receipt and handed it to him.

"Thanks for a great night." He kissed my hand.

Butterflies, butterflies, butterflies! "Thank you."

He tapped the roof of my car twice, said, "Goodnight," and walked away.

I started my car and watched him disappear behind the car next to us then sit in his Del Sol. He waved to me from the driver's seat and looked away. As he started the car, I hopped out of my car and quietly closed the door. I had to retaliate after his fake proposal. Little did he know, I knew how to pull off amazing pranks too.

The cool air tousled my hair as I crouched on the ground and skirted around Jessie's car. My heart raced like a kid playing hide and seek. Still ducking low, I neared the driver's side window.

Just under Jessie's window I halted.

One, two, three.

I popped straight up. My hair tossed around my face as I flung my palms against his window and wailed like a dying goat. Yes, a dying goat. And no, no matter how many times Jessie asked me since, I could not recapture that sound.

"Whoa!" Jessie's hands thumped against the roof of the car.

A laugh started in my face, knotted my stomach, and squeezed my eyes so hard tears wet my cheeks. He crossed his arms over his steering wheel and put his head down.

I hobbled to the curb, desperate not to pee my pants, and sat down.

Jessie got out of his car and ran toward me. I stood and sprinted away. We ran behind Barnes & Noble. My flip-flop fell off next to the dumpsters where I stopped and put my hands on my knees. Jessie panted beside me.

I straightened my back and smiled. He grabbed my hands and looked into my eyes.

I looked back and saw my future.

His laugh subsided while both of our chests rose and fell. I looked up at the night sky, took a deep breath to fill my lungs, and exhaled. The breeze moved across my face and swept my hair away from my eyes.

Jessie's cologne smelled like summer rain.

I smiled and analyzed the adventure in his eyes. Before I could say anything he placed his index finger over my lips.

Home, finally home, I thought.

Our eyes closed. Our lips touched. And Orion watched as we kissed under an April sky.

OLD JESSIE. I MISSED HIM.

I closed my eyes and told myself what I'd tell my clients.

It's not about you. His pornography struggle is deeper than that. You need to know it's not about you. You are enough. You are the woman he wanted to marry.

So much for that. Everything I knew, everything I taught others—it didn't help. And I started to question the validity of anything I'd ever said.

Chapter 4 *Taylor*

At 5:09pm on a toasty June afternoon I walked away from Andy's embrace with another $900 in my pocket and a brand new name. A few, what I called innocent, pictures later Andy convinced me to become his top girl, which meant my pictures would go from PG-13 to R pretty quick.

"I love you, Taylor." He ran his fingers through my hair. "I'll take care of you. You're my glamour girl."

His words were love to a wanting heart.

"I'll make you a star." He smiled and put his arm around me. "You are my most beautiful model, you know that?"

I looked down and smiled.

"Hey, why don't you make up a new name?"

"What do you mean?"

"Make up another name so you can separate Taylor from your new life. Then when I put your pictures online no one will be able to find you by your real name."

Online? He didn't mention that before, but I felt strange questioning him. He loved me. He was the first person since Daddy died to even say those words.

So I came up with the name Sadie and left Andy's arms to go back to my empty apartment and stare at the pile of laundry I still didn't know how to wash. Mom never let me do house chores. Not sure why. Maybe she thought I'd find something she didn't want me to see.

I posed for Andy almost two weeks straight and I'd bought so many new clothes that laundry wasn't necessary yet. Not to mention the hangers upon hangers of clothes Andy bought for me. "I want my girl to look like a princess," he'd say. I couldn't deny that. Or anything he said for that matter.

I felt beautiful, loved, and high on life. Oh, and how could I forget? In love for the first time to an older guy with enough stars in his eyes to fill the universe. Pretty cool, considering only two months ago the entire world stepped on the backs of my shoes and made me feel worthless. It's like my "average" beauty and intelligence wasn't worth the world's acknowledgement.

I grabbed my keys and left my apartment in search of my first laundry detergent. When I entered Walgreens, I remembered sitting on the curb talking to Andy and couldn't be more thankful for the decision I made. Easy money, easy job, and I found love.

As I walked down the aisles I noticed my confidence had increased. Finally I raised my shoulders, instead of rushing in and out of stores hoping no one from high school would see me and make fun of me for something.

I made my way down aisle nine, otherwise known as laundry detergent heaven.

"Let's see," I whispered aloud. "Tide, All, Arm & Hammer—why are there so many?"

"Oh, look who it is." A familiar voice rattled my heart.

I turned to see Angela Bright, the girl who spent her high school years being rude to me, standing in the middle of her posse.

"What?" she said. "You work here or something? Don't got much of a life, do ya? Just graduated and spending your life at Walgreens."

Little did she know.

She continued whispering about me as I turned to analyze detergents. Her words slid off my heart like a kid down a Slip and Slide. A few seconds later she walked away with giggly friends, spitting at me with her words. It took all I had not to turn around and spit in her face for real, but Andy's words softened my response. *You're my glamour girl.* I needed to live up to that. Not that I'd have the nerve to spit in her face anyway.

I settled on Tide and went back to my apartment to wash three loads of clothes. I shrank seven shirts and discolored a few more.

Oh well, you live, you learn.

A FEW DAYS LATER WHILE I ADMIRED THE NEW BED ANDY bought me for my apartment, he called to ask if I'd be interested in a sparkling new car.

"Of course," I said, sitting on the floor beside my bed.

"Okay, princess. Only one thing, I need you to do a little video shoot. No biggie. It'll be quick, I promise. You'll get a brand new car, paid off, and an extra $1,500 for a little video."

My heart knotted.

"For me?" His candy-coated words tempted me.

"Are you sure you want me to be in a video?"

"Of course I do, sweetheart. There's no one more beautiful. I told you I'd make you a star, didn't I?"

"Don't you have other models who could do that?"

"They already do. I need someone fresh and young."

I didn't want to lose him. That's the only reason I said yes. The money, the car, the glamour life?those things were nothing compared to my love for Andy. I wanted to please him and I didn't care what it cost me. Eh, scratch that, I needed to please him.

The next day I walked into his house. He gave me lingerie to wear, told me how he wanted me to do my makeup, then positioned me on his couch. A man walked in. Older, like he could've been my dad, only nowhere near as handsome.

I looked at Andy.

He smiled. "You ready?"

"Who's that?" I nodded to the balding man.

"Paul. He's going to be in this one with you."

I gulped. My ears and cheeks burned. Baldy looked me up and down. Andy stood behind the camera.

"Ready in three," he said.

The camera started rolling and Baldy approached me.

He didn't tell me a guy would be in the video with me. But I couldn't say no when he approached me, with that camera in my face and everything, so I pretended to enjoy myself. My heartbeat clogged my ears, softening the music Andy played in the background. The camera, in my face every five seconds, made it hard to hide my tears. Or maybe Andy didn't care about my tears. He ordered me around. Move this way and that. Do this, no, no, wait, do that. Somehow my body listened as my mind imagined my wedding dress stained with my blood. No one would want me now. No one.

The sheets turned crimson and I thought for sure I'd bleed to death. But Andy smiled and reassured me, touching my cheek between takes. "This is so good," he said. "I didn't know you were a virgin."

The room disappeared. Andy disappeared. Memories replayed in my mind. Mom passed out on the living room couch. Her first boyfriend since Daddy died. His breath. The mayonnaise on his mustache. I could see it all like it happened yesterday. He touched me. And I thought for sure he stole my virginity.

Andy tossed a rag in my face. I soaked it with my tears, hoping when I lifted it from my eyes I'd be alone. Free to cry. I tossed the tear-filled cloth to the side of me and looked at Andy. He beamed. Shame and pride tugged my heart. But I gave in to pride. It's easier to give in to pride than to fight it, and at that point, I didn't have the energy to fight anything.

"You didn't tell me you were a virgin," he said, sitting beside me.

I nodded, biting my lip to hold back more tears.

"You'll be fine, sweetheart." He brushed my hair behind my ear and ran his fingers to my chin. "I'll take care of you."

I didn't believe him, but I chose to anyway.

Chapter 5 *Ally*

June in Maryland, at least where I live, is like preparation for weeks of sweat. June usually isn't so bad, but get to July and you long for an air conditioner. Not Verity though, she didn't use central air, even though she had no problem affording it.

Which is why, most times, I chose to meet her somewhere else. Although I regretted it when we were sitting in the café at Barnes & Noble and she said, way too loud, "Jessie and porn? Really?"

A few heads turned. Some tried not to turn their head, but I saw their ears perk up.

"So, what did you do?" Verity said, still loud.

"Be a little quieter," I said through my teeth.

"Sorry," she whispered. "What happened?"

"I freaked out. My emotions are unexplainable, really. I know, funny for a counselor, but it's like nothing makes sense to me." I paused. "I wonder what my co-workers would think of me. I didn't expect this one. I didn't realize how much insecurity I've had all this time. Unless it's new."

"Well, at least he didn't have an affair. And besides, I always told you fairy-tales didn't exist, but you chose to believe Jessie was perfect and your marriage would be, too."

Not in a million years did I think Verity would know more about love than me. I longed for romance my entire life. I read books, so many of them, to know how to be the perfect wife. She made fun of me our entire lives for dreaming of love and marriage. Used to tell me love was nothing more than a choice. "I never thought Jessie was perfect?"

"Yes, you did."

"No, I didn't. I thought he was perfect for me, not perfect. No one is."

"Well, porn isn't that big of a deal. I used to think so, but when we first got married I couldn't stop him from watching it, so I watch it with him now. At least this way I know what he's doing. It's not that bad, really."

I closed my eyes and rubbed my forehead, hoping the perked ears around me couldn't hear our conversation.

"What? You act like I'm crazy or something."

"An understatement."

"Seriously, you should watch it with him."

"That's not an option. I don't condone that stuff and never will. You're probably just doing that to make yourself feel better. Some kind of coping mechanism."

"You make it sound like such a big deal. Every guy looks at other women. It's just the way they are. And I look at other men too. It's natural. You can't get married and expect to never be attracted to other people again. That's unnatural."

I looked over my shoulder to make sure no one heard our conversation. A couple of teenagers looked our way and laughed. Everything I ever knew about love suddenly seemed unrealistic. Lies. I lived in lies. "Okay, I don't want to talk about this with you. We're obviously not on the same page. And I have no desire to be on your page."

"You don't think other men are attractive?"

"I've never thought about it."

"You are lying. What about that guy we saw at Walgreens in Perry Hall? Remember him?"

I squinted my eyes, peeling my brain apart. "Don't think so."

"Yes, you do. Last week when we stopped there on our way to McDonald's, we asked him where they hid the Chapstick, remember?"

"Um, I remember Walgreens and Chapstick, and a guy, but don't remember what he looked like."

My cell phone vibrated in my purse. I shut it off without looking at it.

"How many times has he called?" Verity said.

"Twelve."

I PLACED MY ELBOW ON MY CAR DOOR AND SUPPORTED MY head with my palm, away from the mirror. I couldn't stand my reflection. Work. I didn't want to return to work tomorrow after an extended weekend.

A woman jogged across the street. I analyzed her body from behind. So womanly, like the women on Jessie's computer. Her blonde ponytail swayed back and forth as she disappeared ahead. I cringed and turned up the music on the radio. Country music attempted to disguise my thoughts.

I accelerated and approached the young jogger, longing for her body. Her curves and hips. Maybe if I dyed my hair blonde Jessie wouldn't need to look elsewhere. Of course that wouldn't change the fact that I looked anorexic compared to the women I saw on his computer.

The jogger disappeared from my view, but a part of me wanted to turn around and watch her again, comparing myself to everything about her.

I wanted to jump into Jessie's mind and see what he would think about her.

My sweaty hand slipped around my steering wheel. I turned left onto Box Hills Parkway. The blonde woman jogged through my brain. I rubbed my temple and turned onto our street.

WHEN I WALKED INTO OUR HOUSE I SMELLED ROSES. And I didn't feel a single butterfly. . . .

I tossed my keys on the kitchen counter and noticed dinner on the table. Steam rose from a pile of mashed potatoes, curling through the air, up and around a nice vase of lavender roses. My favorite.

First time Jessie cooked dinner for me. And the first time a sweet gesture of his made me want to cry sad tears. I looked around the room, peered into the dining room and living room. No Jessie. I sat down at the table and shoved a fork full of potatoes in my mouth.

Jessie sat down beside me. "Hi."

I pushed my corn into my potatoes and took another bite. Jessie bowed his head. I almost fell off of my chair. He never prayed in front of me, much less before a meal. My cheeks out-warmed the food and my appetite disappeared. I stood and walked away. Halfway down the hallway I slid my hand against the wall. Tears. Tears. No more tears. Not now.

I walked into our bedroom, flipped the light switch and stared at our bed. So many beautiful nights blew threw my mind like February wind. So cold, yet so alive. I clenched my teeth and bit my lip while I ran my fingers over the comforter. Relieving my weak legs, I climbed into bed and pulled the covers over my head. Clutching the pillow, I buried my face within its feathers. Another sob convulsed my body. Rivulets of tears wet my entire face and pillow. I hoped Jessie couldn't hear me.

THE DOOR OPENED. JESSIE'S SWIFT MOVEMENTS AWAKENED the silence. He changed his clothes as I inched toward the edge of the bed, as far away from his side as possible.

Sheets rustled and the bed dipped. I never noticed how much of a hill I slept on until now. Jessie's hand touched mine. "Ally, I miss you." His finger traced my jaw up to my ear and sent shivers down my neck. Part of me wanted to swat his hand away.

"It's not going to be easy," I said.

"I know, but are we going to get through this?"

I rested on my back and looked at him. The nighttime glow highlighted the white of his eyes as he brushed a hand through his hair. I loved his hair color, and couldn't help but wonder if he felt the same about my mine.

"I have to ask you something," I said.

"Okay."

"How many times have you looked at it? I mean, total?"

"I already told you."

"Did you lie?"

"No." He fidgeted under the covers, eventually landing on his back with his eyes looking toward the ceiling. Then he cleared his throat. "A lot."

I sat up. "You lied to me."

He shook his head.

I wanted to scream in his face. But it didn't seem worth it. Instead, I stood and walked toward the door. "Jessie," I turned. "You promised me.

You never, ever break promises. That's what you told me." A single tear fell off my chin. "That's what you said on our first real date. How, how am I supposed to believe any of your promises were real? Is this real?" I held up my left hand and pointed to my wedding ring. "Was any of it real?"

Jessie stood, hands at his sides, eyes glistening. "You know it was real. I don't need to tell you that."

"How could I believe you even if you did tell me?" I walked out of the bedroom and down the hallway.

His footsteps echoed mine.

I looked at the ceiling in the hallway. "Please leave me alone."

"I can't. You're my wife. We need to talk this out."

I turned. "I need some time to myself, to sort through all this."

"There's no textbook answer to this one, Ally. You need to talk to me. We have to work through this together."

Easy for him to say.

I walked down the hallway to the top of the stairs. The wooden railing beckoned me to run my hand down its back, like I did so many times before. But my heart wanted to turn around and feel Jessie's hand on the small of my own back. Part of me wanted to erase all of the pain and find our love again, but I couldn't get over his dishonesty. I walked down the steps, hands at my sides.

"You always thought I was so perfect," Jessie said, trailing behind me. "I thought if I told you that you'd think less of me. And all those guys you counsel, and your dad, I mean, I didn't want to be categorized as one of them. I wanted to be perfect in your eyes." He paused. "Ally, please. Give me another chance."

"I did. And you lied."

I walked into the living room, Jessie still behind me. Shadows of tree branches floated across the walls, pointing to pictures of a once happy couple. I sunk into the couch and curled up on my side.

Jessie sat down beside my feet. I stared at him, void of emotion. The scent of lavender roses fought its way to my heart. I waited, wondering what he'd say.

The wind cried, filling the dark room. I peered over the couch as a rose petal landed on the table. Life played in slow motion. If only I could've fast-forwarded it. If only I could've skipped to happily ever after. "If only I could rewind and never find out," I said.

"If only I would have told you from day one," Jessie said to my feet.

"If only." A thousand sentences beginning with if only swam through the mucky waters of my heart. So many hopes and dreams. Broken. One minute I had the best marriage in the world, the next ... this.

"Ally, I want to get through this. I'll do whatever it takes."

Only one problem, I had no idea what it would take. I knew what I'd tell my clients, but . . . Jessie and me . . . this wasn't supposed to happen to us.

"I've already put an accountability program on my computer. It will e-mail you all the Web sites I've visited in a week."

"Thanks." Sounded more like a question. "Jess, how many times since the day we met? Don't lie this time. I'm serious. Get it out now and be done."

He inhaled in slow motion. If only I could've found a rewind button.

"At least three times a week," he said. "Sometimes every day."

Pause.

The wind wept.

I stared at Jessie.

All cried out, I could only stare and hope for the nightmare to end.

Chapter 6 *Taylor*

Oh, the money. It flooded in like a tsunami. Andy did what he promised, after only a few weeks, he made me a star. I guess you'd call it that. He posted pictures of me online and the videos, of course, can't forget the videos. People loved me. Men wanted me. They emailed me constantly, but I never saw those. Andy'd tell me about them but, yeah, he'd also respond as me. He thought I'd mess up, whatever that meant. Anyway, I was a star in Andy's eyes and in his wallet's eyes, so I tried to believe it too.

Along with all the attention, I had more money than I knew what to do with. It happened so fast. If it weren't for the intense amount of cash in my purse I might've stopped before it got worse.

Andy held me in his kitchen after another video shoot. The hot June sun sparkled on the tile, warming me even with the air conditioner on.

"My business is really taking off," he said. "Soon we're gonna be so big that we'll have to hire more people. And you know what that means? More money and fame for you. I have no doubt we'll get noticed at the AVN Awards this year."

"AVN Awards?"

"Think Oscars in the adult film industry." He smiled so wide the sun could've hid and the room would've stayed bright. "We're going this year to get our names out there. Maybe next year we'll be working in California and win some awards."

Something about that smile got me every time I doubted my life or myself. Something about that smile flipped my heart like a pancake whenever I felt like I was burning. Something about that smile took my innocence and turned me into a person I didn't know.

Andy twisted the cap of his Cherry Coke. Part of me wanted to run away and go back to real life. But his smile. The attention. The money—especially the money and independence. I couldn't leave it all behind. Finally, my life held some sort of purpose, some sort of significance. And soon everyone would know my name. Well, Sadie's name.

Right then, as his soda fizzed and ran down his throat I made a pact with myself. From then on I'd pretend to be the girl Andy wanted me to be. The wild, but innocent porn star so far from everything I knew.

Like a light switch, I turned on the extrovert and said goodbye to the shy eighteen-year-old girl I used to be. See ya later, Taylor. Hello, Sadie.

Two minutes later Andy lit a cigarette and handed it to me. Pressing the cigarette to my lips, I inhaled. Didn't take long for me to nearly cough my lungs out.

"You never had pot before?" Andy laughed.

Pot? I shook my head, smiled, and inhaled again and again until my lungs were so full of marijuana that my head lightened. The rolled up paper stopped burning when I took a break. So Andy put it back to my lips. I held it and pressed my mouth over it. Two more puffs of air and the world went fuzzy and butterflies flew around the room. "Look." I pointed, bent over in hysterics. "Butterflies."

Andy held his stomach and laughed.

I don't remember what happened after that, except a lot of laughing, but I woke up beside Andy the next morning.

"I promise we didn't have sex," he said. "I wouldn't do that to you."

Wow. So much for good morning.

"I respect you too much."

He made me feel so good. So cherished. Sure, he sold my body and purity to the world, but he loved me. And, yeah, he watched me have sex with other men, but he loved me enough to wait. And oddly, even though I'd given up my body to others, I didn't feel comfortable having sex with Andy.

He reached for my hand. I pulled away and climbed out of bed.

"Where you going?" he asked.

"Shopping." I smiled. "Want to come?"

"Nah, I'll stay here for now. Be back around three, okay?"

I walked away, feeling horrible and excited, wrong and gratified, like my birthday should've been in June. A Gemini. Two people. Yes, two different people. That was me. Living a lie so passionately that I started to believe its reality.

And so I shopped my heart out, trying to spend my problems away. When I came back to Andy at 3:45pm, I didn't feel any better. The problems went away while I swiped my credit card, but returned when Andy's face weakened my knees.

He wrapped his fingers around my arm and pulled me in his front door. "Where were you, huh?"

"Shopping, I told you."

"You're late."

His hand stung my face like I'd jumped twenty feet face first in water. I landed on the floor. He ran toward me and forced me up by my shirt collar. I flinched.

"Be late again." He jerked his face to mine. "And see what happens."

He dropped my shirt collar. I fell to the floor and watched him walk into the living room. My body trembled from my fingers to my lips. Again, I wanted to run. Why couldn't I run?

"Camera rolls in five minutes," he called from the other room. "Get up and get ready. You look like you were hit by fifteen trains."

I obeyed and went upstairs to put on makeup while I gave myself a pep talk.

Get rid of Taylor. You need to be Sadie now. You need to make Andy happy. Whatever it takes. Don't make him mad again. Just be so good that he can't get mad at you.

I went downstairs and met Andy with a smile.

He kissed me on the forehead. "Sorry for blowin' up. I promise that won't happen again." His eyes scanned me up and down. "Gorgeous. Absolutely gorgeous."

I grinned, sliding my invisible Sadie mask over me. She could help me get through another degrading experience. She actually liked this life, the attention, the money and makeup and clothes. So for another few hours I shunned my heart, lived Sadie's dream, and gave in to Andy.

My world revolved around Andy.

Chapter 7 *Ally*

Athunderstorm cooled the humid air as I walked into work on Friday, pushing the present behind me and making myself believe the past could somehow be the future. If only. If only a thousand things.

The front desk, plastered with post-it notes, sat empty. Must be early, I thought.

So far, so good. No emotional breakdowns. No gorgeous women jogged down the street, and I hadn't dwelled on the images that ran through my mind randomly throughout the day.

Lauren walked around the corner with a water bottle. The yellow walls made her smile seem even brighter, like I just walked into spring. Such a sweet girl. Clueless about reality, but then, I guess I could relate. Not too long ago, I was her age, walking down an aisle toward Jessie. I looked at her engagement ring, wondered if her fiancé had a secret life, too. So many people who walked through my office did. So many. So sad.

"You feeling better?" Lauren said, face bright and young, unharmed by marriage.

"I'm fine."

I'm sure that was believable.

She sat in her swivel chair and clicked the computer mouse. "Lots of post-it notes in there for ya."

A teenage boy—with his shoulders down and his hair glued to his forehead—walked out of Mr. Almond's office as I walked into mine. It smelled like paint. Maybe the chemicals would poison me to death if I kept the door closed and inhaled more than usual, I thought. Okay, a little dramatic. I laughed inside. And I'm counseling couples today. God, help me.

Maybe I should pray.

No. Too busy.

I sat down, turned on my computer, and sifted through the post-it note wallpaper on my desk. I missed one day. Only one and I return to a mountain of notes. The computer finally came to life. I typed in my password. JessieLove. My stomach tightened. I ignored it. Needed to focus.

I opened Outlook and watched fifty-six new messages pour into the inbox. The last message popped up. From Jessie. "Not now, Jess. I need to focus."

I looked over my schedule for the day, organized my desk five times, stared out the window, and battled thoughts until someone knocked on the door.

I jumped. "Come in."

"Hey." Lauren peered through the crack. "The Fowlers are here. You ready?"

"Send 'em in."

Here we go.

I stood and walked to the door.

Lauren opened the door and waved her hand toward me. "Right this way."

Mara aged since I saw her two weeks ago. I couldn't believe she convinced Jed to come. I imagined him a little taller, less facial hair or none at all, and dressed like a golfer. Nope. He resembled a short bear with sweat pants and a t-shirt. Was that a ketchup stain?

"Nice to meet you, Jed." I extended my hand.

He shook, nice and quick. No eye contact.

Mara inhaled and closed her eyes.

"Why don't you two have a seat?"

I sat down and wiped my sweaty hands onto my skirt, then looked up at the marriage I needed to save.

"Okay," I said. "Jed, I'm going to give you this piece of carpet. It means you take the floor. When I ask you to hand the carpet to Mara, it's her turn to talk. No one is allowed to speak unless they have the carpet. Make sense?"

He took the carpet square and said nothing.

Mara nodded and crossed her arms.

"Alright, I'll start with a word of prayer." I closed my eyes and bowed my head. "Father, thank You for Your presence in our lives. I pray for wisdom and guidance. May Your peace fill the hearts in this room as we lift our lives to You, for Your will. In Jesus' name, Amen."

My prayers lacked feeling for so long.

"Jed, why don't you start off by telling me why you are here?"

"Isn't it obvious?" He tossed the carpet on to his lap and sneered at Mara.

"What made you decide to come today? Are you purely here for Mara's sake?"

"Yes."

"Okay, why do you think Mara wanted you here?"

"Because I had an affair. I fell in love with another woman. And I'm happy. Okay? I'm here to end this. I want it over and I'm tired of waiting. I'm tired of her nagging. I'm tired of everything about her."

Mara's face turned red, but the circles under her eyes were still dry. Probably all cried out, like me.

"What do you hope to accomplish with this session, Jed?"

"I just want someone else to say it's okay for us to get divorced. I don't want to have an affair. I just want to be finished."

"Finished with what?"

"With this." He waved his hand around Mara. "She's not the person I married and I can't stay married to the person she's become."

I understand. "And who has she become?"

"The woman I married was fun. She didn't care if I ate potato chips during movies. She didn't yell at me for missing a spot when I offered to do the dishes. She kissed me when we gave the kids a bath, instead of telling me it's too crowded in the bathroom. She's become a nagging witch and I can't take it."

"Why do you think she changed?"

He stared at me, blinked twice, looked down, and picked up the carpet square. "I don't know."

"Jed, could you hand Mara the carpet?"

She gently took the carpet from his hands, careful not to look in his direction. "I changed because Jed stopped loving me, a long time ago, way before the affair."

"That's not—" Jed interrupted.

"You'll have a chance to talk in a minute or so," I said. "So, Mara, when did you begin to feel that Jed didn't love you?"

"Maybe two years into our marriage. He started watching television more. Whenever I talked about something on my mind he wouldn't look at me. He just stared at the television from the time he came home from work until his head hit the pillow. I would try to make love to him and he would say, 'I'm too tired.' I tried everything. He just stopped pursuing me."

"And what did you do when he stopped pursuing you?"

"I pursued him more, only to get rejected."

"And how did that make you feel?"

"Alone." A tear finally wet the circles under her eyes.

A sex-hungry woman with blonde hair careened through my mind. I winced and shook the thought. "Mara, could you hand Jed the carpet?"

He took it. "That's not true. I watched television so much because she stopped talking to me. And every night when I walked through the door she had this crabby attitude, like I did something wrong just by walking through the door. She tries to blame it on me, but it was her, her and that attitude of hers."

"Did she ever tell you that she didn't feel loved?"

"Yeah, but it was too late. I already started the affair and just stopped caring about the marriage."

"Do you love her?"

"I loved the woman I married. Not this woman."

Mara played with the edge of her shirt and I thought of Jessie. The last two days. The tears, the broken dreams, the past. Mara's eyes found mine.

I looked at Jed, but saw Jessie.

Come on, Ally, I said inside, forget your heart right now and live from your head. You're here to save this marriage. Don't make it worse.

I slid my emotions to the side and continued, "Jed, do you think you have changed since the day you and Mara got married?"

Mentally, I listed the ways Jessie and I changed over the years. Less pillow fights, but we still had fun. Less time, but we still made love. Everything made sense, everything except his secrets.

I looked back at Jed. "I'm sorry, could you repeat that?"

Mara looked at Jed. He looked at me, eyebrows bent toward his nose. "I just said, 'Yes, but in a good way.'"

"I'm sorry. I'm feeling very ill right now." I lied, like Jessie, to protect myself. The tiniest part of me understood his perspective. Too ashamed to admit the truth.

Well, I am feeling a little lightheaded, I tried to convince myself.

Weird how easy lying could be if you convinced yourself that it was true.

"Are you okay?" Mara interrupted my thoughts.

I almost forgot where I was. "Yes, I'm so sorry. I really don't feel well."

"Maybe we can come back."

"No, no." I couldn't let another marriage fail. "I'm okay, just needed a second to breathe."

Jed's eyebrows didn't change; in fact, they morphed into one line of hair over his eyes.

"So, Jed," I said, "how do you feel you have changed since your wedding day?"

His eyebrows finally separated. The wrinkles on his forehead smoothed. He exhaled and handed the carpet to Mara. "I can't answer that."

Can't? Or won't?

Mara didn't hesitate. "Maybe it is my fault. I was just thinking about it and, well, when I got pregnant the first time I was under a lot of stress. I didn't have energy for anything and I felt so unattractive and boring. Maybe my irritability got the best of me and Jed felt pushed away."

"That could be, Mara, but it takes two to be in a marriage and it takes two to destruct a marriage."

She looked down. "I know." Her eyes looked to her husband. "But I think it started with me."

Maybe Jessie's issues started with me. Maybe I worked too much. Maybe he wanted me home more. Maybe I should have helped him with his marketing business like he wanted. Maybe, maybe, maybe.

I repositioned in my chair. But still, those women, all of them, were blonde and curvy. Maybe he married me because he was infatuated with me, but deep down he wanted a blonde. Why else would he have needed to look at those women almost every day for years?

I refocused my eyes and Jed stood at the door with one hand on the knob.

"I can't do this. I don't want this marriage to work. I want out." He turned, looked at Mara, then me. "And you aren't focused on us anyway. This whole thing is pointless."

The door opened and closed. Jed disappeared.

Mara's eyes danced across the room, eventually catching my gaze. I looked away. Tears burned my eyes like pool water. When I looked back to Mara she smiled. "Thank you, Allyson. You tried. Maybe next week we can talk about coping with divorce."

Ouch. That hurt. Deeper than she'd ever know.

I stood, walked to Mara's chair and put my hand on her shoulder.

Absent words were substituted by Mara's sniffling.

I failed.

The door opened again. I turned and saw Lauren's face between the door and the wall. "Jessie's here, Allyson. He said it's important. I told him you were with a client." She looked at Mara. "I'll send him in when you are finished, unless you—"

"Thanks, Lauren."

I glanced to my left and looked down at the woman I could unfortunately relate to. I wanted to hug her. I wanted her to hug me. I wanted to be someone else. Someone blonde. Someone better. Someone who didn't ruin everything she touched.

Chapter 8 *Taylor*

Marijuana became my best friend. Well, that is until Gianna walked into Andy's house on a cool mid-June morning. June, you never know what to expect.

Andy escorted her to the living room where I sat, drowning myself in Jack Daniels. Yeah, the clock had yet to strike noon, but I needed to be Sadie without that stupid voice in my head jabbering at me to stop. Jabber, jabber, jabber—Sadie never stopped pouring oil on my squeaky fears.

"Have a seat," he said to her, then looked at me. "Taylor, this is Gianna. She's going to be in a few films with you and see how it goes."

I held up the bottle and smiled. "Welcome."

Andy left the room and Gianna sat down like she'd been through the porn thing five-thousand times. She didn't even look at me, just dug in her purse for some kind of treasure.

I laughed. "You got something special in there?"

"You have no idea."

And out she pulled it—there, in a tiny Ziploc bag, my new powdery-white best friend awaited me.

"Want some?" Gianna fought a smile. "This is how I do what I do. It's my little secret."

Anything, anything to take away the pain I would feel in my next video.

She placed a small chunk of white stuff on the glass coffee table and used a fifty-dollar bill to create a line out of the powder. Had to be cocaine, I thought, and took another gulp of Jack. Taylor clawed at the back of my mind, but I ignored her.

Gianna handed me a straw. My hands trembled as I stared at the trimmed white line.

"Snort it," Gianna said, like it was no big deal.

I looked into her eyes. "Do you ever want to get out of this? Do you ever want to stop?"

"I don't think about it. I've been doing this for five years. It's the only thing I know, the only way I know how to make money," she said, drizzled with expletives.

"Do you like doing this?"

"It's not about what I like." She looked away. "It's about what I need."

Andy entered the room again. We quieted our conversation and watched him sit down across from us.

"Enough for me?" he said.

"Probably." Gianna eyed the shaky straw in my hand.

One, two, three, just do it.

And with one quick, deep sniff, I did it.

The dusty drug traveled up my nose like it was made to, easier than I thought. My head rushed, dizzying me. I stared at my feet while Gianna and Andy made another line. They laughed and talked while my throat numbed. I tried to swallow over and over, but it got harder. Thirsty and desperate to get my throat back to life, I got up to get some water. Shivering, I wondered how I could be so cold when I felt so warm inside.

I poured water into a cup. As the stream smoothed into liquid heaven, my life turned from dirt floors to marble in an instant. No more problems. At least while I soared above life in euphoria. I listened to Andy and Gianna talk as I looked through the glass of water to see their distant faces.

I could so get used to this, I thought.

I looked back at my water, suddenly irritated. Selfish jerk, I said, go get your friends a drink.

I poured two more glasses, dreaming about how thankful they'd be when I handed them a drink. They'd love me. Need me, even if only for a second of their life as they sipped from the water and quenched their dry mouths.

When I walked back into the living room, well, all I can say is that life felt like a Hollywood movie, all the bad parts hidden while the good scenes rolled together like Jazz notes. Everything felt good. Everything I once felt shameful about now allured me. My little companion I called "Cola" not only helped me forget reality, but also helped me love the ugly reality around me.

That night, I even enjoyed the bruises Andy created up and down my body when I laughed at him for using the word ignorant instead of rude.

I finally had an escape from the life I never wanted to live.

My friend, Cola.

Chapter 9 *Ally*

Jessie walked into my office as Mara stammered out. Funny, everyone thought I had a picture perfect marriage. If only they knew I never did. Lies, lies, lies. Our marriage foundation rested on a bed of lies.

I thought he was special, different.

"I have another appointment in fifteen minutes." I looked at the clock, realizing I had forty minutes. "Or something like that." I turned my back to him and walked to the window, trying to hold back tears. We married each other less than a decade ago, but I knew him so well that I could imagine his stance. Arms at his sides, rigid jaw, head slightly down, eyes looking up—typical when he's upset. I peeked just to feel right. Right, oh right, I was.

"Ally," he said. "What can I do? I can't work. I can't focus on anything. I'm a mess. You're everything to me. I don't' know what I'd do if you … you know."

"Our marriage is a lie, Jessie. A lie. I mean, you probably went home and looked at other women after you proposed to me."

He shook his head.

I sat down and twisted my chair back and forth. "You did, didn't you?"

"I don't remember. And don't play counselor with me, I'm your husband." Austerity thickened his voice.

I never heard anger in his voice, not toward me, not like that. He sat in front of me, in the chair Jed Fowler sat in before he walked out.

"What happened to best friends? To faithfulness?" I wondered aloud.

He slammed his palms on my desk. I jumped. Flashbacks of Step-Dad hitting Mom screamed tortuous thoughts about marriage.

Jessie shifted in his seat. "Sorry. But we're still best friends. I don't care what you say, we are."

I wanted to believe him, but I couldn't without questioning his words, all of them.

"Look, you teach people this stuff all the time. You've told me in the past you felt sorry for men because of all this. What happened to that?"

"Not you, Jess. Not you. I thought you were different."

"I'm a man, Ally. I'm not God."

Wow. His words felt like warm water to a frostbitten heart. "You lied. It's not even those girls"—was it?—"it's the fact that you lied. And you lied again after you promised not to lie. It doesn't even make sense. I believed everything you said for years, Jess. Years. Now I can't figure out if anything about us was real."

"Everything was real."

I bit my lip. "No. You were sneaking around obsessed with other women while we were dating, engaged, married."

The word *married* echoed in the room as we stared at each other. I looked out the window. Tree branches waved their bright green leaves at me, against a cloudy backdrop. Maybe I overreacted, I thought. Maybe Verity had a point. They're just dirty pictures, it's not like he cheated.

But he did. He did and he lied.

Pressure swelled in my chest. Pictures of women congested my thoughts.

The springs in Jessie's chair squeaked. His pants swooshed behind me until I saw his reflection in the window, beside mine.

I faced him, cheeks wet with broken dreams. He didn't feel like much of a lover anymore, but he was right, he was still my best friend. And I needed him.

His arms opened. I curled into his chest and pressed my forehead into his body. He sighed. I pulled away, unable to go through with it.

Someone knocked on the door. Probably my next appointment. I didn't move or speak. I couldn't. There's nothing I wanted more than to be comforted by my best friend, but I wanted nothing to do with my husband. It didn't make sense.

Nothing made sense anymore.

MY CELL PHONE RANG THE SECOND I GOT INTO MY CAR. I ignored it and turned the keys in the ignition, wondering how I made it through the day without a breakdown. Thankfully my last few clients were new and more interested in spilling their stories than listening to me.

I pulled out of the parking lot onto Emmorton Road and saw her. Same woman as before. Blonde ponytail taunting me as it swung back and forth and out of view. I turned down a side street to follow her. Perched on my steering wheel, I drove by and analyzed her body. Jealous. So jealous and I hated it. I'd never felt so crazy in my life.

I passed her, turned around and drove by again.

"Wow. I'm losing it. I'm really, really losing it."

I slouched into my seat. Then I saw her face. Only one word for that face: beautiful. She was beautiful—not me. Not in a million years did I think I'd care about this stuff. I'd always felt so secure with Jessie. But maybe my security was my naivety, I reasoned. But I'm not naïve. Maybe I'm just blind.

I stopped at a red light and thought of the first words Jessie's dad said to me. I don't know how I could have been so stupid. I should have believed him, but Jessie encouraged me, held my hand, told me he'd always stand beside me.

You know how the sky looks just after sunset? The colors fade to navy, almost grey, while the clouds float under the stars. That's how the sky looked when Jessie took me to meet his father for the first time. Except just before we reached his house the edges of the clouds turned black.

Jessie knocked on his dad's front door. No one answered. He knocked harder. Paint chips crackled and fell off the peeling door. A sparrow flapped out of view, leaving a silence so thick I couldn't imagine breaking through it.

Wham! The door thrust open, porch boards creaked.

Jessie's father stood in the doorway. His eyes hardly opened as they stared me down. "Who's this?"

Jessie shifted his balance from one leg to the other and wrapped his arm around me. "Sir, this is my fiancée, Allyson."

Veins covered his father's black eyes like tree branches. My hands shook and I couldn't stop blinking. For a few seconds I managed not to breathe, afraid of what might happen if I drew more attention to myself.

Jessie's arm slipped from behind me and took my hand. "Sir, we are going to be married soon. I thought you should meet her first."

"This isn't the right one for you." His father stood, hand twisting the doorknob.

"Actually, she is."

Eyes of death ran up and down my body. "You're not marrying her with my permission. You need a gorgeous wife." He surveyed me again. "She's okay, but not gorgeous."

Jessie's chest rose and fell like he'd been running for his life. I squeezed his hand. He looked at me. My eyes begged him to take us back to the car. And without a word, he consented.

Before we reached the steps the door slammed. I jumped.

Jessie stopped, held my face in his hands and said, "Listen to me, Ally, you are everything I ever wanted to marry. Don't let him get to you. He doesn't even like me and I'm his own son. We don't have to talk to him for the rest of our lives if he wants to be like that, you hear me?"

I nodded.

Romance was enough. I didn't need anything else. One look at Jessie and I didn't care about the world. All I wanted was more of him. To wake up next to him every day for the rest of my life.

He was all I needed.

A car horn beeped. I came back to reality and accelerated, wondering how long the light shined green and how long I sat spaced out.

When I turned onto our street I wanted to turn around. I didn't want to go home. Not yet. Too much to think about and process before I could face Jessie again.

I slowed down in front of our mocha-colored duplex and glanced at the cherry tree in our front yard.

A bouncy blonde hurried down the pathway—my pathway—clutching her purse as her sun-streaked hair shielded her face. I stopped, trying to make sense of what I saw.

The woman drove off and I wilted in my seat. I should've seen it coming. He liked blondes all along. His dad probably knew that. His dad probably knew our marriage would be ruined because I could never be gorgeous enough, too.

I got out of my car and walked to the house, not in a hurry to tell Jessie I saw his other woman leave our house. Our house.

I opened the door. Jessie looked at me from the dining room table, surrounded by folders and papers.

"We're done," I said, a single tear on my lip. "I can't do this."

"What are you talking about?"

"What is wrong with me? How can you even ask that?" I sniffed. "So much for wanting to start over, right? So much for not being able to live without me. I'm sorry I'm not gorgeous." I ran off, hoping Jessie wouldn't follow. I'd never felt so ugly in my life. In every way. And I didn't want Jessie's eyes on my imperfections.

But he followed. "What did I do?"

Digging through the closet, I ignored him. The soundtrack of my life stopped playing. A deadly silence permeated the room. I piled shirts on the bed, then jeans, trousers, socks. Jessie grabbed my arm. I twisted away.

He swept my clothes into his arms and threw them back into the closet. "You're not leaving."

"You can't tell me what to do." I stared up at his darkened eyes. "You did this. Not me."

"Ally, we can work this out."

"Work what out? What's the point when you have Barbie? Why not just marry her? Oh, what? Barbie's not intelligent enough for you? You just like the sex, isn't that right?"

He exhaled. "What are you talking about?"

"I saw her, Jessie. I saw her leaving the house right before I pulled up. Are you really that stupid?"

He sighed. "She was my client's wife. She just dropped off a file for her husband. Didn't even step in the door."

"I can't believe you. She was prettier than me, wasn't she? Gorgeous, wasn't she? I'm sorry I can't be that for you." I knelt down in the closet and picked up my clothes. "I'm done."

"Oh, Ally. Stop. You are beautiful to me, in every way. I didn't have an affair with that woman. You have to believe me. I barely even said a word to her."

I threw clothes on the bed.

Jessie stood in front of me and glided his hands down my arms, pleading with his eyes.

"How can I ever believe you? How?"

Chapter 10 *Taylor*

Cola got me through the next few weeks, although I had to keep taking more to feel the effects, and the more I took the more paranoid I became. Like marijuana, only worse.

Andy sent me to a local clinic to get tested for diseases. I went, not knowing what in the world the tests were for, but found out soon after that I contracted Chlamydia. Already. I didn't even know what Chlamydia was.

"That's okay," Andy told me over the phone. "We'll shoot with Gianna for a few days. Take your antibiotics and you'll be back to work in no time."

What a star, I thought. Thrilling lifestyle.

To cope with the good news, I spent the night with Cola. But I got so fearful of Mom finding me that I duct-taped clothes to my windows so no one could see in. I taped and taped and taped my entire apartment until I ran out of tape.

I didn't want anyone to kidnap me. And the more I taped, the more I knew that the trees outside my window were spying on me and telling Mom everything. After I finally covered every window, I looked at my television and knew it had some kind of video camera lodged in there, watching my every move. So I draped a blanket over it.

"Yes," I whispered.

After outsmarting the spies and checking the lock on my front door a hundred times, I curled up in a ball on my bed and thought about everything. I thought about Taylor and Sadie. I compared their lives, wondering who was dealt the worst cards.

"Get out of this," Taylor said.

"No, you need the money. You need Andy. You're nothing without him," Sadie argued back.

The two of them bickered aloud until I realized I was having a conversation with myself. I laughed so hard I literally peed my pants. The pee burned so bad because my body had been so torn and stretched. I looked at the ceiling as my laugh turned to weeping. Life felt like one of those mirror mazes at the amusement park. Nowhere to turn but to Andy, and he only shoved me in front of a camera so he could make money off me.

I pulled my damp legs to my chest and cried like I did when I saw Daddy's dead body in a casket. My weeping continued even when my eyes had no more tears to give. So I wept with dry eyes until I fell asleep.

But even my dreams tormented me.

THE NEXT MORNING I WOKE UP CRAVING COLA, BUT STAYED in bed and stared at the ceiling instead. Andy called several times, but I didn't pick up. Instead I thought about running away. I wanted to stop doing drugs, stop making porn movies, and get back to being Taylor, the girl no one knew. But I thought for sure Andy would kill me if he found me. So I needed a plan, a good plan.

Yeah, I just didn't know what that plan would be. I didn't know anyone else. No one cared. Mom hadn't picked up her phone since I left, except that one time her boyfriend hung up on me. And after being fondled by one too many of her boyfriends, I didn't care to go back there.

I looked around the room for an answer.

And on my dresser, five feet away, Cola begged to drown my sorrow.

"I can take you above life, make everything golden," Cola said.

No, no. I couldn't. But I wanted to. I really, really wanted to.

I stood and walked to the dresser. Cola stared up at me, longing to be inside of me, like everyone else. But no one, not one person, ever wanted to be inside my heart.

I snatched Cola from my dresser. "Why do you use me?" I cried. "Why do you pretend to care? What kind of best friend are you?"

I threw Cola on the floor and collapsed onto my knees. "Why do I still want you? Why do I still want Andy?" I pounded the floor, crying until I couldn't breathe.

Everything felt numb, from my hands to my heart. Life seemed pointless, but I needed to keep going. I couldn't let Andy down. Maybe, I thought, maybe he'll let me stop. Maybe I can work behind the scenes with him instead. Happily ever after, right?

Couldn't hurt to ask.

Chapter 11 *Ally*

Toes in the blades of grass, I sat in our backyard and watched the lush trees sway above me, kissed by golden streaks of sunlight. The weeks, so fast, carried me into the future, a future so unknown, so different and divested of a life once filled with love—true, romantic, unbridled love.

Jessie stepped outside in yesterday's clothes and a smile. Two weeks passed since I saw that woman leave our house. And I chose to believe him, even if he lied. Sometimes, like then, it felt better to believe a lie than to question it.

He sat beside me. "I feel good about the future."

I forced a smile.

"I feel like we're finally starting to get somewhere."

I didn't. And even though I decided to believe him about that girl hopping away from our house, I still wondered sometimes if she shared my husband with me. The thought gave me chills.

"Hey." He took my hand. "I'd like to take you out to dinner tonight."

I nodded. Jessie squeezed my shoulder and stood, walked away, then came back with a bowl of Raisin Bran. Out of the corner of my eye I watched him inhale the cereal. The spoon clanked against his teeth and milk dripped down his chin. I never noticed how loud he chewed before.

I stood and walked through the glass doors into our dining room. Jessie's computer screen laughed at me.

I imagined going out with him tonight and hoped for the energy to smile. Just as long as our waitress wasn't a blonde with perfect curves, I'd be okay.

Footsteps tapped behind me, then stopped. Jessie's arms wrapped around me. The warmth of his neck heated mine. Flesh to flesh, I cringed inside. The sound of his breath, his chest rising and falling against my back, I couldn't take it.

My own marriage suffocated me, stealing my breath with every thought of the past, of what we were supposed to be, not what we'd become.

I pulled away and headed for the shower.

As I opened the bathroom door a familiar smile enticed me. I closed my eyes. There, on the backs of my eyelids I saw him. Sean Kensington. High school sweetheart. First date. Prom date. Best friend, all those years, until Jessie. He would've taken care of me, unlike Jessie. He wouldn't have lied. He adored me, everything about me. Brown hair and all.

Maybe I married the wrong person.

I turned the faucet in the bathtub. I knew I shouldn't, but I allowed thoughts of Sean to entertain me. Water gushed and swirled around the tub. I turned and looked in the mirror. My eyes, my hair—Jessie made me hate it all. But Sean. . . .

Sean adored me.

JESSIE OPENED THE DOOR TO OUR FAVORITE RESTAURANT and I walked inside, scanning the room for blonde women.

Coast clear.

His hand reached for mine. I put my hand in my pocket.

"How many?" The coal-haired hostess said.

"Two," Jessie said.

She handed us a pager with flashing red lights. "It'll be about twenty minutes."

Jessie led me to the other side of the room and we sat down on a bench. His eyes were on me. My eyes were on my shoes.

"You okay?" Jessie said, brushing my hair behind my ear.

I nodded.

Laughing people mocked our silence. How I wanted to laugh. I looked at Jessie. He snapped his head, quick. My heart plummeted. I looked across the room and saw her straight blonde hair soft on her shoulders, curves in all the right places, model height. Jessie's eyes were on me. Mine were on the girl I caught him staring at. This can't be happening, I thought. "Were you staring at her?"

"Who?"

I pointed and watched his eyes scan the girl's body.

"No, I wasn't."

"When did you turn into such a liar?" I said loud enough to slice the laugher in the room.

People stared. My hands trembled. I shook my head, scrunching my face to avoid tears. Then I stood and walked out. He followed and tugged my arm. I shrugged him away and jogged across the parking lot. Clammy June air dried my cheeks. I could almost smell the salty Chesapeake Bay. Jessie jogged behind me. A gamut of beautiful memories clung to my mind. Our memories. Our past. Out of breath, I stopped beside the car and turned to him.

His eyes moved back and forth across my face. "Please. Don't do this."

"Don't lie to me. Were you looking at her?"

His shoulders dropped.

Another tear trailed my nose. "Were you attracted to her?"

"Don't ask me something like that."

"Tell me."

"Yes. I was attracted to her, okay? I didn't mean to look at her. She just caught my eye and you happened to look at me right when I saw her. I didn't stare at her like you think."

"Why am I not enough to keep your attention?" I opened the car door, sat down, and slammed the door in his face. The car shuddered.

He walked around the car, head down, and sat in the driver's seat. "You can't expect me to not see people, Ally."

I stared out the window, avoiding everything about him. "I want to go home."

"But—"

"Now."

JESSIE PULLED INTO THE GARAGE. I JUMPED OUT BEFORE

he turned the car off. My knees weakened. My pulse felt non-existent, yet at the same time, too fast. I turned to Jessie just before I reached the door.

No words.

Not a single word came to mind.

For years we sat in silence, speechless, unable to find words to describe how we felt. Now, silence reminded me of death and not a single word could awaken it.

I went inside and sat down on the living room floor, back against the couch, knees pulled to my chest. Jessie slumped into the couch a few feet away from me. I didn't know why, it didn't make sense, but I wanted him to hold me. I wanted him closer.

I glanced at his feet. His hand moved toward my shoulder. I pulled away. I didn't want him to touch me. But I did. Oh, I didn't know. Addled by all of it, by the fall of my life, my marriage, I couldn't do anything but stare into space and try to make sense of the puzzle in my head.

I needed to fix it. I needed to use what I'd learned in school, in all those years of counseling, and fix my marriage.

I draped my arms over my knees and put my head down.

Jessie sighed.

It's possible, I thought. I could've married the wrong person. His dad always said that. Maybe he was right. Maybe we were infatuated and made a stupid decision. But the past, all of those memories, all of those beautiful memories, they had to be real.

I peered up at Jess—elbow on the arm of the couch, fingers weaved in and out of his hair.

He sat up. "Talk to me."

"About what?"

"Tell me what's on your mind."

"I just want to be the most beautiful woman in the world to you."

Silence quickened the pulse in my ears. The clock ticked as background noise. Tick, tock, tick, tock. Now I knew what people meant when they talked about deafening silence. I wanted to rip the clock off the wall before it split my eardrums. I wanted to close my ears, turn off my heart, receive nothing about the silence, but it settled in the room.

And it hurt.

"Why aren't you saying anything?" I finally said.

"I don't want to lie."

"So, I'm not the most beautiful woman to you?"

"Don't ask me things like that."

"What do you think is more beautiful than me? What qualities?"

He breathed heavily, lips pursed tight and unwilling to budge. The silence stung. I'd never been so torn in my entire life. It's like someone took the perfectly together puzzle of my life and threw it on the floor, leaving every piece to fend for itself. And now I didn't know where to start. It seemed like ninety-percent of the pieces disappeared.

"You can tell me." I already knew anyway.

"I don't know."

"Please."

"Blonde hair, blue eyes, tall—I don't know. Please don't make me say this, Ally. I don't want to hurt you."

If I already knew, his words shouldn't have been so offensive. "Give me a person."

His jittery eyes scanned my face.

"Name someone you think is more beautiful than me."

"I'm not doing that."

"Please."

"Why?"

"Please."

"Ally, I don't think like that. I don't compare you to people. There is no most beautiful to me. There are too many different kinds of beautiful to say that. But you are beautiful to me. I swear it. You are."

"Is that supposed to make me feel better? The fact that you think hundreds of women are beautiful? That you can't tell me I'm number one in your eyes?"

"I don't know. It's not possible."

"Who's more beautiful than me?"

"Anna Lafferty."

Anna from our first apartment building? I gasped for air and let out a deep sob.

Jessie reached for me.

"So, you think Anna is more beautiful than me?"

"Yes, she's more beautiful than you."

I looked into his eyes, tears covering my face.

Nothing could describe that kind of pain, that kind of moment in a marriage.

Jessie held my hand.

I slipped my hand from his and walked away. I asked, I know. But it still hurt. Part of me hoped he'd tell me that no one in the world surpassed me in his eyes, but I guess I needed to hear the truth, even though I regretted it.

As I climbed the stairs to bed I thought about Sean and the one hundred what ifs that went along with him. But for some reason, I knew I couldn't fall asleep in another bed. Wishing I were callous to the pain, I stared at the ceiling as I reclined into my pillow. Ensnared by my own marriage.

Chapter 12 *Taylor*

I went to the library to learn about Chlamydia. That's when I realized it could cause infertility. I sighed, relieved. One less thing to worry about.

I left the library, bought a hot dog drenched in nacho cheese from 7-eleven, and sat in my car, picking apart the hot dog and barely eating it. Chlamydia didn't seem so glamorous, so worth the money. But maybe I wouldn't get it again.

Disgusted, I tossed the hot dog in the plastic 7-eleven bag and looked at the radio. I remembered the day I left Walgreens, belting my happy heart out to Aerosmith. Now, my radio hadn't been turned on for weeks. My heart wanted nothing to do with music. It reminded me of Daddy, of my lonely high school years and my insatiable desire to be someone. To leave a mark in the world.

I drove away from 7-eleven, thinking about my mark. Porn. Blood. Chlamydia. Cola. Money. Yeah, some mark.

This life seemed so light, so easy, so undeniably easy.

"What can you give me?" I said to the chill in my car, hoping Sadie would answer.

She did. Her words floated on the coolness in my car, landing on my heart and soothing my worries. Her icy presence had a way of reassuring me, of making me follow her toward another life, a life she promised to be better. "You will be someone," she said. "You just have to get through the hard parts first. This life can be great. You will be sexy, wanted, and rich."

"Okay," I said. "I'll ride this rollercoaster to the end."

There had to be something better at the end. I mean, that's what rollercoaster's do. They go up and down, thrill you, terrify you, wrap your hair around your face so you can barely see, and then they end. And you feel better for having chosen to ride. You realize if you had left the park without riding, you would've regretted it.

They teach you that you can handle so much more than you think, and at the end, it's worth it.

Chapter 13 *Ally*

I walked into Mom's house. Burnt bacon filled my nose. Must've learned that from her, I thought. Always rushing around, never doing anything with one hundred percent of me. Maybe that's how I treated my marriage. I walked through the living room and into the kitchen. No one. I walked halfway down the basement steps. "Mom?"

The Price is Right played around the corner.

Mom walked to the bottom of the steps with a basket of clothes on her hip and an old burp cloth turned rag on her shoulder. She smiled. "How was your date with Jessie?"

"Good." I lied. Again. "Rushed breakfast?"

She laughed and winked. "Can you tell?"

Mom walked upstairs behind me. Pictures scaled the wall next to the stairs, filled with so much joy it hurt. Even after all Dad did to Mom—to me—I couldn't help but wish he would've stayed. Maybe he left to be with another woman.

I stopped and looked at a photograph so alive it could almost breathe. My wedding day. Smiles painted brighter than film could capture. I ran my fingertips along the frame. Blinded. I was so blinded back then.

"You okay?" Mom said.

I nodded and walked upstairs.

"Something on your mind?" she said as I followed her into the kitchen. "Hey, how about some crab cakes?"

I rested my elbows on the counter and sighed.

"You can talk to me, you know."

"Yes, I know."

"Speaking of which, there's something I need to tell you." She walked into the dining room and sat down. "Sit."

I obeyed. "Mom, you don't need to. I'm just tired that's all. We don't need to bring up the past again."

She played with fake sunflowers in the centerpiece. "I think you—"

"Mom, I found porn on Jessie's computer." There. I got it out. And it felt good. Maybe she and I could relate for once. Maybe she could hold me and tell me how horrible the pain was for her, how she got over it—or didn't she? I looked up at her face.

She brought her hands together and pressed them against her lips.

"I need to know something, Mom. Why didn't you leave?"

"Remember when we were looking for a wedding dress and I wanted to tell you something?"

I nodded.

"I should have just told you then, before your wedding. It's my biggest regret." She paused. "When your father left it wasn't his fault."

"I saw the magazines. I know I was young, but I remember it so clear."

"You might hate me after I say this, but I need to tell you the truth. If you don't want to talk to me for a few—"

"What, Mom?"

"When you were little, I had an affair. Your dad never did anything wrong. I just fell for someone else." She practically destroyed the artificial sunflower in her hand. "It was your step-dad. Eventually your dad found out and talked me into trying to work it out, for you. I tried, Ally, God knows I tried, but I just didn't love your dad anymore. We weren't right for each other. I wasn't happy. I'm happy now. That's what matters."

I couldn't breathe. Or think. I didn't even know who I was anymore. I looked back and forth. Mom's voice faded into a buzzing sound. I imagined Dad on the front lawn, turning back to my little face in the window.

I needed to get away. Now.

"Ally," Mom said. "I didn't mean to hurt you."

"But what about the magazines?"

"Please sit."

"I'm not sitting. Say what you need to say."

"I brought home magazines for your father one day hoping it would make him want something else and leave, so I didn't have to. He wouldn't even touch the things. But when you were about three years old, I told him that the affair started before you were born and—."

"Don't tell me." I paced the room, blinking back tears. "He's not my father. Tell me my step-dad is not my father."

"He's not. But I lied to your dad. I told him that you weren't his daughter. He wanted to stay at first, but after awhile he said he couldn't handle looking at you. So he left. And that's what I wanted." Tears tripped over her cracked lips. "I'm so sorry, Ally. I don't deserve your forgiveness, but I had to tell you. I don't want you thinking your dad was—"

I bolted out of the house, not willing to give her the pleasure of seeing my face again. Ever. Like a piece of trash tossed underneath moving vehicles, I wondered when I'd stop getting flung around, and finally, come to rest safely in the grass.

I didn't know who I was, much less whose life I'd been living. So I sat in my car and begged God to take me back to the lies, back to the golden life where everything appeared perfect.

Chapter 14 *Taylor*

Another day passed, another day alone in my apartment. No Andy. But he called and checked on me a few times a day. My cell phone rang for the third time today.

"You taking your meds?" Andy said. No hello.

"Yup."

"Okay, you're going to be back next week. I've got a few photo sessions I want to do with you."

I sighed, grateful to be freed from a video shoot for once.

"I'm going to set up a Web site for you."

"For me?"

"Yes, only you. I'm going to post pictures and videos on there. I have a feeling we're going to make a lot of money off of it. People are responding to you like crazy."

As much as I wanted to stop being Sadie, it felt sort of nice to know people were "responding" to me. People calling me pretty, wanting to see my pictures—I liked that. Maybe Angela and her friends would see them and be jealous. Maybe I'd end up on an MTV reality show, all glitzy and happy and famous.

"Did you hear me?" Andy said.

"No, I'm sorry."

"You need to stop spacing and listen. I said now would be a good time to get breast implants."

Breast implants? Uh, the thought hadn't crossed my mind.

"I know you can afford it. I pay you more than enough."

Except most of my money went to Cola or Jack. "Yeah. I don't want breast implants though."

"I didn't ask what you wanted, sweetheart."

A woman giggled in the background.

"Who's that?" I said.

"Gianna. We just finished a shoot and she's waiting for her driver."

She giggled some more, like they were cheek to cheek or something.

"Okay, well I don't really see the need for breast implants."

"Trust me, there's a need. I'll get everything set up for you, all you have to do is show up."

No sense in arguing. Maybe I'd look good anyway. Maybe he really did know what he was doing. After all, he only wanted the best for me. He wanted to make me famous and happy, filled to the brim with a life of glamour and fun and jealous ex-classmates.

Sounded good to me.

I hung up the phone with Andy and his giggly companion.

I placed the phone in my purse and decided on a spontaneous drive. I felt good today. Better than usual. And sort of hopeful about my future again. Up and down, on and off, it never ended. I couldn't figure out what to feel or think most of the time, but today, today I felt like I could fly.

I left my apartment and opened my car door, humming R. Kelly's song, picturing Michael Jordan and Bugs Bunny in my head, and feeling high on life again, without the help of Cola.

I drove around singing and sticking my head out the window. Windows down, sunroof opened, the hot July breeze tangled my hair. I thought about Ocean City, Maryland. The beach. The smell of salty shores and crabs covered in Old Bay seasoning. Smooth, warm sand under my toes. Without another thought, I drove south, heading toward the Chesapeake Bay Bridge that would take me to the sandy strip.

My cell phone rang.

Andy.

I hit End. My phone sang *Free Fallin'* as it turned off.

And I smiled.

Chapter 15 *Ally*

I walked into my house. Jessie's muffled laugh traveled down the stairs. I needed him. Regardless of our issues, I needed him.

As I walked upstairs Jessie's words sharpened. When I reached the top I leaned my head against the bedroom door. Another voice landed on my ears. "She can't expect you not to look at stuff, man," Tim said. "Just don't tell her if it bothers her."

I pressed my ear as close as I could to the crack in the door.

"Verity watches it with me," Tim said. "She actually likes it. And I'm telling ya, sex has been better since she has."

I couldn't believe what I heard.

"Yeah," Jessie said. "I don't know. You know Ally has a past filled with that stuff."

I opened the door.

Jessie's arms fell to his sides. He looked at the phone on the bed then back to me.

"Hi, Tim," I said, eyes stabbing Jessie. "Ally here." I picked up the phone. "Just so you know, Verity isn't crazy about that stuff. She only does it because you don't love her enough to stop."

Click. I tossed the phone back on the bed.

Jessie inhaled and crossed his arms.

I shook my head. "What?"

He unfolded his arms and threw his hands in the air. "You take this stuff too seriously."

"Right. You make it sound like I'm crazy and if it weren't for me and my craziness you'd watch that stuff every night."

He looked down.

"Look at me."

Clenched jaw, he looked at me.

"Have you looked at anything since the day I found out?"

"No." He sat on the bed.

"Not online, not in person, not in magazines?"

"I don't think it's wise for me to tell you every detail."

"Wise or not, I deserve to know."

He fell back onto the bed. "Not online and not in magazines. In person, yes."

"What do you mean?"

"I drove passed a billboard today on my way to OfficeMax. Does this really make you feel better?"

"Nothing can, but I need to know the truth. Did you think about her?"

"Yes."

My lungs hurt, like they didn't have enough room in my chest to breathe. "What did you think?"

"I just wondered what it would be like, Ally. Don't ask details. Listen, you need to realize that every man deals with this at some point. At least I want to get rid of it. At least I'm not like Tim."

"Don't even play that card. You are like Tim. To me you are no different. Fantasizing about some woman on a billboard is no different than watching those vi—" I shook my head, unable to finish my sentence.

Jessie sat up.

I looked at him, waiting, hoping for the bad dream to be over, over for good. "I have another fertility appointment Monday before work, and you know what I'm thinking?"

He shook his head.

"I'm hoping I'll never be able to get pregnant." I looked at the door and back to Jess. "I just can't imagine."

He flopped back onto the bed.

So much for wanting him to comfort me. So much for wanting to tell him about Dad and ask him what I should do.

I couldn't trust him with even the smallest part of me, much less my heart.

I walked out of the bedroom and to the hallway, feeling so unloved, deceived, ripped apart in the most scandalous ways.

Why me, Lord, why me?

I'm sure God didn't hear me anyway. And if He did, He ignored me for all the times I ignored Him.

Jessie walked into the hallway. "There's something else I need to tell you."

Chapter 16 *Taylor*

O cean City, Maryland welcomed me, complete with flooding rain. Figures. I drove up and down Coastal Highway, peering to the left and right, at the Chesapeake Bay, then the Atlantic Ocean, waiting for the sun to dry the rain.

I drove for an hour but the rain didn't dry. So I pulled over, rubbed my eyes, and turned my cell phone back on.

New voicemail.

I dialed *86 and listened.

"Taylor, Andy here. Just checking in on you. Give me a call when you wake up, I have something to ask you."

"Taylor, Andy again. I'm starting to worry. Your phone has been off for over two hours."

"I'm coming over. It's been four hours and I haven't heard back."

Oh, no.

My jaw stiffened like it did after a date with Cola. I reached into my purse, hoping I remembered to bring Cola, just in case. But I found nothing except shimmery lip-gloss, rosy blush (I can't live without blush), and enough cash to buy a new wardrobe or fifty more grams of Cola.

I started to call Andy back, but hung up. Before I put the phone down, it rang. I stared at his name on the screen. He'd never believe I drove to Ocean City alone. I could feel the back of his hand on my cheek already.

The phone went to my voicemail as I drove a few minutes and considered driving home, then parked my car near the sandy shore and got out to feel the sand between my toes.

Rain drizzled, dampening my head and eyelashes. I walked down a narrow path. Tall grass decorated with water beads waved to me as I walked by.

And then, I turned the corner and the Atlantic Ocean reached its vast arms out to me, telling me to come and stay awhile.

Only a handful of people were scattered on the beach. Too rainy. A good thing, considering I didn't want to be around many people, especially men. And especially men who might recognize me by my pictures or videos.

I sat a few feet away from the foamy shore and watched the waves crash against each other. The wind cooled my cheeks and chapped my lips. One after another, waves rolled to my feet. How could something so peaceful come from two things crashing into each other?

I took my shoes off and tucked my feet into the warm, gritty sand.

More waves collided, hushing me into a trance.

I analyzed the landless horizon, wondering how so many atoms could come together and form something so beautiful without a higher power. Recent memories of science class, evolution theories and all, floated across my mind. I wished my thoughts could've come together as easy as hydrogen and oxygen.

A big bang, I thought, staring at the hazy sky. A big bang couldn't have created all of this. Every color in the sky, every wave that crashes—there's no way.

It didn't make sense to me. But then again, neither did God.

My phone rang again. The beauty of technology. Cell phones always interrupted good moments in life.

I picked it up.

Silence.

"Taylor?" Andy's strained voice echoed against the *shhhh, shhhh, shhhh* of the ocean.

"Yeah."

"Yeah? Where are you? I've been to your apartment. I've been driving around everywhere worried sick. I thought you were dead."

"I'm okay."

"You don't run off without telling me where you are, you hear me? What if something happened to you?"

"Yeah, what if? What if I died and you couldn't use my body to make money?" I pulled my feet out of the sand and sandwiched my cell phone between my neck and head.

"Don't talk like that," he said, garnished with expletives.

For the next three minutes and nineteen seconds Andy told me what a horrible actress (by actress he meant porn star) I was and that I needed to get breast implants if I wanted to make something of myself. Oh, he went on and on, flattering me with empty words. "I'm only trying to encourage you," he said. "You need to be the best. You want to be the best, don't you? Don't you want to be known for something?"

His words made sense. I did want to be known for something. But as his words bounced around my head, they cartwheeled off my heart. The frothy shore teased me, telling me there's something more to life, something deeper than what I knew. But the reality of the sea felt untouchable—too illogical and unknown, too strange to trust. It didn't make sense to me. But Andy's words did.

Chapter 17 *Ally*

Jessie stood in the hallway, shoulders down, unable to look at my face. I knew what he was about to tell me. He slept with another woman. Probably the woman I saw skipping away from the house the other day.

He nodded to the bedroom. "Can we sit down?"

"I'd rather not right now."

"I want to be honest with you."

I nodded, swallowed, waited.

"I lied the other night." He exhaled. "I've watched videos and I've bought magazines."

"Did you have an affair?"

"I've looked at magazines, videos, stuff on the Internet, TV. . . ."

"And no affair? How do I know you are telling the truth?"

He looked down. "Do you realize how hard it is to be a man in this world? Do you even know what I have to deal with? I hate this stuff. I've tried to break out of it since the day it came into my life. It doesn't work. It just comes back."

"Do you realize how hard it is to be me? To feel like you'll never measure up unless you get a thousand plastic surgeries and make yourself look like another person?"

"What am I supposed to do? Every movie we watch has something in it. I can't even walk through the grocery store line without seeing something. And even if I don't dwell on the image, it pops up later. And then another, and then another until I give in and look for more."

"Do you ever, just once, think about what it's like to be me right now?"

"I'm opening up to you. Can't you see that?"

I nodded my head and chewed the inside of my cheek.

He rubbed his forehead.

I looked away.

"Are we going to get through this?" he said.

I played with my wedding ring. The diamond caught sunrays from the windows. I wish I could be as bright and reflective of beauty, I thought. Really, I'd just give anything to feel alive again. To stick my head out a car window and laugh until my jeans are too big.

I remembered the night Jessie proposed.

ON A HUMID SATURDAY IN JULY, WHEN JESSIE AND I WERE so in love we ignored conflict, he picked me up for our usual date.

I opened my apartment door and he beamed with a rose held between his teeth. "Happy three months." He handed me the rose.

I took it, wondering if he'd finally say it. A few weeks into our relationship he told me that he had never told any woman that he loved her. He wanted to save that for his wife. Every day I waited with a fear inside that he'd never say it and I'd end up single again, wondering if God wanted me to wake up alone for the rest of my life. "So, where are we going?" I pried.

"You need to learn to like surprises."

"And you need to learn to surprise me."

"Oh, what are you saying? My attempts weren't successful?"

I smiled and sat down, waiting for him to close the car door. He didn't. He got down on one knee beside me and took my hand, smiling that adventurous smile of his.

"How's this for a surprise?" he said.

I laughed. "Yeah, right. We've been here before, remember? Remember the fear in your eyes when I got even?"

He squeezed my hand. "Allyson, since the day I first saw you in Barnes & Noble I knew you were different. I don't know what it is, but that first time I held your hand, I can't even explain it, but you . . ." He looked down at our hands. "Shoot, what am I saying?"

"Are you being serious, Jessie?"

When he looked up at me again I knew he wasn't kidding. Jessie is a prankster. We both are, but when he's serious his entire face relaxes and his eyes don't dart around as much.

He stared at me. When he blinked again, his eyes were wet. "Allyson, I had this all planned for later, I had a speech and I can't remember it." He paused, looked to the left then back at me. "It doesn't matter. Just know that I love you and I'm a better man because of it. You've changed me. You've completed me like no other women ever could. I can't imagine my life without you."

I glanced down and saw a diamond ring in Jessie's right hand. I blinked about eight thousand times in one minute, wiped my eyes with my right hand, and looked at the ring again. "You're serious!"

"Allyson, say you'll marry me."

I jumped up to hug him and hit my head on the roof of the car. His eyes lightened when I managed to get out of the car and stoop down next to him. "Yes, yes, a thousand times, yes."

He held me and started talking again. I didn't hear him. "Just stop talking right now. I don't know what you're saying."

He smiled. There on the gravel, sitting beside his car, we planned our future.

Minutes turned to hours, timed by the multihued sky. When the colors dimmed our faces and the streetlights lit our eyes, Jessie stood and took my hand. I waited in front of him, both hands in his, and there in the gloaming silence he brushed my hair behind my ear and whispered three words I longed to hear.

"I love you."

We never left the parking lot.

JESSIE LEANED AGAINST THE BEDROOM DOORFRAME, rubbing his thumbs into his palms. And I missed him. I missed the fun— laughing in bed so loud we'd disturb the neighbors, jumping in his arms when he walked through the door, splashing each other while we washed dishes.

I missed old Jessie.
This wasn't what I signed up for.

Chapter 18 *Taylor*

I guess I deserved the bruises. I shouldn't have gone to Ocean City without telling Andy. He cared about me like no one else. And I failed him.

Alone in my bedroom, I listened to the sound of the air conditioner as Cola stared at me from my dresser. I'm not sure why, but I didn't want him this time. I wanted to try to handle my problems on my own, or maybe I wanted to wallow in my bad mood and I feared Cola would make me feel too good. He did so effortlessly. Always made me forget my problems, but never helped me deal with them. Then, after a date with him I'd wake up to the same problems. I guess that's how Cola became my best friend.

Drip, drip. Water drummed from the bathroom. No matter how hard I tried, I couldn't get the sink to completely turn off. So I learned to deal with the sound and turn it into something peaceful and soothing.

Kind of like what I had become.

I turned to my side and stared out the window. Orange lights flickered by my window, almost to the beat of the dripping water. Summer air, I could smell it even with the windows closed. Crickets talked, adding to the tempo of the drips.

Reminded me of the night Daddy kissed me before he died.

He cupped my face in his hands, looked me right in the eyes and said, "I love you, princess. Don't you forget it."

I smiled as he kissed my cheek and patted my head. He got into his car that sweaty August day and blew me one last kiss.

I didn't know a drunk driver would take Daddy's life twenty minutes later. If so I would've kissed him a thousand times and told him even more times how much I loved him. Instead, I smiled and selfishly soaked in his love.

Years afterward, I wondered if Kenny Eckhart knew he'd ripped a daddy from a four-year-old little girl. I still had his address, still wanted to write him and tell him he took Daddy from me, but I figured he knew and didn't care, otherwise he would've looked at me the day we went to court.

The orange lights, the buzzing air conditioner, the dripping water, all of it hushed me into a daze.

I could barely keep my eyes open. When I saw Daddy's face on the backs of my eyelids I begged sleep to take me away and never let me wake up.

Chapter 19 *Ally*

After Jessie and I had no more words for each other we went to bed, and in the middle of the night I woke up to a ghastly snore resonating from his mouth. I peered over his body and squinted my eyes. Only one in the morning.

Rolling to my side, I tugged the covers up to my chin and sniffed. Something touched my shoulder.

"You okay?" Jessie.

I picked up his hand and placed it on his chest.

So tired of marriage, so tired of the way I felt when I looked at him. Part of me longed for the past, the other part of me longed for a future without him. Yet, in some cleft of my heart I wanted to be with him.

But I felt so inadequate. Always comparing myself to her—the woman on his computer screen, the woman I saw jogging. I couldn't even undress around him without thinking of every flaw on my body. I locked the door when I showered to make sure he wouldn't catch a glimpse of me. My security and confidence vanished the day I discovered his secret and I hated the way it made me go crazy.

He touched my shoulder again.

Only a few weeks ago I would've been nuzzled into his chest, wetting his shirt as I told him the truth about Dad. Funny, the man I thought to be unfaithful turned out to be faithful, and the man I imagined would never betray me broke me to pieces.

Life can be so different when you're not living in lies.

Jessie snored again. I wished I had his ability to fall asleep within two seconds.

I should've caught his lies. Being a counselor, I should've seen it coming.

I tugged the covers, hoping to wake him. He stopped snoring and rolled toward me.

"Hey," he whispered.

I twisted my wedding ring. Bono's face flashed in my mind. Jessie's glistening eyes watched me as I strained my heart and looked at him. The lyrics of *With or Without You* rang in my head.

"What are you thinking?" Jessie said.

A laugh almost escaped my lips, but instead came out as a huff. "Nothing," I said. "Just song lyrics in my head."

"Which one?"

"With or Without You."

Jessie turned over on his back. I listened to the sound of his breath, wondering if I'd ever want to make love again.

"So," he said. "You can't live without me?"

"I don't know."

"Ally, I love you. I might have issues sometimes, but I still love you, always have."

"What about faithfulness?"

"I messed up."

I closed my eyes. Raindrops tapped the window, dampening the mood and arousing the silence. Jessie rolled over. Sadness rose from his breath. My eyes glazed over. Memories flashed in my mind like fireflies.

I looked at the ceiling again. Jessie's breathing heavied. I closed my stinging eyes and hoped for rest, unhindered rest. No nightmares, no endless thoughts tiring my heart and wrestling my mind until dawn, no dreams of what ifs, no more bitter droplets on my pillow. Rest, just rest.

Too awake to sleep, too tired to move, I stared at the ceiling and listened to Jessie's rhythmic snore, wondering if he dreamt about some other woman as I watched shadows dance across the walls. So juvenile, Ally, I told myself. But I still wondered.

His snoring matched the tempo of the rain.

And I wondered.

THE EIGHT-LETTER WORD BURNED MY HEART AS I ROLLED
over to an empty bed the next morning. Marriage. I told myself all kinds of
things, like, "If I would've known this before he put that ring on my finger
I would had never said yes." And then I thought of Sean again.

I shouldn't have gotten married so fast, I thought.

Sean and I knew each other inside and out. Best friends for seven
years. He wouldn't have treated me this way. He would've protected me.
He would've been faithful his entire life. I should've listened to him when
he told me Jessie was a hoax. But alas, I followed a whirlwind of emotions,
never consulting my mind.

I got out of bed and heard something downstairs. It sounded like Jessie
was still home, but I thought he had a meeting. I stopped and listened.

Click, click.

My stomach sank to my knees, but I kept walking down the stairs.
When I reached the middle of the steps Jessie clicked a screen away, turned
to me, and stumbled over words. My face, I'm sure, said it all. I turned and
ran upstairs and into our bedroom.

He didn't follow.

And that made my anger rise to heights I never imagined.

I locked the door, raided everything in the closet and shoved clumps of
clothes into a duffel bag. When I reached for my shoes I heard the garage
door open. I flew to the window and sure enough, Jessie's car backed down
the driveway and onto the street.

Broken, I couldn't move, not even an inch. Forget the clothes, forget
running away, he already did it for me. I dropped to my knees.

An hour swept by and my tears never dried up. Jessie never came home.
And I couldn't have been more confused. Alone, I wept, longing for Sean
to rescue me and help me live happily every after. Longing for anything,
anything but my stifling wedding vows.

The phone rang.

Chapter 20 *Taylor*

Dreams of Daddy vanished when I opened my eyes and saw Andy hovering over my bed.

"You look so beautiful when you sleep," he said. "Like an angel."

I almost asked how he got into my apartment, but then I remembered he had a spare key since I moved in. Just in case, he'd always say. I guess this was a *just in case* kind of moment.

"I want to take you out to breakfast." He stroked my hair.

"What for?"

"Does a guy need a reason to take his girlfriend out to breakfast?"

"Girlfriend?"

"Isn't that what you are?"

"Well, I figured, but you never said it in such an official way before."

"Well, girlfriend, get ready to go out for breakfast. I'll wait in the living room."

In such good spirits today, huh? I thought. I kinda liked the way it sounded. Girlfriend. No one ever called me that in my life. The same secure feeling you get when strapping on a seat belt, that's kinda the way I felt when he called me his girlfriend. Secure, no matter how bumpy the ride.

I took a shower, painted, curled, primped, and hair sprayed myself super fast, then met Andy in the living room of my apartment.

He held out his hand.

I took it.

I started to walk to the front door, but he stopped and pulled me toward him. After a long kiss, he cradled my head in his hands, like Daddy.

"You are mine," he said with gentle creases around his eyes, then pulled a tiny scarlet box from his pocket. "This is for you." He held out the box. I feared the contents. I wasn't ready for marriage, not yet, not now. He extended his arm so the box almost touched my stomach. "Open it."

Trying to smile, I opened the box and an enormous pink stone winked at me.

"I just wanted to show you how much I care." He pulled the ring from its temporary home and placed it on my right hand ring finger.

Amazed at its sparkling beauty and relieved that it wasn't on my left hand, I laughed. "Thanks, Andy. It's so pretty."

His chin raised a few inches, making him appear taller. I slipped my hand into his and we walked into the stairwell.

The second we opened the door to leave the apartment complex, his hand left mine. As usual. He never held my hand in public, never acted like he loved me in public. I thought the girlfriend thing would change that, or maybe the ring on my finger, but no. He turned into businessman and turned off the romance.

I'm not good enough to be seen with, not pretty enough, I kept telling myself. Maybe if I got breast implants, maybe then he'd love me in public.

He turned up the music, wound the windows down, and drove me to Bob Evans while I told myself I'd do it. I'd do anything to be perfect, to be beautiful and "complete" as Andy said so many times before.

Finally, I decided to get breast implants.

For the sake of completion.

Chapter 21 *Ally*

I let the phone ring a few times, so Jessie wouldn't think I wanted to talk
to him. Meanwhile I sniffed my crying away and dried my eyes.
On the fifth ring I answered the phone.

"May I speak with Allyson, please?" the voice said.

I paused, nearly wilting to the floor again. Jessie didn't call.

"Hello?" The stranger's voice said again.

"If you're trying to sell something, I'm not interested."

"Wait, wait, I'm not trying to sell something." He paused. "Ally, this is
D—" His voice broke and trailed off. "This is Edward Kay, your, your—"

Edward Kay? The name spun through my head a few times before it
finally sunk in. "I know who you are."

"Can I meet with you for lunch?"

I didn't know how to talk to him, what to say, what he knew. "Sure.
Where? When?"

"Are you free tomorrow?"

"Well, tomorrow is Sunday and I have a bunch of things to do at
church, but maybe Monday?"

"That sounds good."

On second thought, I didn't really want to go to church or lead a bible
study. "Actually, I may be able to do tomorrow."

"No, no. You go on to church. I'll see you Monday around sunset or so.
We'll meet after dinner instead. How about we meet at the park?"

"Which one?"

"You'll know." I thought I heard him sniffle.

We hung up and I remembered the little park in Baltimore. Double
Rock Park. I remembered splashing in the creek, catching minnows and

crayfish, hopping rocks and eating ice cream at the picnic tables. Dad took me there every Saturday for our "Daddy, daughter date."

I smiled.

What would I say to him after all these years of hating him?

I couldn't imagine Monday, but I really, really wanted it to come.

I finally set the phone down, wondering if I'd call him Dad. What an awkward situation.

I sat on the bed, tired from the emotional concoction the day stewed, and heard the garage door open.

Just when I felt okay about Jessie being gone, he came back.

Chapter 22 *Taylor*

Andy looked at me over scrambled eggs, toast, sausage, bacon, and orange juice.

"If you think it's good for me," I said. "I'd like to get the implants now."

"Good for you?" He laughed. "It'll make you a ten. Well," he picked a sausage link up with his index finger and thumb, took a bite, and continued, "there is one other thing."

My heart picked up a few paces or skipped a few beats, I couldn't tell.

"You should probably have your teeth whitened, get some hair extensions to about here"—he motioned to his elbow—"and I was thinking we could get you some Pilate videos to tone up your stomach muscles."

Um, so much for one other thing.

"But we'll do all that after the breast implants, that's the most important." He took another bite of sausage.

He tossed around those words like nothing while he chomped on a greasy link of cooked pig.

I raised my fork to take a bite of my eggs, but Andy gently pushed my hand down.

"It's time you start eating better. I don't want to see you get fat on me." He laughed, shoving another forkful of fat in his mouth.

I placed my fork on top of my plate and folded my hands in my lap. As I leaned back in my chair I watched Andy. Forkful after forkful, he ate. Forkful after forkful, I watched. And all I could think about was Daddy.

I didn't believe in prayers. And I didn't believe people went somewhere when they died. I figured they closed their eyes and said goodbye forever. Nothing next. No reincarnation. No heaven. No hell. Just darkness.

But I talked to Daddy that day, making myself believe that somehow, somewhere he heard me.

As Andy signed the check I ended my conversation with Daddy.

"If you could, Daddy," I said in my head. "Please, please rescue me. I don't know how to get out. One minute I love it, the next I hate everything about my life and all that I've become."

Andy smiled and nodded for me to get up and follow him to the car. I knew what was next. I knew why he didn't want me to eat. He wanted me to be ready for my next great film. My next great chance to become a star. Except it'd been weeks and no sign of stardom had shown up yet.

Oh, well.

I stood and followed Andy.

Time to pretend again.

Chapter 23 *Ally*

Jessie never opened the bedroom door.

The numbers on the clock turned and turned until I heard the garage door open again, ten minutes later. I scrambled to the bedroom window.

There went Jessie's car. Again.

I ran to the phone and dialed his number.

Ring. Ring. Ring. Ring.

"Hello, you've reached?"

Click.

The sound of his voice could've just as well been the sound of a siren screeching in my ear. Annoying and painful.

That's it, I thought. I'm done.

I went into the bathroom, rinsed my face and reapplied makeup. Lots of makeup. I curled my hair a little, went back to the bedroom and slipped on my favorite silky dress, a great necklace and a set of blue sapphire earrings to match, and a pair of lacey heels.

Yes, I wanted to make an impression. I wanted to be noticed since my husband obviously didn't care.

On my way to my car I passed the dining room table and without thinking twice I took my rings off my finger and put them right in front of Jessie's usual chair. No note. No regrets. Nothing.

And I knew exactly where I needed to go.

I KNEW WHERE SEAN WORKED SO IT WASN'T DIFFICULT TO find him. Still not married or tied down, he worked late nights at Recher

Theatre in Towson.

I parked my car in the nearby Barnes & Noble parking lot. Yes, there's pretty much a Barnes & Noble everywhere in Maryland.

Chin up, shoulders back, feeling the best I'd felt in days, I walked down Towson streets until I reached Recher Theatre. Unable to go in, I meandered outside for a while. Maybe Sean would come out and see me. Yet, I feared what would happen if he did.

I slinked down and sat against the wall of the theatre. Don't be mistaken by the name, it's mostly a music venue. Sometimes comedians show up, but mostly bands. People walked by me. Happy couples. Not-so-happy singles. Hands linked. Hands in pockets. I analyzed the love around me, remembering Sean, remembering Jessie before all of this.

Sean walked through the doors.

Thump. Thump.

My heart, my hands, my neck, everything throbbed. Everything rocked inside of me. My world was turning upside down and I didn't know if I wanted to stop it.

Smiling brighter than ever, Sean reached his arms out and I hesitantly walked into his embrace. Images from high school brushed through my mind as his hand touched my back. The smell of his cologne, still the same, took me back to nights of stargazing on the roof of his car. Happiness, I thought. I was happy then.

"So, how've you been?" he said. "It's been so long."

"I'm doing great."

Sean didn't shy away from my eyes. He looked right into them. I thought for sure he saw through my mask, but he didn't say anything. He just smiled, ran a hand over his shorter than short hair, and led me back to the bench.

Butterflies invaded my insides, but they didn't feel the same as the night I met Jessie. They felt like an invasion, pure and simple. But I tossed the truth aside and told myself to sit next to Sean.

He sat a few feet away from me and took my hand.

"No rings," he said, still holding my hand.

"Separation."

"I'm sorry." He shook his head. "What happened?"

"Not worth talking about."

He inched closer to me.

My insides shivered.

And closer.

From my toes to my cheeks, my body heated. *What am I doing?* ran through my mind a few times, but I ignored it. My husband doesn't care, I told myself. He doesn't want me. Doesn't love me. I'm not good enough.

Not.

Good.

Enough.

Sean's hand touched my knee. His other arm wrapped around my shoulders and pulled me into his chest. "Whatever he did or said isn't right, Allyson. You are beautiful. Inside and out. You deserved better."

Honey, sweet, sweet, honey to my broken heart. I couldn't help but notice, though, the d on the end of deserve. Jessie was becoming my past.

And I didn't like it.

But I wanted to feel loved and Sean could provide that. He thought I was the most beautiful woman in the world from the day I met him. Probably still did.

To be sure, I asked.

He smiled. A serious, joy-worn smile. "Allyson, you shouldn't need to ask that question."

"But I am asking," I said. "Do you think I'm beautiful?"

"The most beautiful."

"More beautiful than a blonde?"

"Who needs to ask that? You define beauty, anything else is nowhere near the kind of beauty you are. Look at you." He waved his hand up and down in front of me. "You're perfect."

Dripping, sweet sugar to my ears.

His cotton candy words seeped into my heart. Maybe I did marry the wrong person, I thought. People tried to warn me. Jessie's own father tried to warn me.

A car beeped.

Sean and I jumped, then laughed and laughed until his face ended up two inches from mine.

With only thick summer air between us, his lips begged me to come closer.

You're perfect.

My eyelids closed.

In the silence of a split second, I pictured Jessie's face. I pictured our wedding vows, our appointments with fertility specialists, our first arguments and makeup nights, our spontaneous road trips. Like flashes of memories at the close of life, my marriage flashed before its end.

And Sean's breath warmed my face.

Chapter 24 *Taylor*

After a few hours of being Sadie, I left Andy's house with another $800 and a yearning for Cola. My insides, down there, burned so bad I could hardly walk. If I didn't know any better, I'd had said my bladder was about to fall out of my body along with everything else.

When I got home that day, I turned on the television, grabbed Cola, and primed a line to snort away my problems. Before I gave in, I noticed a lingerie ad on television. I thought of the fame Andy promised me.

Glancing down at Cola, I pictured Daddy. I wondered if somehow he could see me, and if so, what he thought of Sadie.

A tear rolled down my cheek and soaked into the powdery white line.

I cupped my head in my hands and pulled my hair until more tears watered my eyes.

No one loves me, I said inside. Daddy, I wish you didn't leave me here. All Mom's boyfriends touching me, now this. None of this would've happened if you were still with me.

I pictured Mom's first boyfriend after Daddy died. The way he smelled sour, like beer and sweat. The way he swaggered into my bedroom at night and made me do things no little kid should be forced to do.

Now, I wanted to die. No part of me wanted to live. I had nothing to live for. Nothing except Andy and porn, and a second life that ripped my insides from my cervix to my heart. No one loved me. No one ever would.

I know what to do, I thought.

I hurried to the dining room and pulled my cell phone from my purse. I searched for Gianna's number and called.

Two rings and she picked up.

"Look who it is," she said.

"Hey, I need to talk to someone, can I come over?"

"Why not? I just got off work. What time will you be here?"

Ugh, work. The word tormented me.

I wrote down directions to her $3,000 a month apartment in Canton and hung up the phone.

Within ten minutes I headed south on I-95. If only I knew just how south I was really headed.

GIANNA WELCOMED ME WITH A HUG AND IMMEDIATELY handed me a joint. I shook my head.

She smirked and walked away. "Close the door, would ya?"

I shut the door and followed her into the living room. Her apartment seemed so feminine and dainty, like a classy young businesswoman lived there. White couches, silk rose petals on the glass coffee table, no television, shelves of books—you would never guess a porn star lived there.

"So, what's going on? Need some tips or something?" She sat on the couch and pulled her knees to her chest.

I sat across from her on the loveseat. "Um, actually I want to ask you a question."

She smiled. Or tried to.

"Do you ever want to stop doing this stuff?" I said.

She sunk into the couch, cross-legged, and inhaled more pot. "By this stuff, do you mean pot?"

"Porn."

"Well, you know, I like to think of it as adult entertainment. I'm an ac-tress, not a porn star. And no, I don't ever want to stop. Sometimes I did in the beginning, but"—she held up the joint—"this gets me through it. And I need the money. Bad."

"Yeah." I thought of Cola.

"I've learned to think of it as destiny."

Destiny?

"It's art, you know."

I nodded without looking up, hoping for a tiny piece of encouragement somewhere under her words.

"What?"

I looked up, half-smiled.

"Well, it may not be *Forrest Gump* or anything, but some of it can be very creative and fun. Very beautiful."

There's no way she experienced the same thing I did—the ripping and bleeding, the laxatives and bruises. Beautiful was not in porn's dictionary, at least not in mine.

"Look, just think of it this way, you are helping tons of marriages and families."

"I am?"

"Of course you are. Think of all the marriages that use adult entertainment to spice up their lives. That's gotta count for something, right?" She swept her long hair behind her ear.

I touched the sofa. "Is this silk?"

"Oh yeah, everything I own is silk. Well, like, almost everything."

She stood and walked into the kitchen, strutting as if her living room turned into a runway when I blinked. I looked over my shoulder as she rummaged through a cabinet and snatched a bag of Cooler Ranch Doritos.

She popped the top of the bag open and walked back into the living room. "Want some?" She held the bag toward me.

"No, thanks."

"Munchies." She laughed and handed me the last of the joint in her hand.

Why not? Wash away the bad dreams and imagine a better life for a little while.

Within an hour we were both high, hungry, and laughing about how wonderful the porn industry was and how we'd soon be stars together. Gianna and Sadie. The best of the best. They'd never find someone better. Ever.

We lounged.

We laughed.

And we lied.

We were so good at it.

Chapter 25 *Ally*

Sean's lips, inches from mine, assaulted my marriage. And I let them. Eyes closed, I waited for him to kiss me.

"Ally?" A familiar voice said.

I jerked away from Sean's face and looked in front of me. Tim licked his lips. I knew he couldn't wait to tell Verity what he saw. I looked back at Sean. He looked at me, then Tim.

"Do you know this guy?" Sean said.

I nodded and said to Tim, "It's not what you think."

"Right," he said, and walked away.

Of all people, of all times.

I stood and literally ran from Sean's perplexed gaze. Must've been quite a sight to the college students walking around Towson. But I had to catch Tim before he called Verity, before he told Jessie.

I caught up to Tim in front of Barnes & Noble.

"Look, I'm not going to tell Jessie." He stopped walking and looked at me. "That's for you to do, if you think it's important enough."

"I know what you're getting at, but this isn't what you think."

"Okay, whatever. Your life, your problems. But I don't feel sorry for you, not at all."

I walked away and called Verity. No answer.

Tim crossed the street and walked toward the parking lot. My heart climbed higher in my chest with every step he took. Please, don't tell Jessie, I said to him in my head over and over.

I still cared about my marriage, about Jessie. Maybe Tim saved me from making a mistake I didn't need to make.

I went home and thought of how I could make everything better, how

I could be the wife Jessie needed.

Within a half hour of thinking, I came up with a list.

Dye my hair blonde. Buy lingerie. Cook a romantic dinner. Be around more. Stop being so irritable around my time of the month. Have sex like the kind I saw in the movies he liked.

I realized I needed to work harder to be the wife he wanted. Then I'd feel the way Sean made me feel—wanted and beautiful. I figured I didn't try hard enough in the past. People needed to change sometimes to be the right person for their spouse. I told my client's that all the time. And it's true. Sometimes we have to sacrifice parts of ourselves for another person.

So, I convinced myself that's what I needed to do, no matter how wrong I felt about making myself into a porn star.

THE NEXT DAY I SKIPPED CHURCH AND WENT TO THE salon, telling myself that my marriage was more important. $193.26 later I climbed on top of the world and enjoyed the view.

When I got into my car I pulled the visor down and admired myself. I never, ever thought I'd look right as a blonde, but did I ever! Not to mention the beautiful hairstyle. I never had layers before, never bothered with my curly mess. Nothing could tame my hair. But now I had straight, blonde, silky hair and I looked exactly like the models Jessie liked.

On the way home I saw a tanning salon and didn't think twice. I parked my car and went inside. After signing up I sat down in the waiting area and smiled at the young girls in the room. Trying not to blush, I picked up People magazine and drowned myself in celebrity gossip.

Every now and then I'd look up at the girls around me and say to myself, "What are you doing here? You don't belong here."

But I convinced myself that I did belong there and so did the young girls around me. We had a right to feel good about ourselves, especially in a world that pushes this kind of stuff. I needed to be beautiful like Jessie wanted in order to fix my marriage. Change, that's what needed to happen to make my marriage thrive again.

I admired the fashion trends of famous actresses and took mental notes so I knew what to buy.

"Allyson, you can go in now."

I stood, tiny eye goggles in my hand, lotion in the other.

SEXINESS. THAT'S WHAT I COVETED. CONVICTION AFTER conviction tried to stop me. This isn't right. You're being immodest. Sexiness isn't beauty. This should only be exposed for your husband. You're turning your back on God.

I didn't listen. If I needed to turn my back on God to fix my marriage, then so be it. Plus, maybe the convictions weren't convictions. Maybe they were signs of legalism in my heart.

Are you sure you're trying to fix your marriage and not your selfish desire to be the most beautiful woman in the world?

The question stabbed me, but I ignored it along with everything else. Following Jesus under those circumstances would only worsen things. And I didn't know what Jesus would do anyway, it's not like He had to worry about being beautiful to His husband. I needed to believe in myself on this one.

So, believing in myself I went as I signed on to an online lingerie shop and searched for things Jessie liked on those other women.

But something happened.

With each skimpy garment of lingerie I saw, I also saw a half-naked woman posing in it. And every time I clicked on a new picture I analyzed her body, up and down, even using the zoom in tool to look closer. I know, I know, insane, crazy—I hated myself for being so insecure, but I couldn't help it.

My shoulders wilted.

My heart stopped racing with excitement and thudded with jealousy.

With every girl, every click, I sunk further into myself. My eyes glazed over as I compared myself to the models on the screen. They're airbrushed, I told myself, striving and striving and striving for a beauty that would be defied by age.

Well, they do make age-defying creams, I thought and then slouched into my chair even more.

Why, God? Why couldn't you have made me to be what he wanted? Why'd you do this to me?

"The first time you cry out to God in months and this is what you say?" I reamed myself. "You're not good enough to talk to God. You're not good enough for anyone."

I never knew words silently glued together in my head could form mallets and pound my soul to death. Until then.

Discouraged with no one but half-naked models staring at me, I did the only thing I thought would make me feel better.

I bought $482 worth of lingerie online and then cried alone in bed, wondering where Jessie went and if he'd ever come back so I could actually use the $695.25 makeover I bought.

When I remembered my meeting with Dad tomorrow I calmed my crying and watched the clock.

No matter how many sheep I counted, I couldn't sleep.

Chapter 26 *Taylor*

Gianna and I became best friends. We did movies together. Hung out on off time. And even shared Andy. We joked and told everyone we were Siamese twins. After she introduced me to LSD I actually hallucinated that we were joined at the hip and even tried to cut her off my body with a kitchen knife.

Not a good night.

But for the most part, life seemed better with her attached to me. Someone understood. Someone cared. Someone needed me as much as I needed her. We sorta used each other like drugs, to get by, to forget how much we hated "work," even though Gianna would never admit that. She prided herself (and me) as the best adult entertainment actresses to ever exist. She assured me that one day we'd stop doing adult movies and become real movie stars.

I sunk into her fantasyland. It sounded so appealing, so much better than reality. So, together we lived in a make-believe world as reality tore us to pieces.

Literally.

"YOU COMING?" GIANNA LOOKED AT ME FROM ANDY'S front door after another long night.

I couldn't resist her mischievous smile, but Andy grabbed my arm.

"I need you to stay here tonight," he said.

"But?"

He squeezed my arm tighter and I knew what he meant. Shut up and listen or I'll turn you black and blue until you pass out. I learned my lesson last time. Better to shut up and listen than to try to get my way.

I tilted my head and gave Gianna the look. She knew what it meant. Every now and then Andy would have a bad day and make one of us stay behind while he forced us to do whatever he asked.

Gianna waved goodbye.

The door closed behind her.

Andy smacked my face. "Don't you ever give me that look again."

Had too much vodka? I wanted to say, but shut up and listen seemed like a better idea.

Andy shoved me toward the steps. "Go upstairs and wait in my bedroom. I'll be up in a second."

Obeying, I trailed the steps and went into his bedroom. I sat on the bed and stared at the blank white walls, wondering what happened to my childhood dream. When life felt like a blank wall that anything could be painted on. Now, someone else painted the wall black for me and I could only sit back and watch.

Andy entered the room with fire in his eyes.

He shoved me on the bed and pulled a gun from his pocket. The cold barrel pressed into my cheek.

"Listen to every word I say or I'll pull this trigger."

Paralyzed, I waited for his orders. I never saw him use a gun before. But when Andy did drugs, watch out! I never knew what to expect. He hadn't had sex with me yet—maybe afraid of Chlamydia or whatever—but I thought for sure he'd try to now.

Without turning around, Andy looked at me and said, "Come in, guys."

I watched the bedroom door open. Two white guys and a black guy walked in, wasted, with the same smell and swagger as Mom's boyfriends. Laughing and acting stupid, they called me names I only heard when I filmed movies. My insides tied themselves into knots. My body tensed. And I wanted, so badly wanted, Cola, but I'd have to get through this one alone.

Andy waved the gun in front of my face and whispered, "Loosen up."

For the next two hours he gave orders, turning me into an object once again. While tossed around, beaten, strangled, and forced to have sex with men I never met before, I stared at white walls. I tried to block out the pain, both inside and out.

But it stung and ached every time I breathed.

I tried to hold my breath.

I thought he loved me. I thought he wanted to be with me forever. To take care of me. Help me become someone special.

But the gun against my flesh told me otherwise.

I wanted to curl up in a ball. But I couldn't. Andy made sure I couldn't. So the rest of the night shredded every last piece of the girl I used to be. Sadie laughed and had fun being abused while Taylor vanished behind the fun, curled up inside, and watched white walls until they turned black.

I WOKE UP IN ANDY'S BATHROOM ACHING FROM HEAD-to-toe. I glanced around the room and noticed dried blood painted on my legs and hands. I couldn't part my feet, couldn't separate my hands, which I realized were tied together and roped around the back of the toilet.

Sadie laughed.

Taylor died in that moment, while Sadie laughed again, an icy, liberating, unruly laugh.

Andy opened the bathroom door. "What is going on in here?"

I laughed.

"I'm serious, Taylor. You're not allowed to leave this house until you show me that I can trust you."

"Stop calling me, Taylor."

"I'm not calling you girlfriend. Not unless you prove you are worthy of the title."

"I didn't mean that." I rolled my eyes. "My name is Sadie."

"Right. Well, Sadie, until I can trust you I'm watching every move you make." He turned to leave the bathroom. "Oh," he turned back to me, "don't roll your eyes at me."

He closed the door and I rolled my eyes.

"I'll be back in three hours," he said from behind the door. "You'll need to get ready for a video."

I looked at the blood on my knees and laughed.

I'll never understand the word star in porn star. Doesn't even make sense.

I laid my head on the tile floor and for the next few hours I dreamt of getting back at Andy.

Chapter 27 *Ally*

Jessie finally came home. He pulled into the garage the same time I pulled out to meet with Dad. Without looking at him, I drove off. Enough emotions clouded my vision because of Dad. I didn't need a heated conversation with Jessie. Besides, I didn't know how to tell him about Sean.

I drove down our street wondering why Jessie married me in the first place, but then stuffed my crinkled thoughts away and opted for better thoughts, like what Dad would smell like, what he'd look like, if he'd have the same gentle eyes and crooked smile.

For thirty-five minutes I pictured his face and carried conversations with him in my head while sweat covered my body. And I even blasted the air conditioner.

When I parked at Double Rock Park I scanned the parking lot and all the cars. No one. Strange for a summer day. I turned the car off and leaned forward to peer around a set of bushes, but saw only empty picnic tables. No one around except a family on the playground.

I watched the husband run up and down a slide with two toddlers, looked like twins. The wife, standing by with a pregnant belly, laughed with her hand over her mouth. Picture perfect. Even blonde.

"Why do you hate me so much, God? What did I do?" I said to the clouds.

I settled into my seat and stared at the family on the playground, wondering if I'd ever have kids, wondering if Mr. and Mrs. Perfect were living a lie too. Did her husband laugh with her and the kids all day and then slip down stairs while she slept to masturbate while drooling over images of other women?

Probably, I thought.

Probably made me feel better. I counseled enough married couples to realize that probably wasn't unrealistic.

I looked out the car window as a rusty car pulled up next to me.

Dad?

I turned away, pretending not to see. Pretending. Pretending. So much pretending. I never realized how much I pretended until now.

I looked back and didn't see him.

Guess it wasn't Dad anyway.

I wiped my hands on my skirt to dry the sweat, then turned back to the other car.

A man's face appeared at my window.

I jumped back and screamed, but no sound came from my mouth. With my hand over my heart I looked into the man's eyes. He smiled, a crooked smile that creased the gentle lines around his eyes.

Daddy.

My heart softened, but thumped louder and faster. I could do nothing but sit there and stare at him. Little Ally. I felt like little Ally again, waiting for Daddy to scoop me up and tell me he loved me, to tell me he never left, that my life wasn't a nightmare.

I looked down at my hands, clasped on my lap, then back to Dad. Watery eyes stared back at me. And he never looked away from my eyes no matter how many times my eyes darted across his face.

I looked at his hair, his face, his lips, his eyes—and I saw myself. He pointed to the door handle. I laughed and blinked a few times, then grabbed my purse and opened the door. He pointed to the ignition.

Oh, the keys.

The way I felt when Jessie and I met, all those butterflies—the good kind—came back. And made their presence well known.

I got out of the car and stood next to Dad. He looked the same, save a few gray hairs.

When I closed the door I stood and waited for him to say something.

He said nothing. Just smiled.

I repositioned my purse on my shoulder and looked at my toenails, then back up to his smile again. I wanted to breathe in and out, you know, like they make women on TV do for Lamaze classes, but I needed to make a good impression.

Dad took my hand.

So many thoughts played and paused in my mind. Everything from anger toward Mom to wondering if Dad thought I was pretty.

Thoughts passed, scene after scene, while I avoided Dad's gaze.

Then, shining in the rays of dusk-dyed light, I saw it.

A wedding ring on his left hand ring finger.

I looked into his eyes again. A tear rolled down his cheek and into the stubble on his jaw.

"Allyson, I'm sorry for all these years," he said, squeezing my hand.

Tears burned the backs of my eyes, but I held them in. "You have nothing to be sorry for."

He smiled and nodded.

I cupped his hand in both of mine, but I wanted to wrap my arms around his neck and never let go.

He looked behind him and cleared his throat. "Let's go sit down."

As I followed Dad I stared at the ring on his finger.

We walked in silence until we reached a picnic table. He sat down and I sat across from him. Still unable to meet his gaze, I looked down and pushed my cuticles back.

"You're wondering about my wife, aren't you?"

I looked up.

"I saw you looking at my ring." He seemed to speak softer than I remembered, like a sweet southern man with an exaggerated s and everything.

"Yeah."

He twisted it off his finger and handed it to me. "Look at the engraved words."

"No, no. I'm sorry for prying."

"Look." He held the ring in front of me. "It's okay."

I spun the ring in my fingers and read the words engraved on the ring. *Edward & Jeannie Forever.* Confused, I looked at him for an answer. He smiled and reached for the ring.

"Just because she signed the papers," he said, "doesn't mean I did."

I looked at him, maybe blinked a few times, replayed his words in my head, then handed him his ring.

"I made vows to your mother thirty-seven years ago. She can break them all she wants, but I don't plan to."

"You mean . . . what?"

"I love her, Allyson. That's never changed. Never will."

"But all she's done." I raised my voice. "This. She's lied, betrayed you, she's made a mess of my life. How can you possibly forgive her, much less still love her?"

Dad pointed to the clouds. "Because He forgave me."

I shook my head back and forth. Clouds were the last things I wanted to look at. None of this made sense. Yes, Jesus forgave us. I knew what Dad implied by that. Bible verses were engraved in my head like the names on Dad's ring. Forgive. Seventy times seven. Love is patient and kind. Yes, I knew all the verses that pointed toward selflessness, but Jesus wasn't a doormat!

God couldn't expect me to be faithful to Jess no matter how many times he betrayed me.

Dad put his wedding ring back on. I remembered taking off mine, wanting to give up, to move on, to find someone who treated me better.

How, I screamed inside, how could Dad still wear that ring?

Chapter 28 Taylor

A ndy untied me so I could do my hair and makeup and follow his rules. Thankfully the guy I was supposed to shoot a video with found out he had Gonorrhea and couldn't make it. Sounds bad to be thankful, but any reason was a good reason. Andy shot a few pictures for my Web site, slapped me around for not being sexy enough, then threw me back into his bathroom, tied me up, and rubbed his spit in my hair.

I closed my eyes as bitter saliva clung to my eyelashes and ran down my nose. So much for getting back at him.

Andy walked to the door. "You were horrible tonight."

He spit across the room. It landed on my foot.

"By the way, tomorrow you have an appointment to get breast implants." He stood in the doorway. "I'm not paying for it either. Not after the stunts you've been pulling. I'm taking the money out of your pay until it's paid in full."

I wanted to refuse him or ask him what kind of stunts I'd been pulling. Seriously, I had no idea. But I couldn't ask anything with a scarf stuffed in my mouth and wrapped around my head.

For hours I stared at the ceiling, wondering how I'd escape Andy before my breast implant surgery. Somehow I needed to tell someone and get out of his presence forever. Maybe fly to Canada for a few years until he found another girl he could ruin. Or, I could start over there. Not like anyone in Maryland cared about me anyway.

If only he tied the rope around my neck, I thought. Then I could just strangle myself to death. What's the point of living anyway? I bet I'd have an empty funeral. In fact, I'd probably be tossed in the ground without a casket.

A tear fell off my cheek.

And another.

And another.

I WOKE UP COVERED IN DRIED SPIT AND TEARS, SMELLING like I hadn't showered in months, feeling like I never showered in my life. Andy tugged at the ropes around my body until they were off. He pulled me up by my hair and untied the scarf in my mouth.

Blank and tired, I looked at the ground.

Andy pulled my chin up. "Look at me."

I did.

"All you have to do is listen." His voice, dry and crackly, boomed through the bathroom. "Listen and you will be a lot better off. That's all I ask."

So I listened as he gave me orders. I showered, he watched. I did my makeup, he watched. I put on my shoes, he watched. I got in the car, he watched.

Andy had one rule.

He watched.

Yep, that was the rule. Everything I did was in his view or I didn't do it.

I swear he must've been looking at me out of the corner of his eye while he drove. I contemplated jumping out of the car, but he put me in the backseat and the doors were child locked. A prisoner. A prisoner in a world I never imagined living in.

Andy turned the music up in the car. Elton John's voice calmed me. Norma Jean's name made me shiver. I listened, watching houses, buildings, stores, and trees pass by. She lived her life like a candle in the wind. Never knowing who to cling to when the rain poured down her cheeks. I imagined Marilyn Monroe in my head. White dress, pretty smile. Elton continued to serenade me. His sad words made sense. Too much sense. Loneliness. And even when she died all the papers had to say was that she was found naked.

The song continued, echoing deep in my heart. Never, never in a million years did I think I'd be able to relate to Marilyn Monroe.

Her name bounced off my mind.

From then on I decided to call her Norma and never look at her as the pretty woman in the white dress, but look at her and see something more, something underneath the surface that needed love and help.

I didn't want to end up like her.

More trees blurred by, like my life. I thought of Norma. If she actually wanted to be a sex object. Or if Elton was right. Maybe "they" crawled out of the woodwork and whispered lies in her ear, making her think being a sex object would be glamorous, devoid of pain.

Maybe the money and fame enticed her. Maybe she wanted to feel worthy of love. Maybe singing to Kennedy made her feel valuable. Starving for love, she'd do anything to fill her appetite. Except her choices ate a hole in her stomach, killing her off like AIDS. Inside, under all the glory, maybe her heart pawed for love, but instead was shoved aside and neglected while her smile and curves were adored.

They crawled out of the woodwork to starve a soul so they could feed thousands of hungry sexual appetites.

I wondered if Elton really did see Norma as more than sexual, more than just our Marilyn Monroe.

I wondered if someone saw me like that.

Andy parked the car.

I looked at the large brown building with glass windows. Nothing hospital-like about it. My foot shook so fast the car started to shake.

I looked down and inhaled. Andy got out of the car and walked over to my window. He motioned toward the building, but I didn't see anyone in the windows.

He opened my door and reached for my hand. I pulled away, hoping I'd be left alone with the doctor long enough to spill my story and run away.

Andy forced me to hold his hand and led me inside. Funny, he actually held my hand in public. What an occasion.

The office smelled like rubber gloves and citrus air fresheners. I looked around at empty chairs, then up at the TV mounted on the wall.

I expected a hospital, rules, regulations, stuff like that. I guess I hoped to hide and escape like Leonardo DiCaprio in *Catch Me If You Can*.

Andy made me sit down while he whispered to the girl at the front desk.

I tried to listen, wondering if he tried to crawl out of rotted wood and lie to her too. Make another Marilyn out of her.

After whispers and giggles, he sat down beside me. I picked up a magazine and thumbed through pages. Andy watched TV. I crossed my legs and looked at the celebrities printed on magazine pages, wondering why I ever wanted fame. Being followed, chased, obsessed over?it didn't seem that nice after all.

Andy grabbed my knee. "Stop shaking your foot. It's annoying and childish."

I stopped my foot and continued looking at glossy photos, analyzing bodies, hairstyles, faces that would never be mine, could never be mine, no matter how many surgeries Andy made me endure.

A door opened.

"Sadie," a man said.

I looked up, shaking from my teeth to my foot.

Andy nodded to the man and looked at me. "Ready?"

Chapter 29 *Ally*

D ad and I stopped talking about Mom after my voice rose along with my blood pressure. He steered the conversation toward the little memories we shared. There weren't many, but we remembered all we could until silence broke through our words and left us alone in the stuffy July night.

We stared at each other for a few minutes. Dad's eyes glistened. I looked passed him at the lightening bugs.

"Let's go," he said, standing. "We can do this again sometime soon."

He walked me to my car and hugged me.

I wish I could say it was a magical, happy-ending kind of hug. But it wasn't. Awkward, loose, and quick. We hugged and parted ways.

I'm not sure what I expected, but that wasn't it.

I PULLED INTO THE GARAGE AT HOME AND SAW JESSIE'S car. Opened the door and saw his face, disheveled and unshaven.

Avoiding his eyes, I walked around him. He turned and touched my arm. I glanced at my wedding rings on the dining room table. Thoughts of Dad's faithfulness made my empty stomach churn. I didn't want to put them back on.

Jessie sniffed. "Allyson."

I looked at him, back to the rings, then walked past them both. And I sighed, longing for the day when I wouldn't want to walk by the present anymore.

Jessie wiped his eyes and picked up my rings.

Ignoring him, I went to our bedroom and saw a grey plastic bag on the bed with a note on top. For a few seconds I stared from the doorway, trying to figure out what I ordered. Quietly, I walked to the bed and picked up the note.

To my wife, the only one I've ever loved – You don't need this, send it back. You are perfect the way you are. Your husband, Jessie

The name of the company on the bag caught my eye. I sighed. If Jessie didn't think I needed lingerie then he would have kept his eyes on me all those years, instead of those women in lingerie.

He walked into the doorway.

I watched him. He watched me. Somewhere inside I wanted to run up and forgive, truly forgive, and make everything better. Somewhere underneath my desire to scream at him I still wanted his hands to caress my face and tell me everything would be okay. But forgiveness Band-Aids wouldn't work in this case. The wound cut too far into me. So far I wondered if it'd ever stop bleeding.

Jessie put his hand on the doorknob and looked down. I folded his note in my hands. His neatly marked words disappeared behind paper. I thought of my marriage. My neatly marked marriage, disappearing behind this crazy reality.

I wanted to say something to Jess. But the betrayal, the other women, the anger and sadness, all of it stacked in front of my forgiveness like solid bricks. Unbreakable, towering, solid bricks.

Too much pride stood on my side of the wall. I knew that. I did. But I didn't care. Humility seemed so far from reach, so pointless, that I couldn't bring myself to think about it, much less ask God for it. Especially after what Jessie did.

Before his downfall, a man's heart is proud, but humility comes before honor.

Jessie took a step. I looked up. He dried his tears on his sleeve. Silence climbed higher, clogging our marriage like thick fog.

I don't even know what humility means right now, God. I can forgive, but I will never be able to forget this. And I can't live with this pain.

"I have a problem. I'm sorry I brought you into this," Jessie plunged the silence. "Maybe you should've married Sean like he always said."

My eye twitched.

He looked up.

I looked down.

"Why should I take anything you say seriously after you ran off for days when I caught you salivating over porn again?" I said. "I mean, what were you thinking, Jess? Begging me to work through it, then looking at it again, so soon?"

"Didn't you get my note?" he said.

I shook my head.

"I came back that day and left a note on the kitchen counter for you saying I talked to Pastor Dave. That's where I went after you came downstairs. And I wasn't looking at porn. An ad popped up on the side of my screen and I lingered on it, but it startled me when you came downstairs. I knew you wouldn't believe that I didn't find it on purpose. Anyway, I went to see Pastor Dave and he told me about a men's retreat over the weekend. It was for addictions." He swung his arms. "So I went."

Ah, so this is the humility. Isn't it, God?

I analyzed my bare ring finger.

Trapped at the end of a dead end road with no way to turn back, I sat on the bed and looked at Jess, hoping he'd break through the walls around me and carry me to the other side, carry me to himself.

But he just stood there.

I pressed my fingers together and made a heart with my hands.

A heart.

All I ever wanted in life was to fall in love, be married, have children, and live a passionate romance unknown to the world. I wanted to prove that even through trials marriages could be beautiful, romantic, and conquering amidst a thousand enemies. But I didn't expect this trial. Porn was the last thing I expected. Lies, porn, adultery, more lies—it shouldn't have ended up this way.

"If I knew this," I thought aloud. "I wouldn't have gotten married."

Jessie's shoulders dropped. The orange glow from the streetlight underlined his lips and jaw and drew a delicate sparkle in his eyes. I traced his highlighted jaw with my eyes and squinted to hold back tears.

Sullen and droopy, Jessie's presence chased the light from the room, leaving us with that hollow, numbing silence when hope seems hopeless and marriages seem marriageless, leaving his eyes with no sparkle, only a shadow so alive it hid the whites of his eyes and everything else in the room.

He reached for the doorknob. My heart reached up from my chest, grabbed my throat, and shoved a heavy sob into the colorless room.

A streak of my steel blue cry saturated the room, but Jessie didn't care.

His hand hit the doorknob and my heart hit the floor.

"I hate this," I said between sobs.

I wanted him to stay.

The door closed, bouncing my cry back to me and twirling it around the empty room.

I fell back on the bed and cried to the ceiling, "Why Jessie? Why my Jessie?"

Chapter 30 *Taylor*

D r. McNear sat down at a table across from Andy and me. "No need to be scared," his words echoed in the fluorescent-lit room. "Andy has brought many of his girls"—his girls?—"to me in the past and I have taken good care of them all." He looked at Andy. "Haven't I, Andy?"

Andy nodded. "Of course you have, Len."

Interesting?a first name basis relationship.

"So, what cup size are we looking for this time?" Dr. McNear stared at my breasts, then my face. "She's a beautiful one, natural-looking too." His eyes gazed down again. "I'd recommend no bigger than a C-cup for her."

Andy put his hands on the doctor's desk and smiled. "A C-cup, huh? I was thinking D. I want her to be a ten and I think if she had those, man, the cash would pour in."

I couldn't stop shaking my foot. Escape seemed impossible. I should have known he knew the surgeon personally, just like he knew Dr. Majewski, who prescribed me "legal" drugs to get through scenes. And yeah, he was definitely aware of the situation.

Anything, anything at all to make more money. That's just how Andy was. All about money. Which is great because most men in the world fall for the little traps he plasters online. And porn keeps on keeping on. So does Andy.

"Okay," Andy interrupted my thoughts. "D it is."

Well. Glad I had a say.

Dr. McNear showed me some pictures, explained the procedure, but I didn't listen. I didn't care. And since when do you get implants the same day you choose your size? Creepy place.

Andy never left my side, even as the anesthesia blurred my vision and dulled their laughs. Even during the surgery, which I hoped I'd never wake from, Andy probably laughed alongside Dr. McNear.

I woke up to the two of them talking about someone named Bridget. I can't even describe the pain I felt, but I'll give it a shot.

My unwanted plastic implants were high on my chest, so high I couldn't see over them, and they were so tight I thought for sure I'd never be able to move my arms again. The nausea crept up slowly. Didn't notice it at first, but once my eyes adjusted to the light and Andy's laugh surged through my brain, gravity could've stopped and the spinning in my head could've kept Earth on track. Yeah, it was that bad.

"Looks like she's up," McNear said, clinking metal objects across the room.

"How soon till we can leave?" Andy said.

"Give her about an hour or so and it'll be fine," McNear said. "Here, take these. I know you are aware of these things, but I have to give them to you to keep myself out of trouble." Footsteps trailed away and stopped. "Throw them out if you want."

"You giving her pain pills or what?" Andy said, muffled by the sound of crinkling paper.

More footsteps. "Here." Paper ripped. "I'll put the prescription in your name. She may be in extreme pain for a few days since we went under the muscle, so you may want to use one of those. If not,"?another rip?"use one of these."

"How long until she can work again?"

"I'd say six weeks. You won't want them to look swollen for films anyway, it'll be too noticeable."

The more the anesthesia wore off the more I wanted to crawl into a hole and die. Imagine being sliced opened, pried apart, and sewn back together while being awake. That's how I felt. And I had a sick feeling those pills from McNear would rattle their way into Andy's mouth and never touch mine.

Chapter 31 *Ally*

Cars drove by, casting shadows on the bedroom ceiling as I remembered the day Jessie and I said *I always will* instead of *I do.*

Mom held my hand. We stood outside the wooden doors, waiting to walk down the aisle. Music stopped. The doors opened. And my stomach waltzed right up to my chest. I squeezed Mom's hand tighter as the violins slowly came to full resonance to the tune of Kenny G's *Going Home.*

Mom guided me down the aisle. I forgot I was walking, breathing, or even living.

So many faces smiled at me. Reality came back. I bit my lip and swallowed. Then I saw him. Hands clasped in front of him, he smiled sweetly. Nothing in the room existed when he smiled. I looked down. My dress shimmered and glided over white rose petals. Mom stopped. I stopped. The time had finally come. I closed my eyes, then looked at my soon-to-be husband.

Mom gave me away and Jessie took my hand. My eyes warmed, preparing to cry the most joyful tears they'd ever cry. And they did. So much that I can't remember any words or vows or anything else until Pastor Dave said, "I now pronounce you husband and wife. Jessie Graham, you may kiss your beautiful bride."

Our lips touched and I didn't mind the surveying audience.

That kiss was unlike any kiss we ever had and any other we ever will have. It stands on its own. Untouched and filled with so much promise, so much hope, but yet not an ounce of expectancy. It was the present. And it was the best present I ever had.

"And so," Jessie whispered. "Life begins."

MY TEARS SUBSIDED AS I WALLOWED IN MEMORIES AND stared into space.

Jessie opened the door and stood in the doorway. "Allyson, I love you. I'm tired of this space between us. It kills me." He stepped in the room. "I hate myself. I hate everything about myself for what I did to you."

He looked different from the man I married that day. More tired, more real. Old Jessie, I knew him. New Jessie was just that. New and unfamiliar. I didn't like unfamiliar. Too risky.

"Allyson, do you hear me?"

I looked up. Jessie stood in front of me, lips relaxed and lonely.

Hold me, Jess. Just hold me, I silently said to him, hoping he'd catch the ESP. I don't have the strength to tell you I need you.

He stood there as lifeless as my fried blonde hair.

A tear fell from my cheek to the bed—our bed—soaking into the same feathers that cushioned our love on our honeymoon.

Hold me, Jess.

He didn't hear me. He didn't know. And I couldn't tell him. I wasn't sure if I actually wanted him to or not.

I sat up.

His hand touched my cheek and stayed there.

I put my hand over his. "I don't know what to do."

He wiped my face and sat down. "Let me fix this, Ally. Let me try."

"Why did you do this to us?"

"I don't know why I'm so stupid." He put his hand on my knee. "I thought it would go away when I married you."

I wanted to ask him a million questions. Do you think I'm beautiful? Do you love me? Really, really love me? Do you think of other women when we're together? Do you stare at blondes when you're out for a walk? What do you see when I'm not around? Why do you want them? Why don't you want me instead?

But the more the questions piled up in the silence, the harder I cried. Jessie held me in his arms, a strange relief considering half of me wanted him as far away as possible. His affection brought shades of scarlet to the room, a shade I hadn't seen for some time.

His fingers danced on my face and played with my hair.

"I love you," he said.

I closed my eyes and leaned my forehead against his.

He placed one hand on my neck and the other on my hand, and then his lips, with delicate purpose, touched mine. A car swooshed by. And like a candle lit after being smothered for so long, I kissed him back, so eager to be illuminated, no matter how dim the light.

He moved closer and wrapped one arm around my hip. His other hand smoothed over my face. I leaned into him, cradling his neck as he kissed my shoulders, my neck, my cheek, sending chills to every part of me, but warming me all the same.

So many thoughts raced through my head. The images, the blondes, they pestered me, haunted me, tried to ruin our moment.

Jessie's index finger pressed against my lips, hushing my thoughts.

Okay. If anything, I'd pretend. I'd pretend none of this happened so I could make love to my husband, get over the past, and forgive even if I'd never forget.

He kissed me.

I let him.

His fingers traced my jaw, pulling my chin to his as he pressed his face against mine. Those fingers soothed me, they swept me away from reality for a few minutes, just a few minutes, as we kissed in the ribbons of moonlight shining from our bay window.

We kissed and touched and kissed some more.

Fireworks of every color burst in the room for the first time in weeks as we made love in the shadows of a summer night.

It would be romantic, perfect, and so Cinderella-like to say that the other women never showed up in my mind that night. But they did.

Sorry, but this is reality I'm sharing. And those women danced around my reality the entire night. Even in my dreams.

Chapter 32 *Taylor*

Unfortunately, I knew Andy too well. He never gave me a pain pill no matter how many times I screamed my bronchial tubes out in the bathroom. He did fling the door open once to say, "Shut up or I'll kill you," and cuss me out. Lovely, I know.

He also brought me stale bread and told me to drink water from the sink, which I couldn't get to until the third day after my surgery, but I did manage to pull myself into the bathtub to run cold water over my aching chest. I kept myself well hydrated by drinking water from the tub's faucet. Easier than pulling myself to a standing position, I guess.

So I stayed there, in the bathtub, cringing and twisting as I tried my hardest to endure the five-thousand bees stinging my chest. Every now and then I'd pass out from the pain. Or I'd throw up on myself and choke on the bile. But I never left the tub so I wouldn't have to move much if I needed a drink. Plus I liked being near ice water in case my watermelons needed a cool down.

The only time Andy gave me a Percocet was when he took me (a week later) to get my stitches removed. Guess he wanted me to be loopy so I didn't spill the truth. Like I would anyway. I bet McNear would've laughed and given Andy a high five.

No, thanks. I'd rather have kept silent and planned my escape for some other time. Some other time when Andy wouldn't be watching me.

On the way home from my check up Andy turned to me while we stopped at a red light. "Will I ever be able to trust you?"

I wanted to spit in his face. And maybe my eyes screamed so, because Andy looked back at the red light disgusted, rolling his eyes and shaking his head. There used to be a sparkle in his eyes. A promise of hope.

The light turned green. I looked at the door handle next to me, wishing it didn't have a child lock. An idea sparked. At the next red light I'd scream and pound the window until someone noticed and called 911.

Andy slowed at the next red light and came to a stop. His thumb drummed the steering wheel and his eyes never left the road. He looked too peaceful to be doing what he did to me.

He turned up the music.

Aerosmith.

Yeah, the same song as before.

Andy accelerated.

I couldn't help it. A tear sunk into the skin on my face, melting the last of my hope. Which wasn't much. Steven Tyler belted lyrics through the speakers. I didn't sing this time. And wasn't sure if I ever would again. Not to mention my implants. I could hardly move my lungs without feeling like my chest caught fire.

Andy stopped at another red light.

Tears coated my face like makeup. Through the blur I looked at the car beside us and saw hope. I blinked my eyes. No way. Maybe Daddy finally heard me. Maybe there was hope.

The cop beside us turned and looked at me. I looked up at zoned out Andy, then back to the cop. Here's my chance.

Chapter 33 *Ally*

After Jessie and I finished making fireworks, he held me as I snuggled on his chest. Like old times. Except the real old times weren't clouded by bad times, but that's fine, for some reason I thought maybe we'd make it through, maybe I'd trust him again.

"Thank you," Jessie said sweetening the silence with his love.

"For what?"

He picked up my arm and put it on his chest. "Want tickles?"

Tickles were our thing. Well, my thing. I don't know why but when Jess ran his fingers up and down my arm, no matter how bad the day, no matter how much I couldn't get to sleep, those tickles soothed me into some of the best nights of sleep I've ever had. They made me feel loved, safe. "Sure," I said, resting my hand on the pillow above his shoulder, my fingers caught in the tangles of his hair.

He tickled me and tickled me and tickled me. But no matter how many tickles, I couldn't fall asleep. And I couldn't stop thinking about his words. "Yes, she's more beautiful than you." I'd rather be haunted by Jacob Marley than those words. A thousand Jacob Marley's suffocating me in a room the size of my leg would be better, so much better, than the evocative frost of those words.

I shivered.

"You okay?" Jessie said.

I turned to my back and looked over at him.

"Can I ask you a question?" he said.

I nodded.

"Why didn't you marry Sean?"

Uh, what?

One word. Tim.

"I mean"—he rubbed this bridge of his nose, right between his eyes—"he always loved you, treated you so nice, and you chose me. Why did you choose me over him?"

I licked my lips, a hundred and fifty percent unsure of what to say. I didn't know the answer to that question. I never thought about it like that. But now, if Jess asked me, if he saw Sean's love for me too, then maybe I did marry the wrong person.

I took a deep breath, exhaled in a rush.

For so long I believed in soul-mates. You found the one person you were made for and married them. No exceptions. No mistakes. But now I wondered. Perhaps mistakes were possible. Perhaps you could choose someone and settle and in turn, miss out on your soul-mate, the best one for you.

"Are you okay?" Jessie asked.

I nodded, this time a no.

"What? Would you rather be with him?"

Inside some chamber of my heart I didn't know existed, my love for Jessie and the pain he caused fused together and swelled until my chest wall felt like it would burst open. I don't know how else to explain that feeling. My heart wanted to run away, to not feel everything inside. But for some reason running away hurt worse than working it out. And honestly, I hated that. "I don't know, Jess," I said. "I don't know what I want." I couldn't look at him, couldn't stand glassy eyes on a man who rarely cried. His sniffling, my pain, my confused desires, everything all at once pulverized my heart until my chest shook and tears rained down my face.

Jessie tried to hold me. I pushed away. He reached again. I pushed away, wanting him to hold me at the same time. He got on his knees in bed, crossed my arms around my chest and pulled me into him. Wriggling to flee his grip, I wet his t-shirt with my tears. He tugged me closer, his strength fighting my . . . my. . . .

My weakness.

My sobs battled my screams while my twisting and turning battled his love. I suppose I didn't want his love, as much as I needed it. His love terrified me, but it didn't scare me enough. Or maybe I was tired.

I collapsed into him and cried until my head shrieked in pain and my lungs begged me to stop. He held me the entire time, rubbing my back, kissing my head, sometimes crying with me.

As my eyes dried up and my lungs thanked me, I thought of Dad. So badly, so, so badly I wanted to tell Jess about Dad. Explain everything, tell him that it wasn't just his issues that were making me turn into a stranger, but also Mom's lie exposed.

A stranger to my own life. Or perhaps my life had become a stranger to me.

I wanted to cry again. Jessie's hand still stroked my hair, pulling damp pieces from my cheeks. I wiped my face, sunk into the bed, and pressed my face into the pillow.

Jessie cuddled into me. "You went to see him, didn't you?"

Chapter 34 *Taylor*

A drenaline ran through my veins and crawled into my hands. I pounded and pounded the window, screaming so loud I could've stopped the wind right in its tracks.

I didn't bother to look at Andy. My eyes fixed themselves on the cop until his eyes turned from wonder to concern. Then I turned to Andy. And his Freddy Kruger smile stopped my breath.

Oh, no. Daddy if you hear me, help.

Andy kept smiling. For the life of me I couldn't figure out why his face beamed, now, of all moments.

The cop tapped on the passenger window, right there in the middle of traffic.

Andy winded the window down.

Out of breath, I looked back and forth, from cop to Andy, Andy to cop, until the officer spoke. "What's going on, Andy?"

You have got to be kidding me, I said to myself, feeling like a melodramatic child.

I tried to stop the gush of tears, if anything to prevent the ache in my chest from getting worse. But I couldn't. I freaked out, screamed, "No," shook my body back and forth like a crazy person, wailed, "No," some more.

I "lost my beans" as Daddy used to say. For once, I could relate to the bulging-eyed man I sat with in the Psych Ward at GBMC when Mom brought me there after my first suicide attempt. A good girl. People always thought of me as the quiet, good girl. They didn't know how bad I wanted to die after Mom's boyfriends touched me. They didn't know I hid behind good grades and plastic smiles when everything about me felt dirty, like now. No safe place, no clean place, just filth and lies and bruises, and I couldn't take it anymore.

Every man except Daddy only wanted me for my body. There were tons of bodies in the world; I didn't understand what was so special about mine.

Andy explained away my problems. Explained my drug problem, my overdose (which never happened) on painkillers after my breast implant surgery, my battle with Syphilis (not true). And the cop, who I could hear amidst my freak out attack, said, "Yeah, I've seen her in your work. She's good. But I didn't know she was like this." He laughed. Yeah, laughed. Then smiled and winked. "Guess I'll watch your other girls from now on."

Andy smiled and shrugged, wound up the window, accelerated out of the officer's view and drove me back to his house in the most horrifying silence I've ever experienced.

I looked out the window at the trees, the birds, the air, the clouds floating under a baby blue sky, and that's when I officially realized there could never be a Creator. Not in a world like this. God wouldn't let this happen to me if He cared about me. Unless He liked to see kids abused and prostitutes die of AIDS and orphans die without ever helping them.

It didn't make sense.

The only thing that made sense was the non-existence of this absent God.

So I started to believe, so strongly, in nothing.

I CAN'T EXPLAIN WHAT HAPPENED TO ANDY AFTER MY moment of insanity. But he stopped locking me in the bathroom and pampered me again. He didn't let me go back to my apartment though. And he made me get out of the lease until he could trust me again.

"What can I do to make you trust me?" I asked.

He slapped me for asking, so I didn't ask again.

I did eight more video shoots in the next two weeks, complete with new boobs. That made a total of thirty-six Internet movies in just a few months of being a porn whore (my name for it). And I don't know if it was my plastic body or what, but Andy's status in the amateur porn industry soared. He sent my pictures and movies to huge agencies and one day Zayta Fontayne—she worked with some big deal agency—called him. And it was a big deal. So much that Andy hung up with her and jumped up and down like a kid in his living room.

"She loves you," he screeched like a teen boy whose voice hadn't deepened. "And she loves me."

I sat on the couch, erasing my daily nightmares with pot, as Andy paced the living room talking of how rich he'd be. Marijuana smoke snaked through the air in front of my face. Andy ran up to me, shook my shoulders in a playful way, and said, "Thank you." I saw that same glimmer in his eyes that I saw on day one.

Finally he sat down and explained to me the deal. "Apparently their director left after they decided condoms weren't necessary anymore. I guess some of them leave it up to the actors now, whether they want to wear one or not. So after he left they got another guy, then another, and now they need someone else. They saw our stuff, loved my directing, loved your abilities and looks, and now they want us to move down there and sign a contract. They're not a huge agency, not mainstream, but they are bigger than us."

I puffed another trail of smoke. "Move out where?"

"Florida. Seems like mainstream porn is getting bigger in Florida. And Zayta said she'd take care of you." His smile annoyed me. "She knows her stuff, knows this industry like she was born to work in it. And she said she hasn't seen talent and beauty like yours in a while."

I scratched my head and fluffed my hair.

"I told you I'd make you a star."

"Thanks."

Andy went into the kitchen and came back with two wine glasses and a bottle of wine. Interesting choice for a porn director, but whatever. Nothing made sense anymore. Nothing except nothing.

"I don't want to move to Florida." I scooted my wine glass to the side.

"Taylor, do you realize you can make more money under Zayta's wing? She's got a lot more experience and I have no doubt that we'll see her in the big agencies one day. Not to mention you'll get more respect. You'll do fewer movies a year for more money." He stood, then sat down next to me.

"They have pretty high standards, you know. This is your big chance."

I looked away from him, wanting to pull my hair out. The last place I wanted to be was in some unknown state where dozens of porn people lived. I wanted to get out of this world and find something else. I just didn't know how anymore, or where I'd go, or who would want me.

I imagined going back to Mom but, yeah, that wouldn't happen. Not to mention the fact that her boyfriend probably saw my, um, work. And I didn't want to find out what kind of doors that'd open.

"How long until we do that?" I said.

"She said they would give us about six weeks to get our stuff together, move down there, get settled in and sign the contract, then show me the money baby!" He stood up and imitated Cuba Gooding. "Say it with me," he said. "Show me the money."

No, thanks.

I played with my earring and stared at my shaking foot. I could play calm so well until I realized how bad my foot vibrated, then my voice would follow, getting all shaky and everything.

I stopped my foot and looked up. Took all I had to remain calm.

Andy sat down beside me. "You're not telling me you want to turn this offer down, are you?" He rubbed my cheek with the back of his hand, disgustingly nice.

"I don't know."

"You really don't have a choice, Sadie girl." His pitch went down an octave, not a good sign, unless you want your flesh bruised. "This is our chance, without you I'm nothing. They want both of us. They don't even care about Gianna, Sunny, and Kelli. They want you. Just you. Don't you realize what this means?"

Gianna. I missed her. I missed having someone who understood. Only thing Andy understood about me was how much money he could get out of me, and the size of my body. He even had my wrist measurements memorized. Six inches even.

He walked across the room, sipped his wine, and looked at me. "This is your future." He set the glass on his fireplace mantle. "You could be famous, you know?"

He did have a point. Maybe one day I'd end up at Gianna's favorite agency, with the pros. She dreamed of being there. Yeah, dreamed. I'm not making that up. She raved about them all the time. Said they would take great care of her. Not sure about the agency's name, I never cared to remember. But I did remember that their actresses weren't allowed to do drugs on the set. You could pick and choose the types of films you did and didn't do. Really you could be more in control and that's what she liked. That sounded good to me. No longer would I be a puppet. And I could rise to fame and meet Justin Timberlake or Rob Thomas. Definitely a bonus. Maybe Rob Thomas would whisk me away and show me a better life.

Yeah, right. What kind of normal guy would want me—a Chlamydia-infested porn star?

Well, I thought. If I'm gonna do porn I might as well get famous doing it.

Andy smiled, rubbed my chin. "I knew you'd soften up."

He walked out of the room again. I sucked the life out of my joint. I never imagined I'd smoke pot, much less snort coke and have sex on camera. Images of myself as a little girl showed up in my dreams all the time. I'd run and play and splash in puddles. Then I'd wake up and wish I could go back to that time of my life.

Nothing about doing what I did felt right, but I didn't know anything about right, or left, or anything. So I had to learn to make myself believe I liked doing what I did. Mind over matter, I'd tell myself. No other way to deal with it, so I let Sadie get angry, have power trips, and use porn like a drug to get what she wanted—attention, success, power. Some days I actually enjoyed it.

Although if I really thought about it I didn't like the idea of other men looking at me like that, especially married men, but I didn't think about it too much. I let it be what it was, and figured their addictions were their problems anyway, not mine.

Besides, I had enough problems of my own.

Chapter 35 *Ally*

I fidgeted with the covers, trying my best not to look in Jessie's eyes. He asked again. "Have you seen Sean?"

"Would it bother you?"

"So you did?"

"Would it matter?"

He shook his head. "I already have my answer."

I pulled the sheets to my chest and turned to my side, away from his accusing eyes. Yes, I saw Sean, but Jessie didn't know the truth. He didn't know that I couldn't kiss Sean because I desperately loved my husband. I didn't want him to know the truth. I wanted him to fight for me.

But he followed my lead and rolled over.

No fight. No begging. No tears.

I twisted the sheets in my hands and scrunched my face. Minutes piled on top of each other as I silently cried, and soon enough Jessie's rhythmic snore told me how much he cared.

Tired of crying, I watched shadows of tree branches quiver in the room as I tried to think of a plan. Either to get my marriage back together or allow it to crumble. Neither felt good right now, but I needed to choose one and run with it.

I WOKE UP THE NEXT MORNING FOR WORK WITH NO resolve, no plan, and no feelings toward anything at all. I figured I'd wait and see what Jessie did. See if he truly wanted to stop looking at porn. See if maybe he'd fight for me, chase after me, something.

I placed our marriage in his hands and went about my day.

LAUREN GREETED ME AT WORK, DOUBLE LOOKED AT ME, AND pretended not to have done so. I forgot I dyed my hair until then. People must've thought my brain departed from me. Definitely a justifiable thought. I've never been the type to wear loads of makeup or accessories, never dyed my hair until then, and I certainly would've never had silky straight hair smoothed back into a low ponytail.

Times change, people change, I reasoned.

I walked into my office and saw my desk. Covered in Post-It notes. Again. I needed to find another way for Lauren to keep me "posted."

I stuck all the notes together and put them to the side, then went through my emails, trying my best to forget about my disastrous marriage. Every now and then a note from Jessie popped up, but I didn't read any of them.

Before I finished responding to emails Lauren stuck her head through the door to prepare me for my first client. A new woman. Sarah Donahue. Her husband refused to come, but she wanted to talk to someone to find out how to restore her marriage. Not sure she came to the right person, but anyway. . . .

She walked in the room, a beautiful, beautiful smile across her face. A little surprised, I walked over to her and shook her hand.

"Sorry I'm a little late." Gentleness glided off her voice. "Derek was arguing with me as I walked out the door."

By the softness of her voice, the sweetness in her eyes, I couldn't think of a reason her husband would argue with her. But I figured I'd find out soon enough.

We sat down, prayed, then she told me about her history with Derek.

"We were high school sweethearts," she said with a smooth smile. "We fell in love my junior year and the romance between us was always there. He was always sweet and gentle, always held doors open for me, gave me cute little gifts, all that." She placed her hand over her mouth and cleared her throat. "Excuse me."

"When did things change?"

"Oh, well, we got married when I turned twenty. He was twenty-one. And everything was perfect for a while even though we were so young.

Everyone thought we'd fail, but we had a great start to our marriage." She counted on her fingers. "About nine months into our marriage I found pornographic magazines hidden in the basement."

My half-smile weakened.

"He denied they were his. And I believed him. He's always been a nice guy, you know? Really sweet, sensitive, he even cried when we watched romantic movies together. So," she laughed sweetly, "you can imagine how much of a shock this was to me."

"How did you feel when you found out? Besides shock, I mean."

"Honestly, I know his struggle with porn isn't about me, so I didn't worry about it too much. I told him I loved him and I'd help him get through it, but he never admitted to doing it." She looked down. "Then I found 900 numbers on our phone bill and I confronted him, but he didn't seem to mind. He told me he needed to release his stress and it was the only thing that worked."

I nodded, speechless.

"Well, he's only gotten worse. I think he might be sleeping with another woman, but I don't know for sure. And our romance is gone. He barely looks at me when we eat dinner. He'd rather eat on the couch while he watches TV."

I shifted in my chair. "How do you feel about this?"

She shrugged. "I think it's not me that's the problem. He's got some issues deep down that have nothing to do with me, but what hurts me the most is that he's turned his back on God." Finally, a sign of sadness crept into her eyes. "I told him I'd always be there for him. And I'll always love him, adultery or no adultery. But I want him to turn back to God. It kills me to see him try to fight this alone."

Her words. I can't even explain what they did to me. My heart almost exploded and flooded my eyes. But the young woman in front of me hadn't a tear in her eye. She sparkled with a love so bright she didn't need to smile. I could see her smile in her eyes. And I wanted that. I wanted that even more than I wanted the physical beauty Jessie admired all those years.

I wanted to ask her how she did it. How she loved someone like that, someone running around with other women and staring at naked girls. But I couldn't ask my client for advice, not unless I wanted a new job.

"You seem very joyful amidst this," I said.

"Yes." She smiled. "You're probably wondering why I'm here, right?"
I nodded.

"I promised him I wouldn't tell anyone. I don't want to embarrass him.
But I needed to talk to someone about it."

"I see." I longed for the joy in her eyes. "So you are absolutely okay with
the way Derek is treating you?"

"No. I'm not okay, but I will fight for him even if he doesn't want me."
She clasped her hands in her lap and smiled. "I love him. I really, really
do. Just because he wants to cheat, doesn't mean I'll stop being faithful." I
thought of Dad and cringed inside. "I'd die for Derek." She looked down.
"And so I am."

"You are dying for him now, you mean?"

"Yes. Every day." She paused. "I'm not going to lie. This hurts. It's the
worst thing I've ever experienced. My heart feels dead at times. I have insecurities and I often want to look like other women. Sometimes I struggle
with wanting to blow up at him, or walk out, or cheat on him too." She
shook her head. "It's not easy."

"What do you think keeps you from doing those things to Derek?"

"Jesus," she said without hesitation. "It's like St. Therese said, 'Since
Jesus has gone back to heaven, I can only follow Him by the path He has
traced.'"

"You must love your husband a lot," I said, wondering how little I loved
my own.

"Yes. But I love God more. And He fills me. He fills me so much that
my husband can empty me and I'll never dry up."

This woman's joy flushed my face. My body tensed. I couldn't be around
her anymore. She flaunted her happiness and it annoyed me. Her smile and
her immense love for God and her husband. Yes, it seemed admirable. I
suppose. I couldn't help but think her words were lies though. She had to
be holding a mask over her face. She wanted me to believe she didn't cry
herself to sleep at night, but she probably did. No one could be that joyful
while being a doormat.

There's no way, I thought. Absolutely no way a woman could be joyful
in these circumstances.

Our time was up. Thankfully. I couldn't listen to her talk about her profound love anymore. But next time she came in my office I'd surely peel away her mask and reveal her true colors. Surely.

Chapter 36 *Taylor*

Two weeks passed since Andy received that call from Zayta. And that's all he talked about. We're gonna be stars this; we're gonna be stars that. Nauseated me beyond belief.

We didn't expect to meet Zayta until we got to Florida, but she called on July thirtieth and told us she'd be coming to visit. "I want to prepare both of you, make sure you know everything you need to know before you get here," she said to Andy.

And when she knocked on Andy's door two days later on a sweltering August afternoon, she didn't just seem professional and confident, it emanated from her words, her gestures, her posture, her astounding beauty and intelligence. I never met a woman so perfect.

She wasn't like the others girls I met. She was a woman. Clarity lived in her eyes and speech. She wasn't rolling up dollar bills like me. She was clean, sophisticated, and beautiful. How she managed all that and did porn, I had no idea.

We talked in the living room for a while. Andy's eyes never left Zayta. Mine never left the floor, except to watch him drool over her. She explained terms I never heard of and taught me how to contort my body into the most awkward and painful positions. "It'll get easier," she said.

She taught Andy how to use a light meter and a more professional camera. Yeah, she brought supplies. It was like porn orientation. I thought of Walgreens, wishing I'd turned around that day—May twenty-fourth?and applied there instead.

After Zayta's four-hour explanation of the serious side of porn, she sat next to me on Andy's couch and said, "You need to remember, this is a business. You get what you want out of it, and leave the rest."

I looked down. That sounded fun and all, but what about Andy? He didn't let me manage myself and make my own decisions, much less take what I want and leave the rest.

Zayta picked up my purse from the couch and scooped my things out. I reached out to stop her, but put my hand in my lap instead.

She pulled out Cola. "This," she said, "has got to go."

"Oh, I'm not addicted or anything."

She put Cola in her bag. "Sweetie, when people are addicted they don't know they are. And even if you aren't, we need to be careful." She picked up my marijuana. "You have no reason for this either. I'm not going to take it, but you need to stop doing this stuff if you want to take your job seriously. There are some girls who manage to stay with big agencies while snorting crack, but not a lot. Better to be safe than sorry."

I listened to Zayta, trying to retain everything she told me, like how to talk to fans, how to talk with directors and producers and costars. She knew a lot, and I trusted her. Andy always told me he'd make me a star, but I found out he only wanted to use me for his own success. Zayta, on the other hand, truly cared about my own success. At least I thought so.

Andy left the room for a bathroom break.

I looked at Zayta. "So, you really like making porn?"

"Oh, honey," she said, flipping her hair behind her shoulder. "I don't just like making porn, I love it. And there's a lot more to it than that. You must learn how to play the game, but when you do, you'll make it." She leaned toward me. "Is Andy a suitcase pimp?"

I pushed my neck forward and crumpled my face. "A what?"

She laughed. "Is he using you or hurting you, baby doll?"

I knew what she asked, but I pretended not to understand. If Andy ever found out I snitched, I'd be lost. No one would want me after this. I'd be alone. Again.

Zayta steered the conversation, so eloquently, in another direction when Andy strolled back in the room. His eyes were a little pink and glazed over.

"I'm serious you two," Zayta said. "Give up the drugs if you want to make it in this business."

"But," I said without realizing it, "how can someone possibly get through a scene without being high? How can someone get through the blood and bruises and pain without something to help them forget what they're doing?"

Zayta smiled. Her ocean-blue eyes smiled too. "Well, first," she said. "You must learn to love this business. And I'll show you how."

This girl was only four years older than me and rich. Diamonds in her ears, on her neck, wrists, fingers. She didn't look run down like Gianna and the other girls I knew. She beamed with class and brains and she dressed the part. Tailored business suit, pretty black heels, perfect hair despite the humidity, subtle makeup—she stood out in the porn world, and I yearned to be like her.

According to her I could be, if I followed her advice and soaked in "the beauty of porn." I hoped she wouldn't prove me wrong and that Florida would be different, that I'd feel better about my life and "take control" as she said.

Zayta left for the night to stay at the Marriott in Baltimore, while Andy pampered me all night. He washed my feet, painted my toenails, brushed my hair, and even let me go shopping without him.

Guess he knew I feared him so much that I'd return without spilling the truth about him. And I did come back, ten minutes before my curfew, without talking to a single person. Except the guy—sorry, my fan—who recognized me from my Web site. I told him he had the wrong girl and walked away, fast.

Anyway, I'm not sure why Andy decided to pamper me, but it wasn't a bad start to my new future.

Chapter 37 *Ally*

An intense migraine irritated me for days and days. I didn't eat right, sleep right, or do much of anything right since Jessie asked me about Sean. He never mentioned it after that, which made me think about it every day. Even if I did cheat, he shouldn't have cared. He cheated first!

Okay, I said to myself. Calm down.

I stopped at a red light on my way to visit Dad, rubbed my temples, and turned some classical music on the radio.

My cell phone rang.

"Ally, are you still coming over tonight?" Verity said.

"Yeah, is that a problem?"

"Most certainly not. My fine, fine lady, how's everything going today?"

"Eh, it's going."

"You've always been such a chipper one, you and that melancholic personality of yours. That's okay," she laughed, "leave it to me to bring color to life."

"Man, you are so encouraging."

"Sure am. Well, I'll make sure dinner is ready by six then. Where are you now?"

"Left work early to meet with someone. I'll be there soon."

I hung up, giving her no time to ask who I left work to meet with. I know what her little mind thought. Same thing Jessie thought. And I didn't care. Soon I'd be ready to explain Dad and they'd understand that I may have almost kissed Sean, but I wasn't having an affair. And honestly, I didn't think I could even if I wanted to. I still loved my Jessie.

DAD GREETED ME WITH A HUG, MUCH WARMER THAN our first meeting, and ushered me into his tiny rancher. I followed him to the living room. The walls were white and bare, not a thing hung on them. The couch stood out like a homeless person at the Grammys. Holes, stains, pieces of cushion playing peek-a-boo—you name it, the couch had it.

I sat on the mismatched love seat instead.

"I'll get some lemonade for you," Dad said, disappearing around the corner.

He came back, smiling, and handed me a glass of homemade lemonade with bits of lemon in it. I tasted it, and wow. Pretty good.

"How have you been the last few weeks?" He sat the arm of the couch.

"Okay, how about you?"

He nodded. "I'm getting by."

"Can I ask you a question?" I almost called him Dad, but still didn't feel right about that. I didn't feel right about calling him by his name either. So I skipped that part altogether.

His upturned lips and gentle eyes urged me to go on.

"How can you stay faithful to someone who hasn't wanted to be with you for years and still wants nothing to do with you?"

He ran his fingers along the rim of his glass.

"I mean, doesn't it hurt? Wouldn't you rather move on and be happy?"

He tilted his head and looked at the ground. "Well, Ally, I guess the problem is that I'd only be happy with your mother."

"But how? How could you be happy with someone who's ruined your life?"

"I don't think of it that way."

"Then how do you think of it?"

"I think of it as her ruining her own life."

Interesting. And confusing. Too many enigmas in my head. "How do you make this seem so easy?"

"It's not easy, but it's worth it."

I covered my mouth with my hand and leaned forward.

"What's wrong?" he said.

"Nothing. I'm okay."

"Your secrets are safe with me, Ally."

"Oh, I know. I'm okay though. Really." I took another sip of lemonade. "So, what have you been doing all these years?"

"Nothing very exciting." He laughed. "I stayed close in case your mom ever changed her mind, but I've given her the space she asked for. I've run my own business hanging wallpaper and painting."

I looked at his bare walls.

He smiled. "I'm easy pleasy. No need to waste money on my own house, no one looks at it except me anyway. And now you." He tapped his glass. "I'm glad you're here."

"Yeah, it's weird. Isn't it?"

He nodded. "Weird in a good way. I don't know how I ever believed you weren't my baby, you've always had my eyes and hair, well, until now."

"Oh." I pulled a piece of my hair in front of my face. "This."

"I like it natural. You're too beautiful for all that unnatural stuff."

"Yeah, tell that to my husband."

Dad knew. I could tell he knew.

"I'll make sure to tell him when I meet him," he said. "What's he like?"

I didn't know how to answer his question. But for the sake of conversation I talked about old Jessie like he never turned into new Jessie. By the end of my description, when I said he was the most charming man I knew, I wanted to run out of Dad's house in tears.

"Sounds like a good man," Dad said after he finished his lemonade.

I didn't argue. Didn't want to tell the truth. And Dad left it alone, filling the conversation with small talk, but I only half-listened. All I could think about was Jessie. Every thought of him came with a picture of a nude woman, and every picture of a nude woman came with an undeniable urge to throw up my lemonade.

I TILTED MY CHAIR BACK IN VERITY'S HOT, NON-AIR-conditioned kitchen.

Her hair glistened in the sunlight from her kitchen windows. "You're not seeing Sean, are you?"

I rolled my eyes.

"Don't give me that," she said. "Are you?"

"I don't want to say who I was with, Ver, but it wasn't Sean. Leave. It. Alone." There aren't enough fingers and toes to count how many times I've said that to her and how many times she refused to listen.

"Wait. You're telling me you have changed your wardrobe, dyed your hair, and started an affair with someone I've never heard of, all for no reason?"

"I never said I did any of those things."

"God gave me two eyeballs and a brain. The brain might be small but I know how to use it, pal. I'm not stupid."

I rubbed my head. My stomach sloshed lemonade up to my chest again. Anxiety. Too much anxiety.

Verity stooped beside me. "You okay?"

I sat completely still and didn't say a word. But Verity said many. And I tuned most of them out. After a few seconds that felt like minutes my stomach calmed, but my headache didn't lessen.

"Do you have anything I can take for my headache?"

"Man, you're a mess." She walked away. "I'll get ya something."

I stared at her crazy walls and furniture, but that made my nausea come back. So I closed my eyes and sunk into my chair.

"Here." Verity stuck out her hands, one holding a water bottle, the other two pills. "Take these."

I took the pills from her hand, put them on my tongue, and washed them down with water.

"What's going on?" she asked.

"Headache. It's killing me. Making me feel like I need to throw up."

"You pregnant?"

I managed to laugh. "Don't think so. Jessie and I haven't touched each other in months, save one time recently and I wasn't ovulating at the time."

"Maybe you have brain cancer."

"That's not funny."

"When did you get so serious?"

"Maybe when my life started to crumble to the ground."

"Okay. Maybe we should watch a movie, get your mind off everything."

I agreed and let her pick the movie. My head hurt too much to care. And what movie did she choose? The very movie Jessie and I named our top romantic movie of all time. And every second of it reminded me of him.

My headache eased halfway through the movie, but the nausea didn't subside until I ate. Verity assured me that I'd get a positive line on a pregnancy test and I wanted to prove her wrong. So we drove to Rite-Aid, bought one, and went back to her house.

"So, what do I get if I'm right?" she said, rubbing her hands together.

"You pick." I knew she wouldn't be right anyway. Jessie and I tried for years to have children. We tried every infertility treatment you can imagine. Nothing. And I knew my ovulation times better than I knew my husband, so no worries there either.

"If I win, you need to watch porn with Jessie and see if you enjoy it."

I raised my eyebrows. "What is wrong with you?"

"Just saying. Don't be so touchy."

"Do you even realize how much pain this has caused me?"

"Yeah, yeah." She nudged me into the bathroom and walked away. "Take the test already, would ya?"

Chapter 38 *Taylor*

Zayta took me shopping and helped me pick out a new wardrobe. She also taught me how to strut my stuff in public and act like a star. I never got so much attention from men in my life. Taylor fell further and further away and Sadie took control, just like Zayta hoped. I kind of liked it.

By the time she went back to Florida, Andy didn't know what to do with me. I turned into a power-driven woman, instead of a shy little girl. Even the makeup tips she gave me made a difference. Little Taylor piled on blush and eyeliner, but Sadie, womanly, beautiful Sadie knew how to make less look like more.

I now understood the art of manipulation and I knew it would take me far in the business. And I didn't want Cola much anymore. Every now and then I'd crave a line so bad I'd shake, but I'd smoke some Kine Bud to get over it. For the most part, it worked. But I didn't know how I'd give up smoking weed or drinking. It helped me get through scenes and the pain of my insides being torn.

After a shoot on a hot weekday morning—I rarely knew what day it was—blood dripped down my legs and I knew I wouldn't be able to go to the bathroom for at least a week.

I walked to the corner of the room where the clean up rags were lumped in a pile and picked one up. After cleaning myself I tossed the rag aside.

Andy walked up to me. "This'll probably be your last day of work until we get down there."

Fine with me, I thought. "Kay. I'm gonna go get dressed."

"So long as you are ready in two hours. I've got a few things to do with

Gianna and then it'll be your turn again."

I SHOWERED FOR A LONG TIME, AS ALWAYS. NO MATTER how hard I scrubbed I never felt clean. I had to go to the bathroom so bad, but after a lot of my movies I couldn't go to the bathroom for days. Too sore, too painful.

After my shower I did my hair, makeup, and got dressed again. I learned to do all those things without looking in the mirror. Too hard to look at myself. Made me think of Taylor and I didn't like that. But once I had makeup and nice clothes on I couldn't find Taylor in the mirror, just Sadie, so I'd be good to go.

I sat on Andy's bed and wondered how many people had sex on it, how many people lost their life on it, how many people got AIDS on it, and wondered if I'd be next.

I looked down at my hand. I forgot I grabbed a bottle of Malibu Coconut Rum. Came natural, I guess.

I took a drink. Straight. The liquid smoothed down my throat and heated my chest.

"Daddy, are you there?" I said to the wall.

Sometimes porn appealed to me. Sometimes the power, the money, the attention, the pretty things—what can I say?—they appealed to me. But other times I wondered if I'd ever be married. There's no way a nice— keyword nice—man would marry me.

And finding another job with this as my only employment. Right. Gianna told me she tried to leave the business once. "The only place that would hire me," she said, "was McDonald's, and I wasn't about to do that." She even had a college degree. So she came back to porn for the money and the glam. Yeah, there's some glam to it. But it's on the surface, unless you're strong like Zayta.

I didn't think I could be like her. Unless she hid her pain behind a smile. Definitely possible. I knew all about hiding.

I took another drink of rum. My brain lightened, but my thoughts gained more weight. And the more weight they gained the more I realized I wanted out of porn. Maybe Zayta really loved her job, maybe she wasn't hurting and broken and raped, maybe she didn't want to get married and have children and be a normal person. But I did.

I set my rum down. I missed the shy girl I used to be. The girl no one noticed or accepted. I didn't like strong, opinionated Sadie. I mean, people accepted me now, but only to use me like a drug. I looked at Andy's laptop across the room and imagined my Web site.

I exhaled and looked at my feet.

I took my heels off and eyed the bedroom doorway.

If I tiptoe while he's filming, I thought, he'll never hear me leave.

Chapter 39 *Ally*

I sat the pregnancy test on the bathroom counter and ignored it, hoping I'd prove Verity wrong again. God knew I couldn't handle a baby right now. He wouldn't do that to me. Or maybe He would. Mother Teresa's words coursed my mind, *I know God will not give me anything I can't handle. I just wish He didn't trust me so much.*

"I can't be like them," I said to God. "I can't be faithful to someone who cheats. It's not possible for me. You know it's not."

I didn't want to look at the test. I wanted to hear God's voice first, or feel peace drip from heaven and seep into my heart. But nothing. I hadn't heard from God in months. I didn't even know what hear from God meant, but I knew it didn't happen.

Bang, bang, rattle, rattle, bang!

"What on earth are you doing?" I said to the bathroom door.

Verity laughed. "Open up. I want to see."

"Hold on."

I walked over to the test. *Please, God, if you still care about me don't make me have a baby right now.*

Never in a trillion years did I think I'd say that, not after we depleted our savings account for infertility treatments.

I inhaled, held my breath, and looked at the test. Oh, the nausea.

Then I saw it. One line. Only one line. I exhaled. Relieved. So relieved.

But sad at the same time. Part of me wanted to know I could have a baby, even if it was the wrong time. But maybe God finally answered my prayers. Maybe He knew I couldn't handle it.

"Oh, no," I said.

"What?" Verity shook the door handle. "I knew it!"

I opened the door. "It's positive, Ver."

Her bottom lip fell. "No way!"

"Just kidding." I bent over in hysterics. "No, it's negative."

"You jerk!"

We sat on the floor laughing and reminiscing childhood pranks we pulled on our neighbors.

"Remember," she said, "the time we peed in a measuring cup and poured it on my brother's bed after he woke up?"

"Yeah. And your mom knew it was us. I couldn't come over for a week."

"Hee-larious! Oh, oh, remember the time you scared the living daylights out of Jessie?"

"Which time? There were so many."

"Back when you guys lived in your old apartment. Remember when he left to get us some ice cream and you snuck out back and hid behind the dumpster."

"Oh, that was hilarious. I popped out and wailed in front of his car like a crazy person." I could barely breathe from laughing so hard. "And he slammed on the breaks and screamed. He thought I was a loony homeless woman."

Verity's spiraling red hair hid her face as she hunched over and tried to speak, but only laughter left her lips. I held my stomach and laughed with her as I pictured Jessie's face the night we met.

I imagined going home and planning an amazing prank that would lead to passionate kisses and love. But I didn't think Jess would receive it. And I didn't think I had enough love to give right now.

Anyway, it felt good, so good, to laugh.

FOUR DAYS PASSED AND MY NAUSEA WORSENED. MY PERIOD never showed up, although it could've been late. I never had regular cycles.

I tried to ignore the pregnancy signs.

The test was negative, the test was negative, I kept telling myself.

To be sure, I decided to take another one. Again. In private, without telling Verity a word.

I bought one exactly a week after taking the previous one. It'll be false, I convinced myself. It had to be false.

I brought the test home, shoved it in my dresser drawer, and ignored it.

Last time I saw Dad he encouraged me to start writing in a journal. He said it helped him get through tough times with Mom and maybe it'd help me sort my thoughts too. Me? I'm not one for writing. For business, that's one thing. But personal stuff? I like to keep that inside, which is exactly why I thought it'd be a good idea to write things out.

I went downstairs, curled up on the couch, turned on Jazz music, and touched pen to paper.

Nothing.

I stared at the blank page where my pen met its blankness, and I waited. But nothing spurned my hand to scribble on those lines.

So I waited.

I DON'T KNOW HOW IT STARTED. MY PEN WROTE WITHOUT me prompting and before I knew it I wrote a letter to God. My first letter to Him. Ever. Honestly, I didn't want to. But I had no one else to talk to. No one else to spill everything to. He knew it all anyway.

Dear God,

I really thought loneliness would hurt worse than the pain of loving him, but sadly, it feels better. What does that mean? Was I right when I believed marriage would cause me to suffer my entire life? Were my fears viable?

Is this what you want from me? To love those who hurt me? Okay, I know you suffered and I shouldn't complain, but why him, God? Is it because he's the only person I ever loved this much? Is it because he was the only person that could break me this much? Why Jessie, God?

I love him so much, and yet, what was once the greatest pleasure in the world has become the greatest pain. Why have you allowed this to happen? Please tell me WHY JESSIE?!

I can't bear the thought of what he did. It's so hard to give him grace and love him anyway. *This pain is something I never could have imagined.*

God, why would you allow this? I want my Jessie back. How can I ever rid thoughts of him enjoying and desiring other women? How?

I know marriages are supposed to be filled with love and grace and forgiveness. I know that's pleasing to you. But I'm sorry, I can't please you right now. I can't please anyone. I feel dead.

There's nothing left in me to give. I want to love him, even if he desires other women forever, but I have never been so broken in my life.

Sometimes I hate him. I'm sorry. But I love him so much that the idea of what he did makes me hate him. How could someone jeopardize such a special, unique romance? Are you trying to show us that there's nothing special and unique, that we're just like everyone else?

God, why did I believe it? Why did I fall for the deception that he wasn't like other men? Why did I have those stupid romantic notions?

Help me. It's so hard for me to love him.

I feel empty inside without him, yet better at the same time. I don't understand that. Why Jessie?

His touch no longer pleases me. It's as though the slightest touch from him sends shocks of fear and sorrow throughout my body, right to my heart. His eyes no longer bring peace, but uncertainty and anxiety. When our eyes lock, I literally shake from emotions I can't even decipher.

Will it always be this way?

I love who he is. I love his heart and passion and his beauty. Both inward and outward beauty. I love his smile and serenity, but I hate him for what he did. Help me to love him regardless of what he did and continues to do.

I want this battle inside of me to calm. I'm tired.

I know I don't deserve your peace or your help. I know I haven't talked to you in months and I've ignored you so much. But I know I'm a mess. I don't know what else to do. You are the only one who can help, but you're silent.

Please don't be silent anymore. I'm sorry. I'm so sorry for everything.

Love,

Ally

Three pages, front and back, covered with blurred ink from splotches of tears. I wrote my heart out, crying the hardest when I'd write *why Jessie?*

and at the end when I apologized to God.

I nuzzled into the arm of the couch, wetting the white fabric with my tears. "What do I do?"

The floor creaked.

I looked up.

Chapter 40 *Taylor*

I changed into normal clothes and waited until I heard Andy tell Gianna and Mike what to do next. Afraid to make any sound, I crawled backwards down the steps. Step after step I imagined Andy finding me and killing me. Voices quieted. I stopped, luckily at the end of the steps.

"Okay, good," Andy said. "Now, stay right there."

I stood and tiptoed to the door. My neck pulsated with such intensity I thought for sure my veins would explode before I opened the door.

One hand on the door, I twisted.

A little more.

My hand, hot with sweat, pulled the door enough to crack it open.

Tears wet my lashes. If I failed, Andy would probably beat me to death.

I opened the door and shut it behind me without making a sound. I guess we'll see if I can get away with this, I thought. Images, tons of nasty images, lashed my mind as I ran from Andy's front lawn and across the street. The smell of semen and blood mixed together tortured me as I ran. I didn't want to go back to those things.

So I ran. And every time an image or smell or taste smashed into my thoughts I'd run harder and faster until my lungs insisted I stop.

I knew I couldn't call 911 because Andy probably knew all the cops. And I couldn't call anyone else because I didn't have anyone else. So I forced my legs to run even when my lungs begged me to stop.

A cramp twisted my side, but I kept going, running nowhere through yards and yards of grass until I found a Rite-Aid. I slowed down to walk in without drawing attention to myself and walked as fast as possible to the bathroom in the back.

I opened the bathroom door, shut it, locked it, checked to make sure I really did lock it, and then I collapsed on the checkered tile. On my knees with my hands on the floor, I rocked back and forth and panted for air. My body trembled. Tears filled my eyes. And images of Andy beating me to death molested me.

SO TIRED AND DRUNK, I FELL ASLEEP ON RITE-AID'S bathroom floor. I don't think I passed out, but maybe I did. Normally it took more alcohol, but like I said, I was tired, probably running two miles at full-speed without a break.

Anyway, I woke up in the bathroom to a young Halle Berry in a royal blue smock hovering over me, saying something to someone on a cell phone. I could've sworn I locked the door.

Too beat up in too many ways to feel embarrassed, I stayed on the floor and tried to listen to her.

"Yeah, yeah," she said. "Mmmhmm, she looks like she's waking up now."

Our eyes met.

"Alright," she said. "I can do that."

She stared at me. I looked away and pulled my knees to my chest. Pity slithered from her eyes. I didn't want her slimy pity. I wanted reassurance, hope, a light at the end of the tunnel—something positive for once.

She hung up the phone. "My name is Naomi. What's yours?"

"Why?"

She didn't roll her eyes. And she didn't look at me like everyone else. She looked through me. Passed my eyes, passed my body, passed Sadie— she saw me, underneath it all. I could tell by the seriousness of her eyes as she tried to smile. But I couldn't trust her, or anyone for that matter.

Naomi sat down beside me and crossed her legs. "Are you hurt?"

I looked around the room, unable to focus on anything.

"Do you want to talk?"

And I thought Andy would make people look up to me. Now I'm on the bathroom floor in Rite-Aid with some stranger who thinks I've lost my mind.

"Who were you on the phone with?" I asked.

She smiled, lighting her face with dimples. "My roommate, Lee. I asked her if you could stay with us."

"Why do you think I need somewhere to stay?"

"A wild guess. Do you?"

"No."

"Your family around? You running from something?"

"I don't have family."

"What are you running from?"

I looked at the bruises on my knees. "I'm not running from anything."

"Do you need any help?"

"Why would you let me live with you?"

"You answer a lot of questions with questions." She smiled. "I'd want someone to do the same for me if I needed help."

She had to know Andy, I thought. He probably had a reward for anyone who found me.

"Want to know the real reason?" she asked.

I looked at her.

"I'm not trying to scare you away, but I'll tell you."

Chapter 41 *Ally*

Jessie walked over to me. I sat up. Silence made its presence known between us, between our marriage. We never knew what to say anymore. How to get over the awkward hill between us. So Jessie stood in front of me, swaying his arms, clasping his hands, swaying his arms again. His lips parted to speak, but he exhaled without words instead.

He probably wanted me to reach out, tell him I still loved him and break the seven thousand inches of ice between us.

I closed my eyes and inhaled. The silence piled higher between us. I exhaled. Jessie's arms swayed. Hands clasped.

Inhale. Exhale. Inhale. Exhale.

If only he'd pursue me. No, he probably feared my reaction. No matter how much I needed him, I still didn't want him all the time, but I thought maybe, maybe if he reached out to me, through the pain, then I'd be able to see his love and escape my spinning emotions.

With each inhale and exhale, disappointment turned a dial in my mind, making me more upset by the second. I wanted to cry in his arms. Looking back, I know it wasn't rational, but I felt like a piece of trash and I needed my husband to make me feel valued. Instead, he stood there, waiting for me to reach out to him.

I wanted him to fight for me, so I stood up and walked toward the stairs.

When I got to the top I turned around and walked back down. Jessie never moved. I walked across the room, stood millimeters from him, and said with such bitterness, "Why did you do this to us?"

Jessie sighed.

The world stopped.

He didn't say a word, didn't raise a finger, and that made me want to go upstairs and be alone. I closed my eyes and when I opened them a blanket of tears covered both of our faces.

He still wouldn't fight for me.

My body heated and melted onto the floor, where I laid like a crumpled piece of refuse. Jessie's heels clicked by me.

I rocked back and forth, weeping.

He ran his fingers down my back. I trembled.

He sat beside me as I cried and shivered. Nausea revealed its odious presence again. And before I could will it down my throat, tangy yellow phlegm gagged me and landed on the floor. And again. And again.

When my body finished I calmed myself and went upstairs without acknowledging Jess. I walked into our bedroom, grabbed the pregnancy test, and went into the bathroom, shutting the door behind me.

I didn't think much about it. I figured it would be negative again, but after throwing up, I had to be sure. Anxiety could've caused me to throw up, I guess. But it never happened before.

I peed on the stick, slid it onto the back of the toilet. Then I stood, flushed, and waited.

God, if you want to give me a child right now, at least let it be a boy. I don't want to see my girl go through all this.

Jessie knocked on the door. "Ally?"

I glanced at the door. Then the pregnancy test. Then back to the door. The handle twisted.

Jessie opened the door and scanned my face, then the toilet.

His back straightened.

He saw it.

I picked up the test. Two obvious lines affirmed Verity's suspicion. Pregnant. Finally pregnant. At the worst possible time.

Jessie took the test from my hands. Well acquainted with them himself, he knew what two lines spelled. P-R-E-G-N-A-N-C-Y.

Hand over my mouth, I held back tears and laughter. Jessie's lips curled upward in a dithery smile. I watched him watch me.

"Let's not ruin this moment," he said. "For the baby's sake."

The baby.

The BABY.

BABY!

Yes, for the baby's sake, I wrapped my arms around Jessie's neck and cried the first happy tears to trickle down my face in months and months.

Jessie held the back of my head. I reached up to touch his hair, but stopped. Our awkward relationship felt like the beginning all over again. Too timid to make a new step. Only we were so much more natural back then.

He held me and we laughed and cried, peeking at the test every few minutes to make sure two lines were still there.

And they were.

They definitely were.

Chapter 42 *Taylor*

Jesus? I rolled my eyes.

She nodded and brushed her hair behind her ear.

"What did you just say?" I said.

"I think Jesus has His arms around you right now. Holding you and weeping with you."

"Well"—I looked around the bathroom—"I don't see Him."

"He's here."

Figures. I finally get away from the lunacy of Andy and run into a religious fanatic. The cross around her neck, reflecting the overhead lights, suddenly caught my attention. I sighed, wondering why religious people always forced their Jesusy thoughts on people, like that would really make me want to learn more about Him.

"If you don't have family around you can stay with me until you find something else," she said.

"Look," I said, swooping my bangs to the side. "I know you want to do good things because you're a religious person and all, but I don't think it's a good idea for me to live with you. Why would you want that anyway? I could be a lying murderer for all you know. And I could care less about your Jesus. He hasn't showed up in my life before, no point in asking Him to now."

I watched her for a reaction.

"You're not a murderer."

I played with my earring. This girl could be my age, I thought. But she doesn't have a clue about the world. Then again, a few months ago I probably would've said the same thing.

Naomi looked at her watch. "I need to get home." She stood and looked around the room with her hands on her hips. "You're welcome to live in here. Or you can come with me. Up to you."

Well, I had two options. Get caught by Andy or live with Mother Teresa.

I rubbed the light purple marks on my knees. Pictures of Andy's fake smile turned my mind black-and-blue. And to think his smile once lit up my life, even if only for a week.

I analyzed Naomi. So pretty, that soft kind of pretty I could never be, especially after all this. Her innocence reminded me of Joey on Dawson's Creek.

"Well?" she said.

I stood and tugged on my skirt, trying to make it seem longer than it was. Naomi linked her arm around mine. I unlinked us and made sure I stood far enough away that she wouldn't do that again.

I still didn't know why she wanted to help me when I had nothing to give her.

She opened the bathroom door. My heart dived to my knees. Andy's face scarred my mind like a painful tattoo. Naomi walked with confidence. I wondered if she admired herself for doing a good deed. Another person using me to feel good about herself.

"Bye Yolanda. Have a great night." She smiled to the lady standing behind the register as we walked to the front doors.

On a scorching hot August day you'd think it'd be impossible to shiver. But when Naomi opened the doors and the stuffy breeze blew my hair back, chills ran from my neck to my toes. Naomi led me to her silver Honda Civic while my eyes darted around the world, hoping not to see Andy, hoping he didn't have a camera pointed on me from some tower in town.

A shadow approached us from behind, getting smaller as it reached my back.

"Taylor?" the man said.

I froze.

Daddy, save me.

Naomi turned to face Shadow Man. I wanted to shrivel up like the Wicked Witch and melt into nothing.

"Can I help you?" she asked.

I refused to turn around, but Shadow Man walked around me. He wore old man shoes. Andy would never wear loafers. My eyes followed Shadow Man's body from feet to waist and that's when I saw his belt buckle. Many nights in a row that same belt unbuckled inches away from me while I pretended to sleep in bed.

Jack. Mom's boyfriend. I didn't need to look at his face to know. I've seen his body from waist down so many times I could draw it without looking—if I could draw, that is.

Roaming eyes pierced my body. I could feel them lusting over me, drooling at the sight of my body in revealing clothes. Sadie must've slipped into me for a minute, because I spit on his shoes and walked away. Naomi followed. Her Civic beeped and unlocked.

We got in. And she drove. She drove and neither of us said a word. But the radio spoke. *She Talks to Angels* by the Black Crowes blurred my eyes. I listened to Naomi sing along. Doesn't get much better than a Halley Berry-looking Jesus freak listening to Black Crowes, I thought. Life keeps getting stranger.

The sharpness of the acoustic guitar cut through the car. The keyboard's soul mixed with the passion of Chris Robinson's voice, shading the car with gloom. Or maybe it was just me, because Naomi bobbed her head along with the music, closing her eyes and singing along at red lights.

I have to admit, I thought for sure she'd blare some hymns or Jesusy songs when I got in the car. She surprised me. And I allowed myself to like her, starting then.

SOMEHOW I MANAGED TO STAY WITH NAOMI AND HER ROOM-mate Lee—her real name is Phyllis—for two days without seeing Andy. Lee and Naomi weren't like most religious people I met. They never talked about Jesus to me, besides that awkward moment in Rite-Aid. And I noticed that they'd pray before meals when I wasn't eating, but when I sat with them they'd skip that part.

Of course, I knew they paused in their mind and said some sort of thank you by the way they touched their forks and waited to pick them up.

We watched movies every night. Non-religious ones, if you can imagine that! Then Naomi and I would talk until midnight.

The third night I stayed with them, Lee went to bed. Naomi didn't say a word for a few minutes. I wondered if she was praying.

A few seconds later she said, "Wanna talk about it?"

"About what?"

"I'm here if you want to."

I looked down and played with the edge of my skirt, the only piece of clothing I'd worn for days. Naomi offered me a few of her clothes, but they wouldn't fit me. Lee offered too, since we were about the same size, but I didn't want to accept her clothes. Shelter from Andy was enough. More than enough. A miracle, actually.

Naomi smoothed her hair into a ponytail and wrote in her journal. I snooped around when she took a shower and read her journal entries. All of them were written to God. More like love letters. Love letters! To God!

I watched her smile as she wrote. My heart panged with jealousy. Not sure why. I didn't want a love affair with her God, and I didn't even know if I wanted a relationship with anyone anymore. But I did still wonder what a real, loving relationship would be like. I pictured Andy. Part of me wanted to run back to him. At least he loved me sometimes.

Naomi set her journal on the coffee table and pulled her legs onto the couch.

"If I talk to you will you promise not to tell anyone?" I said.

"Only if you promise to trust me."

I swallowed but nothing went down my throat. Too dry. Too hot. "Is the air on?" I stalled, but she nodded and urged me with her eyes to go on. "Um." I shook my foot. "I think I'm going to leave tomorrow."

"Where will you go?"

"My Dad lives in Richmond. I'm going to fly there tomorrow."

"Okay," she said. "What were you running from though?"

Every part of my body, even my hands, ached to tell her. I throbbed all over. No one knew my secret. No one except people in the porn world who could care less about me. Even if Naomi only cared about me to do a good deed, at least she wanted something positive for me. Of course Zayta would swear up and down that she wanted the best for me. You know, stardom and power and fake body parts.

"Girl, are you alright?" Naomi said.

"Sorry." I tapped my fingers on my knee. "Um, what did you say?"

"What were you running from the other day?"

"My ex-boyfriend. He stalks me sometimes." I looked at my knees. "Beats me, too."

She sighed and sat beside me. I inched away.

"I'm sorry you had to go through that. Does your dad know you're coming there?" she said.

"Yes."

"Well, if you want you can come to church with us tomorrow before you go."

"No, thanks." I laughed. "You don't want someone like me in church."

"Why not?"

"You just don't."

Chapter 43 *Ally*

J ournal on my lap, I waited on the couch for Jessie to get home from his appointment with a client.

Dear God,

Thank you for this baby. At first I wanted to throw my fists in the air and ask you a million times why you chose now of all times for us to have a baby. But now I know that it was the perfect time. This baby is helping our marriage heal. I don't know how yet, but I feel closer to him.

It's still hard. Sometimes I feel hopeless. I am trying though. I really am.

My insecurities today:
1.) Naturally, I'm not what Jessie likes physically.
2.) I don't look like those girls on his computer.
3.) I'm afraid my pregnancy will make me look even worse.
4.) I don't dress in those four-inch heels he likes.
5.) My hair is too frizzy.
6.) My lips aren't big enough.
7.) My nose is too big.
8.) You know my physical insecurities from head to toe.
9.) I'm not enough to captivate his heart.

Please help me. Help me to not care if he finds other women attractive. Help me to not care if he likes attributes that I don't have. I want to rest, especially for the baby. More than anything, help me to stop focusing on myself. I'm so tired of myself. I don't want to care about outward beauty. I don't want to need validation from men, even my

husband. I want to find my value only in you. Why is that so hard?
I hear Jessie. Be back soon. Thank you for this baby!
Allyson

JESSIE HELD MY HAND AS WE DROVE TO THE OBGYN OF Upper Chesapeake Hospital. I pretended not to see the provocative billboard we drove passed. But I watched Jessie out of the corner of my eye. He didn't seem to look.

Phew.

I relaxed my back and watched for more billboards.

As we neared our exit on I-695 Jessie squeezed my hand. "I know we said we wouldn't talk about names until we were in the third trimester, but I'm curious to know which ones you like."

"I don't know."

"But maybe it would be nice to have a name chosen for a child, even if we do have a miscarriage."

I slid my hand from his and looked ahead. Normally I would've turned to the right and stared out the window, but I had a paranoia about him seeing a beautiful woman or a sexy billboard. I wanted to make sure I saw what he saw. Maybe I liked torturing myself. Not sure why. Pencils shoved in my eyeballs would've been more bearable than the emotional charley horses I gave myself.

Jessie parked in front of the office building adjacent to the hospital and held my chin. "You excited?"

I allowed myself to smile amidst one of my emotional spasms.

Jessie rubbed my cheek with his thumb and gave me his eyes—romantic, hopeful eyes. For a moment, I bathed in the sunshine of his love without thinking of rain. His eyes, his hand on my face, the tiny baby growing inside of me—I longed to be sodden with the present and not swept away by a flood if Jessie looked at something again.

We walked inside, signed in, and sat in the waiting room until smooth blonde hair walked across the room. Jessie looked at his hands and fidgeted with his keys.

"Allyson Graham? You can follow me." The blonde said.

Are you kidding me, God?

Jessie's eyes darted everywhere but the pretty little blonde's body. We followed her down an off-white hallway covered in pictures of moms and babies. She weighed me. 127lbs. I wondered how much she weighed.

"Is this your first baby?" she asked Jessie.

He stared at the ground and nodded.

She showed him our room and told me to go pee on a stick and test my something-something levels. I didn't listen. I went in the bathroom and looked in the mirror. After waiting a few seconds, I flushed the toilet I never peed in and went to the room where Jessie. His eyes were fixated on his shoes.

Miss Gorgeous asked questions. I answered.

"Your midwife will be in soon." She smiled and left the room.

Jessie pressed his lips together and refused to look at me. I hopped off the exam table and stood in front of him. He stared at my feet.

Thump. Thump. Thump. My heart. In my throat.

Jessie tilted his head and scratched it.

"More beautiful than me, isn't she?" I said.

He huffed.

"It's obvious. You were acting so weird."

"I didn't look at her."

"No?" I laughed. "Well, you sure had fun trying not to look at her. Was she that pretty? So gorgeous you had to fidget with your keys the entire time and stare at your feet."

"No. I mean, I don't know. I just didn't want to make you think I looked at her."

The door opened. My heart flopped around my chest like a fish yearning for water. Jessie looked down.

"Good morning." Our midwife said, tipping her red glasses down. "I'm Lisa. How's everybody feeling today?"

If only she knew.

I skated around her question with a smile. She continued to talk to us, making us excited about the miracle of life inside of me.

After explaining screening tests, healthy foods, and things to avoid she placed her glasses on the tip of her nose and said, "Alrighty, you three. I'll see you in a few weeks."

I looked at Jess. He tried to smile. And together we watched Lisa walk away, her bright red sneakers shining underneath her long blue-checkered dress. Southern, sweet, and quirky?she brought laughter to our tense marriage. For that, I enjoyed her presence.

JESS DIDN'T TALK MUCH ON THE RIDE HOME. WE LISTENED TO music and stared at the cars ahead of us. Flashes of Miss Gorgeous appeared in my mind at random times. I'd tell myself to stop thinking about her, but instead I'd reevaluate her body in detail, then ask myself how I got to be so immature.

By the time we got home I wanted to curl up on the couch and watch a movie or read a book, anything to run away from reality.

In silence, we walked inside.

Jessie checked his email while I sat on the couch. Neither of us knew how to break through the silence anymore. He feared me. I feared reality.

I pulled our beige throw over my legs and peered over the couch at Jessie. He looked up at me with those I'm hurt eyes, like all the life drained from them and he needed my love to fill them back up.

"Can I tell you something?" I said.

He stopped clicking his mouse and walked into the living room.

"You can sit with me."

He sat down near my feet.

"I've been seeing my Dad, Jess."

"What?"

"It's a long story. Basically, Mom told Dad that I wasn't his child to get him to leave. She was having an affair." I choked on words I wished I didn't have to say, ever. "She wanted out, so she lied. Dad left because it hurt too much and he wanted her to choose him. So he waited. And waited. And he's still waiting."

Jessie scooted toward me and pulled my shoulders into his chest. Pressing my head into his neck, I begged myself not to cry. But my emotions surged like an unstoppable volcano, its lava molten and ready to erupt. I squeezed Jessie's arm and wept louder than I ever had in my life.

Childhood memories whirled by like a summer breeze. The smell of freshly cut grass. Dad's tan arms pushing a mower across the lawn as I drew on the sidewalk with chalk. His smile as he looked at me every few minutes. The way he ran to me when he finished and twirled me around the yard.

Each memory shoved Mom's arrow further into my heart.

I covered my salty face with my hands. He cradled me like a baby. And I moaned and cried.

"You know what gets me the most?" I sucked in a mouthful of air. "Do you remember how upset I was that I didn't have a dad to walk me down the aisle?"

Jessie dried a tear as it tripped over his eyelid.

"This is why"—I gasped for air—"it's so hard for me to smile right now. It's not just the porn thing. It's everything." I blinked, trying to see Jess through blurry streaks. "Too many lies."

Chapter 44 *Taylor*

Maybe I felt bad for lying to Naomi. I don't know. Whatever the reason, I went to church with her and Lee. What a wonderful experience. Not. I should've turned around and walked out of the building when I counted the eleventh person to give me a dirty look.

Faces. They looked me up and down, like Andy, only with disapproving eyes.

"Did you see her skirt?" an older woman said.

"Why would someone dress like that in church?" a mom with a baby on her hip said.

"Did you see her hair? Has she ever brushed it?" a younger girl said.

The men didn't say anything, but some of them looked at me like every other man I knew. They couldn't get past my plastic chest to see my bleeding heart.

Naomi ushered me into the sanctuary. And by sanctuary I mean auditorium. Rows and rows of comfy chairs lined up in the humongous room. The stage, lit by overhead lights, had tons of instruments, and what I assumed to be a million choir seats. A large cross hung in the back, glowing with red and orange lights.

I sat down after Naomi, about three rows from the back.

"You are loved," she said.

Loved? Did you see the 922 nasty looks I got when I walked in here? I wanted to say.

Everyone stood and sang songs. Some people raised their hands, others yawned. Naomi closed her eyes and sang. I could barely hear her, but her lips moved with the lyrics. Kinda strange to me. I heard her sing in the car and in her apartment several times and she sounded like Mariah Carey without the high pitch thing. She sang better than most people around me. Everyone sat. A few men collected money in baskets. Then a tall man with a suit and tie stood behind the podium and prayed. I looked around. Some people prayed, but quite a few stared around the room, looking at others, yawning, analyzing their fingernails—you name it. A guy about my age even played Tetris on his cell phone.

When it came time for the preacher to talk I tried to pay attention, but I couldn't. People's faces distracted and often disturbed me. A few people wore smiles, but a lot of them looked worse than me. Not their clothing, of course. They had sunken faces—broken and sad and so much like me.

What was the point of their religion if they didn't have joy?

I couldn't imagine why so many people gave me dirty looks. Church didn't seem like a holy, authentic place. It seemed like a place for a bunch of people to hide their pain behind fake smiles.

So, I wondered, how could they could judge me?

MAYBE I WAS ONE OF THEM, BUT NOT REALLY. I DIDN'T know Jesus and I didn't want to. I preferred being wrecked and unhappy, instead of wrecked with a mask. I knew masks well. I wore one every time I made porn.

Naomi and I left her church after she tried to introduce me to people. They all ended the conversation to walk away and talk to someone else. Except for February. I'm not kidding you, the guy's name was February, but Naomi called him Feo. Poor guy.

Earthy and real, he was the only person in the entire church to look into my eyes and say, "Nice to meet you, Jen." My name of the moment.

He was also one of the only people without a perfectly pressed outfit. I liked him. Not in that way. He wasn't attractive to me and I didn't want a relationship, especially with a religious person, but his eyes sparkled with something I couldn't describe. Not like Andy's confident twinkle. Something more. Something I couldn't figure out no matter how long I stared at him, so I just gave the credit to Rembrandt.

Anyway, Naomi and I got into her car, and she turned up the music.

Humid air whipped our hair around our faces as we sang together. For once, I felt like a normal nineteen-year-old girl.

Naomi stopped at Rite-Aid to get some snacks and drinks for our trip to Rocks State Park. I waited in the car, hoping to avoid any chance of seeing Andy. When I saw him park beside her car, my body turned to Jell-O. He had another woman with him. The Jell-O turned rock hard. My body tightened all over. Even my eyes tensed. I turned away when he got out of the car, then watched Andy and his woman walk into Rite-Aid holding hands.

My eyes filled with tears, but I could still see them clearly holding hands, their arms swaying back and forth, laughing in the rays of sun.

He held her hand in public.

Naomi opened the car door.

I forced a smile.

"What's wrong?" she asked, eyes open, ears ready to do a good deed.

I shook my head and thought of Andy.

The woman holding his hand looked like me. Only better.

PERRY HALL TO ROCKS STATE PARK IN FALLSTON IS A LONG drive. At least it felt that way after seeing Andy strolling around winking at that gorgeous woman. So annoying.

Naomi sang to her music, everything from Queen to En Vogue, and I spaced out, imagining 501 ways to get back at Andy. Until Naomi walked me down a dirt path through the woods. We walked over rocks, down a few hills, over a bridge, and finally I saw it.

It wasn't a huge waterfall or anything, but it was the only one I'd ever seen in real life. We sat down on a rock in front of the gushing water. Naomi pulled a few snacks and drinks out of her bag and leaned back on her hands.

I loved that she never forced me to talk. She let us live in silence without a hint of awkwardness. She was there. Just there. And I loved that about her.

Hushhh. Hushhh.

I looked up. Beyond the falling water to the baby blue sky. The sun reached through the trees, grabbing everything in its way. Closing my eyes,

I listened. And when I opened them I knew I didn't want revenge. Not with Andy. I loved him too much to treat him the way he treated me.

He needs me, I thought. I can change him. Help him heal.

Streams of water smoothed over rocks, crashed into the brook, and misted my bare feet.

"I need to go back to my Dad tonight," I said.

Naomi looked up. "Oh, I know. Do you need to leave now?"

I nodded. I guess I didn't need to leave right that moment, but I wanted to get back to Andy as soon as possible.

Naomi gathered her things and stood. She gave me a hand to get up, but I pretended not to see it.

We drove down Route 1, this time without music.

"Are you sure you are going to be okay?" Naomi said.

"Yes."

She gave silence room to talk. And whoa, did it talk! I imagined Andy's face when I'd walk up to him and tell him I loved him, no matter what he did to me. If I could show him faithfulness and love, maybe his heart would heal and he'd show the same to me. He had to love me a little. All of those times he played with my hair and told me he loved me—they had to be real moments of love.

We merged onto Harford Road and Naomi crushed the silence.

"Jen," she said. "I know you haven't told me the truth. And I'm not asking you to." She stopped at a red light. "But I know your heart is searching for something to fill you right now. You're looking in the wrong places though."

My chest flushed with heat. "You don't know me."

"No, you're right. I don't know you. But I would love to know the real you, the you behind all of your pain."

I pressed my eyebrows together and clenched my teeth. She didn't know anything about me.

"I'm here. You know where I live, and I'm going to give you my phone number before you get out of this car."

SHE KEPT HER PROMISE. ON A TORN OUT PAPER FORM HER journal, she wrote her number and handed it to me.

"Thanks," I said, stuffing it in my pocket. Not that I'll need it, I thought.

I mumbled something that sounded like a goodbye and got out of her car. I'm sure she had her suspicions about dropping me off at Walgreens, but she didn't put up a fight.

As I walked from her car, I wondered if she felt good about what she did. Not once did she bring up Jesus, at least not in a way most religious people did to me. People always shoved the "Salvation Prayer" in my face. Once I even said the prayer and pretended to believe just to make the person get all crazy and excited.

I felt bad. A little. But Sadie said it, not me.

I walked into Walgreens and went to the bathroom to freshen up. I even bought some makeup with the last few dollars I had in my purse.

After fixing myself up, I walked to Andy's, hoping the other girl wouldn't be there when I showed up. And if so, I'd pretend to love her too. Just to make Andy want me again.

The sun still hadn't set as I walked down back roads, which made me sweat. I wanted to get home before Andy, change my clothes, and put on my I'll-do-anything-for-you smile.

Finally, I made it to his house.

His convertible sparkled in the driveway.

Home. He was home.

Now what?

I turned the front door knob. Locked.

I peered in the house. Not a person in sight. Arms crossed, I sat on his front step and tapped my foot on the pavement.

Chapter 45 *Ally*

A lifetime of psychological study couldn't had prepared me for the emotional up-and-down's Jessie's porn struggle gave me.

After vomiting my heart all over him as we sat on the living room floor, I looked into his eyes and saw my best friend. Not only did he suffer the vomit, but he cried with me, stroked my hair, and listened.

He listened.

And he never said, "But Ally _____" Fill in the blank with any of the following: I'm a good husband, I love you, I'll do anything, do you still love me, are you ever going to get over this, and on the list goes.

Nothing of the sort escaped his lips. Only the subtle hush of his breath.

A pink hue from the sunset saturated the room and our skin. Jessie locked his fingers with mine and led me through the dining room to the back door. He opened the door and I followed him outside. The sweetness of my petunias wrapped around my heart like a gentle vine. With each in-hale, I could breathe again. Really breathe.

Jessie kicked off his shoes. So did I.

Hand in hand, grass tickled our feet as we walked a few yards. Jessie motioned for me to sit. When I did, he sat behind me and circled his arms around my shoulders. Leaning back into his embrace, I gazed at bands of carnation pink and lavender draped across the sky.

Right then I knew what my next journal entry would be about. And I couldn't wait to write it.

LATER THAT NIGHT, I WROTE:

Dearest Jesus,

Thank you for the breath of fresh air. Thank you for helping me to see the truth even when I couldn't feel it. Thank you for Jessie. Please strengthen and encourage him when I so often fail.

When I sat with him in the lawn early this evening, the sweet air all around us, the colors in every direction, the breeze on our faces, I realized that the past doesn't always have to be better than the future, or better yet, the present. I realized that you have given me a choice to live how I want to, even if things around me try to bring me down.

I really do love him . . . I think back to those silly first dates and I can't help but smile. I loved him even then. His heart shined through everything he did, everything he touched, everything he said.

We were connected even then. I remember leaving him the night I met him, screaming in my car like a little girl, and telling you, "I will love him more than anyone ever could, Jesus. Make that always be true."

I want to love him . . . good and bad. I want to love him ALWAYS for who he is, not what he does. I am blessed to call him mine.

Thank you for the moment of rest today. Phew, I needed that! I can't help but think that sunset was just for me.

Yours,
Allyson

EVERYTHING ABOUT THE NEXT DAY WITH JESSIE, FROM breakfast in bed to our afternoon love tangled in sheets, made me smile.

We skipped church and hoped God wouldn't mind. He started it, after all, with His gorgeous handwriting in the sky.

Mmm . . . the way it tingled my spine to hear Jessie laugh, to hear my laugh make love to his. I didn't want the day to end, fearing the future would ruin the present.

Jessie drew my chin toward his face as we lay in bed together after our third pillow fight of the day. "What are you thinking?"

I didn't want to tell him.

The softness of his face creased as he smiled.

My lips attempted a smile.

"You alright?" he said.

"Can I ask you something?"

Jessie brushed my hair behind my ear. "Ask away."

Afraid to ask, to ruin the present, I looked away, hoping Jessie'd leave it be. I didn't think I could handle the truth his answer would bring.

"Ally, if something is bothering you, please ask." He squeezed my hand. "The more you hold in, the more you're going to run. Talk to me."

I inhaled. The comforter rose with my body.

Somewhere inside of my head, my heart, and what felt like my entire existence, there lived an annoying woodpecker of desire. Desire to know things I knew would hurt me. He pecked and pecked and pecked so much that he made every desire feel like a need. An insatiable need that would only be reconciled if I gave in to the pecking, the constant, annoying pecking. And if I did, I knew, I just knew, the pecking would stop.

Or so I hoped.

"Was she prettier than me?" My words came out with a gush of air. Relief and nausea plagued me at once.

Jessie shook his head. "Who?"

"The nurse. Yesterday."

After an exaggerated inhale, Jessie's chest dropped. "Why do you ask questions like this?"

I didn't even care if he lied. I needed a no.

"I already know the answer," I said.

"If you already know the answer, then why do you ask?"

"Guess some part of me wanted you to say you are so captivated by me that you'd never think that in a million years." My lips trembled. "But I know that's not true. Can you just say it? I need to hear the truth."

"Ally, she was more beautiful than you, yes. Physically. Just physically. Why does this matter so much? Don't you und erstand how much I love you, all of you? Not just the physical, but every little detail."

I bit my lip. Something about the way he said beautiful smashed my aching heart to pieces and made the woodpecker go crazy. I never said beautiful. I said pretty. Why did he choose that word?

Beautiful.

Beautiful.

Beautiful.

I never wanted to hear the word again.

Pretending not to care, I touched my hand to Jessie's cheek. "Don't worry about it. This conversation's over." I smiled. "Wanna get a lemon-lime snowball and share it, like old times?"

A weak smile stretched Jessie's lips.

I popped out of bed and threw a pillow at him. "Come on." I tossed another pillow. "Let's stop thinking about this stuff and enjoy the day."

PEOPLE LAUGHED AND TALKED IN LINE, WAITING FOR THEIR refreshing cup of flavored ice. Jessie paid for ours—a medium watermelon, lemon, and lime snowball with marshmallow in a cup on the side for me, and a large spearmint snowball with vanilla ice cream in the middle for him—then he led us to a bench to sit on.

"I wonder how many memories we have that include snowballs." He sat down.

I sat beside him. "Too many. Remember the time we challenged each other to see who could eat the most marshmallow?"

He laughed. "Or the time we had a snowball fight, using our spoons to fling it at each other, and I poured my entire cup on your head."

"Yeah, then the bees came. I about killed you."

He slipped a spoonful of lime green ice onto his tongue. "Well, at least I got you back for all those scares. Your arms were flailing around pretty good, ain't no foolin'."

"Ain't no foolin'?" I laughed. "Is that a new one?"

Crossing his eyes at me, he dribbled ice from the corner of his mouth.

"Nice." I snatched the snowball from his hands and the spoon from his nose. "No more sugar for you."

My best friend. No matter what we'd been through, no matter what we'd go through, no matter how many times I might've wanted to fling my rings at his face, Jessie would always be my best friend.

Chapter 46 *Taylor*

The setting sun warmed my back as I stood and walked to Andy's door. My chest tightened. Holding my breath, I reached out. My knuckles touched the center of the door.

Knock. Knock. Knock.

Even if he had other girls to replace me, he still needed me to make Zayta happy.

My heart slammed against my chest.

I opened the door a little.

Seconds tapped by. And by. And by. Palms against the door, I pushed. Quiet, I told myself. Steady. I peeked my head between the door and its frame.

Slam!

My skull cracked against the doorframe. Lights dizzied my mind. Numb—minus the screwdrivers piercing my temples and neck—my eyes closed. On the ground, face first, I tried to move my arms. Nothing happened. Again, I tried. Nothing.

Once more, someone painted my world black.

BLINDING LIGHT SHOT THROUGH MY EYES, STRAIGHT TO MY head. Shielding my eyes with my hand, I squinted until I saw the TV mounted on the wall. The cool leather under my body told me where I was.

I moaned.

"I see you're awake now, you stupid whore." From behind me, probably sitting on his favorite chair, Andy's voice bruised me.

Love him, I begged myself. He needs your love.

The distinct smell—like wet-grass melting into earthy metal over-tones—of marijuana filled my nose. I breathed in, wishing I could get high from secondhand smoke. Drugs succeeded, most times, in tearing me away from pain, unless I came off the high before I fell asleep. That made every-thing worse.

Cola. My dear friend, Cola, would help me love Andy no matter how much he hated me. A little remained in my purse, enough to get a smooth high. I patted the couch around my body. Did I bring my purse?

"What are you looking for?" Andy's voice crackled. "Where'd you run off to, dirty whore?"

Something slammed into the wall.

I remembered the door smashing my head into the frame. That ex-plains the migraine, I told myself. I wanted to leave, but I needed to help him heal. "I ran," I said, "because I didn't want to do this anymore." Turn-ing my head, I squinted in pain. Andy walked across the room to the man-tle, grabbed a candleholder, and flung it across the room. It shattered over my head. Shards of glass rained over my stomach.

"I knew I couldn't trust you." Andy huffed. "Why did I hire you in the first place?"

"Because you saw dollar signs in my eyes."

Andy pulled a string of names—similar to whore—out of his mouth, his pitch rising with each one. After Zayta called a few weeks ago, he toned down the physical abuse a little—I said a little—and replaced it with full-blown emotional abuse.

"I love you, Andy." My voice shook.

"Whores don't know what love is."

"I know you better than anyone, Andy. I know what makes you flip, what makes you smile, what makes you nervous."

"You don't know anything except how to say yes to everything that comes your way."

Searching his living room without moving my body, I tried to think of an excuse to end the conversation. By the deep tone of Andy's voice and his clenched jaw, I could tell he was high—not the best time to express my devotion to him. He didn't believe he had anything to heal from anyway. Maybe he didn't. Maybe he was just nuts. And maybe I was nuts for trying to help.

Either way, I had to try.

The last days of summer felt like winter, when clouds always hide the sun.

Walls around me caved in. Andy's living room dimmed. His voice—ranting, raving, panting—sprinted through my mind. Lightheaded, I thought for sure I'd faint.

"Do you hear me?" Andy shouted.

My ears rang.

Glancing up, I saw his face turn white then fill with pink. He grabbed an empty Jack Daniels bottle off the coffee table and held it high above his head, like I cared.

"Kill me," I said. "I'm just a piece of trash anyway."

So much for love, I thought.

He flung his arm and the bottle crashed on the wall behind my head. Unmoved, I stared at him, wishing he killed me.

Worthless piece of trash.

He's right, I thought.

Andy charged me and flung my body to the ground.

He landed on top of me, digging his fingernails into my arms.

"Let go!" My veins flushed with heat.

He shoved his elbow into my neck. I gagged and kicked, too worn out to cry.

Tighter and tighter, his fingers squeezed my neck.

Kicking and coughing, I tried to scream.

Andy shoved his slimy tongue down my throat while his fingers squeezed my neck tighter.

Unable to cough, my arms weakened, my legs stopped kicking, and I hoped he'd look into my eyes and realize he loved me too much to hurt me.

But he didn't look into my eyes.

Instead, his lips touched my arm. Twisting away, my body flailed underneath of him. His teeth sunk into my arm and clamped down, sending waves of pain from my arm to my brain to my chest.

He stood and yanked me across the floor by my hair. I let him, wondering if these would be my last moments alive.

Andy threw me into a closet and locked the door. "Stay in there until you're sorry, and I'll let you out," he said from behind the door. "And if you pull this prank again you'll wish you would've killed yourself before my hands get to you."

Norma Jean smiled in my mind.

Curling into a ball, I talked to Daddy. He never talked back, but my heart splattered all over him until silence ran up and down my head like a million ants.

I looked around, hoping I'd find something to hang myself with.

The empty closet snickered at me.

The only end I could see waited for me behind a veil of suicide.

Behind the veil, death would kiss my lips and send me off into a painless oblivion where nothing existed—no gods, no pain, no drugs, no porn, no men, nothing.

That's all I wanted. An end. An escape.

Lifting my arms above my head, I slipped my shirt off and tied it around my neck.

Okay, so that's not gonna work.

I looked down.

By the light under the door something shimmered. I picked the piece of glass up and held it in my palm.

Must be a sign.

Daddy, if heaven exists, if you're there, will I see you after I kill myself? Do dirty whores make it to heaven?

No, I thought. Daddy's not there. And whores definitely wouldn't be accepted in heaven if they aren't accepted in churches. Nothing exists after this, anyway. Nothing except permanent escape from hell.

I pressed the triangle of glass into my wrist.

One, two—

The glass fell to the floor.

Surrounded by darkness I wanted to be swallowed by, I waited a few more minutes to try again.

Running the glass along my arm, I thought of myself. So glamorous, all decked out and Sadie-like. Lost behind it all, Taylor cried in the silence of the closet, but she drifted so far away I couldn't taste her tears. I couldn't feel them swiveling down her cheeks. I wanted to. I wanted her to come out and help me get out of the mess Sadie made of my life.

But Taylor hardly spoke. Nothing new there. Sadie, the dominant one, whispered things in my ear all day, even in my dreams.

"It won't take long. Just make a quick slit over your vein. All the pain will go away in a few minutes and you'll be free. It's the only way," she said.

Glass to vein, I held my breath and counted to ten. A little while longer and I'd be free.

Eternal darkness had to feel better than life. It had to.

I exhaled and held my breath again. This time I'd do it. This time I'd lift the veil.

One.

Two.

I pierced a tiny dot in my skin. In a quiet corner of my mind Taylor held my hand, asking me to stop. But Sadie, so strong and loud, urged my hand forward.

Three.

Pricked. Sliced. Opened.

Blood trickled down my arm and soaked into the fibers of my jean skirt.

I imagined worse. More pain, more blood, more something.

Thick scarlet liquid oozed from my wrist as I held it front of me.

A fire started in my wrist and sizzled up my arm. Hot pokers seared every inch of it, making it harder to stay calm.

Dizzier than I'd ever been, I closed my eyes. Mind over matter, mind over matter, I told myself. But the burning increased and my hand shook.

I held my arm to stop the shaking, but it worsened.

And worsened.

When I thought it couldn't get any worse my vision darkened around the edges.

I screamed out as my hands blurred. But I still saw them, cramped up into claws. I couldn't extend my fingers no matter how hard I tried. And the claws freaked me out so much I thought I'd pee my pants and be found dead in a sea of my own urine. Not the poetic ending I hoped for.

Right then I wanted to live. But my vision disappeared and my pulse slowed. Life leaked out of me. I couldn't do anything about it.

Thump.

Thump.

With every heart beat my brain flung against my forehead, like it would explode into pieces before the agony ended. *Thump.* Slower now, steady. *Thump.* My head, oh the excruciating throbs. My brain pushed and swelled and thudded.

I drew in one last breath and held it as long as I could.

Almost there, I thought. Almost.

Chapter 47 *Ally*

Weeks upon weeks went by. September's wind carried less humidity and the sound of locusts. I listened to them as I drove to work on a crisp Monday morning when Mom popped into my head. Only a small part of me wanted to talk to her, but after Jess and I experienced four straight days of romance like old times, I thought of calling her.

I struggled so much to stay joyful and loving with Jess, but I chose love anyway. And I thought of Dad every time I chose love over myself. If he still loves her, I thought, I should, too. And if I could love Jess through all my doubts and fears, I could love her. I would try to do practical things to keep myself in line. For every negative thought I had about Jessie or our marriage, I'd think of a reason I married him. It's as though I allowed our past to marry our present and create a brighter future.

A few days before, I came out of the shower and saw Jessie hiding something in the closet. His eyes practically flopped out of his head when he saw me. I can't express to you how much I wanted to run over to him and dig through the closet to reveal some great sin of his. But I didn't.

I still don't know what he hid. I left for work while he worked from home, as usual, so the only thing I could stand on was trust.

So, I did. Weak and wobbly as it can be sometimes, I stood on my trust for him. And although I'd barely be able to trust Mom, I thought I should at least try.

But for now, for now I needed to focus on Jessie.

AT WORK, IN BETWEEN A COUNSELING SESSION WITH A teenage girl and Myra, an email from Jessie popped up in the bottom right corner of my computer screen.

Earlier last week he sent me all sorts of romantic messages, so I opened the email expecting the same.

It said:

Dear Ally,

I can barely write this. But I am writing you anyway. I don't want to hide anything from you anymore.

Today as I was working I was hit with an advertisement that was nothing short of sexual :/ . . . One of those Internet ads in the side bar. To cut to the chase, I wasn't strong and my mind went back to the thoughts and images stored in my mind.

I fell Ally, and I hate myself. I hate what I did to you . . . and I hate what pain this will cause you. I need help ... I need your forgiveness and grace. I need this stuff out of my life for good. I need it gone, so we can get back to life. I need it to be finished so my heart won't be weighed down with fear every time I walk out the door or get online.

Please forgive me, sweet Ally. I'm sorry to have ruined that beautiful, free smile you had when we got married. I don't deserve you ... but I need you.

And I love you. I am just so weak still.

Do you love me?
Jessie

Birds chirped in the background of my calm mind. Yes, calm. Guess it happened so many times that the trigger pulled my anger again, but nothing happened. No explosion this time.

Only a longing for strength so deep I had to grip the handles of my chair to keep from falling on the ground.

Why me? ran through my head a time or two, but I didn't care anymore.

More than that, I didn't understand men and why it took so much effort to be devoted to their wives.

"Penises," Verity's voice buzzed in my mind. "Men aren't much more than glorified penises."

That girl tells you how it is. She's the crassest Christian I know, but she loves Jesus so I do my best to overlook it. Although I'd rather not have her annoying words stored in my memory.

I typed, *Yes, I love you.* And hit send.

Then I spun my chair around and looked out the window. Tree branches trembled in the breeze, their leaves shaking like my heart.

Verity's words weren't true. Obviously. Otherwise I wouldn't have married. Then again, maybe if I knew the truth I wouldn't have married him.

Think a positive thought, I told myself, then remembered Jessie's beautiful, servant-hearted spirit. All the times he brought me breakfast in bed. The mornings I woke up to his eyes on my face, his smile in my heart. All the massages he gave me after our evening walks, never once asking for me to return the favor.

Dad randomly interrupted my train of positivity. His faith echoed deep in my heart, begging me to reach for love and faithfulness and never let go, to bind it around my heart and love Jessie through it.

I twisted my chair and reached for the phone, dialed Dad's number, and waited.

"Hey, Ally," Dad said on the other end.

"Dad, I have a question." I just called him Dad for the first time.

"Sure, go ahead."

"I need to know how you've managed to go your entire life without looking at porn. If you really did."

"Wow."

"You don't have to answer if you don't want to. I'm wondering if it's even possible. And if you did, I need to know how."

"Hm. Does Jessie have a problem with it?"

I clicked my pen. "You don't need to answer my question if you don't want to, but I do need to go in a few minutes so I can't talk long."

"I see." He paused. "Well, I saw some as a boy, but not much. And believe me, I see enough driving down the road. A woman doesn't need to be naked and having sex with another man for a man to create pornography in his head, you know?"

I didn't want to know. "So how do you keep yourself from falling into it? Especially since you're single and all."

"Well, I don't really consider myself single, but I keep from lusting by loving Jesus more than myself. Doesn't get much plainer than that. It all flows fr—"

"Okay, okay, I know that. But what do you really do? I mean, practically?"

"Well, Ally." His tone dropped. Still sweet, but more serious. "Not everything in life has an instruction sheet. Sometimes God leads you where He wants you without telling you exactly how to get there." He paused. "But I can tell you this, cutting out my eye helped a great deal."

Someone knocked on the door.

Lauren peeked her smile in the room. "Myra's here."

Nodding, Dad and I said our goodbyes.

I rubbed my eyes. Living without an instruction sheet made no sense to me. There's always a solution to a problem, and therefore a method to solving every problem. Even with God's help, still, there are solutions and answers and ways to make sure things never go wrong.

Myra walked in my office.

There had to be a method to rid lust, heal broken hearts, and fix marriages that don't always want to be fixed. Otherwise my job would be pointless.

Chapter 48 *Taylor*

Obviously, I didn't die.

Instead, I dreamed of kissing Daddy's feet. I couldn't see his face, but I tried over and over. I looked up and his white robe blinded me. So sobbed at his feet as he told me that I'm not a whore. I cried harder. He held out a heart-shaped box and said, "Even if you were a whore, my daughter, you can be with me again if you accept this new heart." I kept telling him I couldn't reach the heart, I didn't know how to accept it, but then I'd get more and more blind.

He never told me how to accept it.

Then his robe turned super bright. I squinted my eyes over and over until I saw a girl's face hovering over me. Brown hair, dark eyes—Naomi?

Every few minutes I'd open my eyes wide and shut them, repeating until I finally saw her the furthest thing from Naomi. Gianna, sitting beside me, her smile whiter than Daddy's robe.

"What in Jupiter did you do to yourself?" She leaned onto my hospital bed.

My lips parted and my breath shook when I exhaled.

Gianna twirled her hair with her fingers. "Hate to break the bad news to you, but you're not dead."

Some news.

"And I've got some more bad news."

My wrist, wrapped in a plastic bandage, caught my attention.

"Do you want to know the news?"

"What is it?" My voice, raspy and dry, surprised me.

"You're pregnant." She huffed and rolled her eyes. "Can you believe that?"

"Um . . . what?"

Grasshoppers danced in my stomach. My stomach. A baby? A baby in my stomach? No, there had to be a mistake.

I looked at Gianna. "Why did they run a pregnancy test? How could they do that if I wasn't awake? Was I awake? I don't remember anything until now."

The light from the window lit her almond eyes. "Beats me." She shrugged. "Maybe an X-Ray?"

I sighed. "I would've known if they ran a test. You're lying."

"It's okay." Gianna patted my arm. "Zayta still wants you in Florida. She doesn't know about the suicide and if she did she'd probably take care of you anyway. And I won't tell anyone about the baby either."

Grasshoppers stopped dancing. And my stomach fizzed like a glass of Sprite, bubbling over and heading for my mouth.

"I'll even go with you to have an abortion." Her teeth sparkled. "I've already had three. It's not that bad, really."

The room fogged over. My mind swung back and forth in a frenzy from wondering how I'd ever be able to have an abortion, to wondering how I'd be able to have a baby, to realizing I would've killed another person if my suicide attempt worked.

Tears built up behind my eyes.

In that moment, right then, I knew I couldn't have an abortion. Adoption, maybe. But not an abortion.

Gianna's voice punched holes in my head for an eternity, then the nurse ushered her out.

AFTER LYING SO MUCH AT THE HOSPITAL, I THOUGHT MY tongue would fry up and turn to ashes, but I managed to walk out of the psych ward a few days later with my entire mouth in tact. Reminded me of the time Mom took me to the psych ward in Baltimore. I tried to kill myself by overdosing on her painkillers and then she forgot to pick me up when I was discharged.

Andy picked me up from the hospital and pretended like nothing happened. I wanted to pound his face into the earth until he reached China.

So much for loving him and playing heart doctor.

We got back to his house.

He opened the car door and actually let me sit in the passengers seat.

Expecting to see Zayta around, I was shocked to walk into Andy's empty house.

"Do you want to rest upstairs?" His eyes never met my face for the first time in the history of his eyes meeting my face.

Without saying a word, I walked up the stairs and into one of the bedrooms for the "porn set."

I reclined on the bed without moving my arms and propped them up on my stomach.

The ceiling blurred as I stared into space. Past memories flipped through my mind, one after another.

The rugged sound of a zipper as Mom's boyfriends unzipped their pants and touched themselves. Warm tears running down my nose as I pretended to sleep.

The stale scent of a school hallway in September. My first crush begged me to have sex with him and yelled, "You're a whore," through the hallway when I denied. Heads turned, my heart ducked inside, and he laughed.

A desire to be adored when Rick, my prom date, forced his body against mine in the bathroom. The nauseating stench of alcohol filled the air between us as my tears landed on the floor. One look at my wet face and Rick kicked the bathroom stall and walked away. The bathroom door slammed my heart and I never saw him again.

Then there's the day I thought life would change. Light sparkled in my heart and eyes as I pulled out of a Walgreens parking lot admiring my reflection in the rearview mirror.

Still, I can feel the sting of ripped skin, the ache in my thighs. I can see red stains on the couch and the lights of a camera filming my trembling lips, my cloaked fear.

I closed my eyes to rid the horrible memories and imagined the bright white robe I saw Daddy wear in my dreams.

My stomach muscles wrestled for food.

And I remembered the baby, the life forming inside of me.

One word entered my mind and lingered there, holding on for the slightest consideration.

Abortion.

Chapter 49 *Ally*

Myra relaxed in a chair across from me, clasped her hands, and tried to make eye contact with me. "He sent me the papers today."

I nodded. "What are you going to do?"

"What else can I do?" She unlocked her fingers and pressed the wrinkles in her skirt. "He doesn't want me anymore. It's over."

Help me fix her marriage. And mine. Show me the method, the answers.

"Have you ever thought of not signing them?" I said.

"Why would I do that? He'll just divorce me anyway."

"Well"—I shifted in my seat—"it will take much longer for the divorce to finalize, and you can keep your rings on, stay faithful, and refuse to be a divorcee no matter what the State says."

The skin around her eyes pulled so tight I imagined it cracking and bleeding.

"If my husband doesn't consider me his wife, then what's the point?"

"The point is. . . ."

My eyes searched Myra's, roaming for an answer, a method, a solution.

"The point is to never give up."

"But why? Why would I do that if he gives up? There is no marriage to fight for anymore. He ruined it. He doesn't want me. If he's not fighting, I don't see why I have to fight. Isn't that just abuse? I don't know what to do. I don't even remember one good thing about our relationship."

"Not one?"

"He's never been the romantic type."

"Why did you marry him?"

"Well, I don't know."

"Think of at least one reason."

Myra paused. And the pause never played again. Her words hid behind the tears forming in her eyes. She knew. I could see it. Somewhere inside of her she still loved him. She just hated that she loved him. I knew the feeling.

I looked around the room. Shelves of books mocked me like the women on Jess's computer. Years of study. Years of hoping to help marriages stay glued together by passion. Suddenly everything seemed less meaningful.

I couldn't fix Myra's marriage.

I couldn't even fix my own.

"Are you okay?" she said.

"I don't have any answers for you." My own words clawed my heart like a vulture after an open wound.

Her eyes widened, tightening the skin around them even more.

"I'm sorry, Myra. I don't think I can help you."

Call it pregnancy hormones. Call it a breakdown. Call it insanity. Whatever you call it, I walked by Myra's twisted face, out the door, passed Lauren's chirpy smile, and right to my car.

Responsible, mature, and oh so gracefully, I put my keys in the ignition and twisted. Again. And again. Oh, yes, and again.

The car mocked me too.

After a few punches on the dashboard, I tried again.

Nothing.

Nothing except Lauren at my car window, her chirpy smile gone south.

SINKING INTO MY SEAT, I CHUCKLED.

Alanis Morissette sang words of irony in my head. I opened the car door and tilted my head toward Lauren.

"What's going on?" she said.

I grabbed my purse from the passenger's seat, twisted the keys from the useless ignition, and got out of my car. "I'm sorry, Lauren. I can't do this anymore. Counseling is not for me. I really have no clue how to do this. Marriages," my voice cracked. "I just don't believe in them like I used to."

She touched my shoulder. "Take some time off. I'll let Mr. Almond know. You just let me know if you want to come back. I won't talk to the other counselors about it."

"Thanks."

I walked home, a few miles down Route 924, and considered a method, a solid way to make love stand when the world's arms keep pushing it down.

I FORGOT.

I completely forgot that Jessie looked at porn again until I walked in the front door and saw my least favorite person to see. Jessie's Dad. Standing in the kitchen with Jessie.

"Look at her." Mr. Graham's eyes surveyed my body. "She's the reason you're having these problems. I told you to marry a beautiful, tall woman. You married the wrong woman, son. Isn't that obvious now?"

Door still open, I flung my keys to the ground and gave Jessie my I-can't-believe-you-could-be-that-stupid look.

Jessie, as dead as his father's heart, stared at me, wordless, then looked at Mr. Graham and shook his head.

"What?" the ogre said. "I only said what's true. You need a woman around here who can keep this place clean. She can't even do that, so what makes you think she'd be able to please you in the bedroom with those average looks?" He swiped dust off an end table and analyzed his finger with disapproval. "If you would listen to me for once, you wouldn't get into these situations you get yourself into."

I walked away, hoping I'd hear Jessie's footsteps behind me.

At the top of the stairs, I paused, waiting for him.

I waited another minute and went into the bathroom, ran hot water, and undressed.

You'd think he would've learned by now to COME AFTER ME!

BY THE TIME I GOT OUT OF THE SHOWER AND PUT ON SOME clothes, it was dark.

Jessie sauntered into the bedroom, head down, shoulders hunched.

"My car didn't start. It's at work." I climbed into bed. "Oh, and by the way, I quit."

"Us or work?" Jessie undressed.

"Huh?"

"What did you quit?"

"Work. I quit work. I'm done."

He didn't look at me. Without a word, he slipped into bed, pulled the covers over his body, turned off the light, and closed his eyes.

Moonbeams casted bands of light on Jessie's face. I could tell by his relaxed features that he needed reassurance from me. He wanted me to tell him everything was okay and that he could talk to me without a shoe flying at his face.

Not in the mood to be the lover, I turned over.

What's so bad about wanting to be loved? I thought. He's the one that hurt me. He's the one that can't keep his eyes off other women. He's the one who invited the ogre over to insult me. And he knows I don't feel comfortable being around that man, much less sharing our most intimate details with him.

I rolled out of bed and walked downstairs, again hoping for Jessie to follow. I knew he wouldn't.

Our library of books, organized by genres and topics, caught my attention. I ran my fingers along the spines. Lord, show me something, some way to fix my marriage. Counseling books, inspirational books, marriage books—none of them stood out to me.

So I tilted my Bible from the rows of books and pulled it out, sat on the couch, and hid my body with our throw.

Palms on either side of the Bible, thumbs on the silver pages, I opened to a random page and scanned for a random verse.

This will be my answer, I thought.

Then render to Caesar's the things that are Caesar's and to God the things that are God's.

Okay, not my answer.

I flipped through the New Testament again, knowing God would show me something this time, a secret to fixing my broken marriage.

Therefore God gave them up in the dishonorable lusts of their hearts to impurity, to the dishonoring of their bodies among themselves, because they exchanged the truth about God for a lie and worshiped and served the creature rather than the Creator, who is blessed forever! Amen.

Apparently God wasn't interested in revealing secrets tonight.

Or maybe He was trying to show me something in those verses.

I reread the words, scanning them for hidden meanings, trying to see what they could mean for me.

Confused, I shut the Bible, opened it up, and turned to a random page again.

I am the true vine, and my Father is the vinedresser. Every branch in me that does not bear fruit he takes away, and every branch that does bear fruit he prunes, that it may bear more fruit. Already you are clean because of the word that I have spoken to you. Abide in me, and I in you. As the branch cannot bear fruit by itself, unless it abides in the vine, neither can you, unless you abide in me. I am the vine; you are the branches. Whoever abides in me and I in him, he it is that bears much fruit, for apart from me you can do nothing.

I closed the Bible and allowed the words to sow seeds of wisdom in my mind. Unsure of whether God gave me the verse or if I happened upon it by chance, I waited for the seeds to grow.

Eyes closed, head propped with pillows, my mind floated back and forth, like a kite caught in a breeze.

I knew I couldn't do anything apart from God. But I guess I tried anyway.

I opened my eyes and stared at the ceiling.

Marriage, in the beginning at least, scooped me off my feet and carried me through a rush of romance. We never thought much of God, and truthfully, I didn't know how to do so as a couple. And most of the time, I didn't want to.

I still didn't.

Chapter 50 *Taylor*

Gianna told me to get health insurance through the medical assistance, so I did and made her come with me to my first appointment to check on the baby. She wouldn't come at first and desperately tried to convince me to have an abortion. It's the only way, she said. I heard those words before and didn't want to hear them anymore, so I told her to either come with me or stay. Either way, I needed to go.

She agreed to go.

After she snorted a line.

We showed up ten minutes late to Lisa's suite on Upper Chesapeake Drive. Honestly, I still hadn't chosen against having an abortion. The visit was sort of my test to see if I could deal with an abortion after hearing the baby's heartbeat. Part of me wished I wouldn't hear a heartbeat.

I signed in at the front desk and walked over to Gianna. The eyes of other women in the room flickered. I could see them out of the corner of my eyes, looking up from their magazines. Faces down, eyes up, they watched me.

I should've worn something more mature, I thought. Like I owned anything mature.

One woman with a soft, pretty way about her glanced at my bare ring finger and back to her magazine.

When I sat down next to Gianna, I thought of the church Naomi took me to, all the people staring and making fun of me. I looked around the room at the different sized bellies, wondering if anyone could love someone enough to look passed the artificial surface and see the pain.

Gianna, unashamed of her life and looks, touched my arm and said, "Don't worry about these nasty looks. These women are just jealous because their husbands have probably seen your porno flicks." She laughed. "Told ya to get an abortion. You'd fit in better with that crowd anyway."

My body melted into the floor.

I knew I should've stopped her from getting high first. Her attitude grew snarkier with each line she snorted.

Most of the women in the room pretended not to hear Gianna's words. Except the one who eyed my absent wedding ring. Her soft beauty disappeared behind a crinkled forehead and evil eyes. She made no effort to hide her stares.

"Taylor Adams," called a young nurse from a hallway door.

Oh, thank you, thank you, thank you.

Clutching my purse to my stomach, I walked passed glistening eyes and turning heads. Gianna followed.

"Wait out here," I whispered.

She exhaled, muttered something under her breath, then walked away.

Without the drugs and porn, she and I would have been good friends, but the surface of our lives, coated with so much junk, kept us from really knowing each other.

"Right this way," the nurse said.

I DIDN'T WANT TO KNOW MY WEIGHT, BUT THE NURSE TOLD me anyway. I'll spare you the details, but let's just say I've never been so skinny in my life.

Lisa finally came in the room. I kept tugging my sleeves to make sure she wouldn't see the scar on my wrist, but I think she saw them anyway.

Her red-rimmed glasses, Hawaiian print dress, and bold sneakers made me laugh.

She leaned me back on the table and squirted cold jelly on my lower abdomen. I flinched.

She laughed. "It'll warm up in a second."

She moved a plastic thing back and forth on my stomach. Static-like sounds came from the device. I held my breath, wondering what the heartbeat would sound like. Maybe the test was a false positive. I didn't feel pregnant.

She looked at the ceiling and squinted her eyes. "Come on, kid. Where are ya?"

The device, held by Lisa's thick fingers, slid across my abdomen, left to right, right to left, then she stopped.

Static disappeared.

I stared at Lisa. She looked at me and smiled.

Galloping horse feet filled the room.

"There you are," Lisa said. "You hear that, Taylor? That's your baby."

Smiling, I listened. I wanted to listen forever.

Yeah, I didn't know the baby's Dad, and I didn't want to either, but still, a heartbeat raced in my womb.

A real heartbeat. A person. A life.

Lisa took the plastic thing away and cleaned the jelly off my skin. I closed my eyes and concentrated. The heartbeat still bounced off the walls of my mind.

I ran my hand across my stomach. Who will raise you?

Lisa gave me some papers, relayed some mandatory information, then hugged me.

She held me so tight I thought she'd never let go.

"I admire you," she said. "You're doing something most people wouldn't do. Stay strong."

She backed away and held a folder to her chest.

My teeth hid under a weak smile. She never did tell me the due date. I'd have an ultrasound later to find out, since I had no idea when I conceived or when I had my last period.

Her glasses fell to the tip of her nose. "Remember, the best road is rarely the easiest."

Nodding, I laughed. I wasn't sure what she meant and I felt dumb asking. She smiled again, patted my knee, and walked out.

My mind centered on thoughts of the baby's heartbeat and adoption. My baby in another woman's arms. It's what needed to happen, but I didn't want to give my little baby up.

Not excited to walk by those sneering women again, I waited, imagining the heartbeat, picturing a little nose and eyes and lips. Imagining my baby, wrapped in blankets, in another woman's arms. Another woman who would be Mommy.

A woman.

I'm still a girl.

I hopped off the examination table and opened the door.

The ring-conscious woman walked by. A scent of juniper and roses walked by with her. She looked me up and down and shook her head.

People never noticed me before. Now they shook their heads in disgust.

I walked by the front desk, figuring I'd make another appointment later if I wanted to, and nodded to Gianna. She stood and followed me to the door.

Every time my heels clinked on the hallway floor I heard the baby's heartbeat. As much as I loved the feeling of bringing something good into the world for once, I didn't think I could do it.

I mean, realistically, abortion seemed like a better option.

Click. Clack. Gallop. Gallop.

My stomach flipped like the leaves on a tree right before a storm comes.

Andy would find out one day, and when he does abortion would be the first thing on his mind.

GIANNA AND I SHOWED UP AT ANDY'S HOUSE. SHE DROPPED me off, probably afraid to come in. I didn't blame her. Andy never scarred her with words and hands like he did me, but I told her everything one day and she kept her distance since then.

Andy stood, hands on his hips, in the hallway to the kitchen as I opened the door.

I turned away, watching the doorknob as I shut the door, hoping to look back and see Andy's eyes turned bright.

His phone rang, but he didn't move. Words rose from his mouth like breath in frosty air. So soft, so chilling that I couldn't understand what he said.

I stood, palms against my tiny skirt, looking at the ground.

Andy stepped forward, cracking the ice between us.

"I'm pregnant." The words came out of my mouth like fire, melting every last inch of ice in the room.

"No, you aren't."

"I heard the heartbeat today."

"Right. Is this supposed to scare me or something?"

"Call the midwife if you don't believe me." I walked toward the steps.

"Well, you're getting an abortion, aren't you?"

"No."

"Zayta found another director. And you're staying here with me." The more words he said, the more his voice raised. "Long story. I'm not getting into details, but you need to get an abortion. I don't want your body getting all stretched out on me."

"I don't want an abortion, Andy."

"What choice do you have? What would you do with a baby? You don't even know how to take care of yourself."

I sat on the bottom step. "I can't have an abortion. I don't know what I'm doing with the baby, but I can't kill it."

"You know, you could do porn while pregnant. Some guys like that. Might be a way for us to get into another avenue."

"I'm not doing that."

"You'll do whatever I tell you to do, baby." His thumb skimmed my cheek. "I'm all you've got."

I stood and looked right into Andy's bloodshot eyes. "You make me do something I don't want to do again and I swear I'll kill myself for good. Me and the baby. And I'll make sure the world knows it's your fault."

Andy laughed. "Right, like that's gonna happen." He scanned my face. His gaze landed on my lips. "And don't ever use that word again."

"What word?"

"Shut up." His palm slapped my mouth and stayed there. Elbow in the air, hand over my mouth, he laughed again. "You have this thing inside of you and your life is going to be over. No one is ever going to take you seriously. Not in this business, not in anything else. I'll make sure of it."

He pushed my face. My neck snapped backward. He stepped away.

I mean, sometimes, even with my walls up, I had an urge to cry. Like Mom's sobs locked behind her door, the tears were still there, just hidden.

But now, now the urge never came when it should have. Forget hidden, they were lost.

And for some reason that hurt even more.

Chapter 51 *Ally*

J essie couldn't come to my next prenatal appointment and boy was I glad. I checked in, sat down, and five seconds later two girls walked in. One of them looked like a smaller version of Angelina Jolie, but the other looked exactly like Jessie's type. You know, tall, curvy, blonde, and pretty much perfect.

She walked over to check in as her Angelina friend sat down on a chair to the left of me, against the wall.

I couldn't help but notice their clothing. The Angelina girl appeared about mid-twenties or so. But the beautiful blonde, she seemed a bit younger, maybe twenty-one at the most. And they dressed like pop stars. Short skirts, high heels, silky straight hair, bangs—you name it.

After Blondie checked in she walked by me. Naturally, I glanced at her ring finger. I assumed she wasn't married, but you know, I wanted to check. She could've been there for a routine checkup, but something told me she was pregnant. Something about the way she timidly walked across the room, shoulders hunched, head down. She didn't carry herself the way she should've based off her looks and style. No confidence existed in her stride.

The other women in the room also stared at the girls. I tried not to be noticeable, but I couldn't help it. I longed for the youth and beauty in that girl, her smooth face and flawless legs, thinking maybe Jessie'd love me if I looked like her.

Then, Angelina's voice jammed pencils in my ear and right to my heart.

"Don't worry about these nasty looks." She smiled at the very pregnant woman across from me. "These women are just jealous because their hus-

221

bands have probably seen your porno flicks." She laughed so cold I wondered if her heart could survive such bitterness. "Told ya to get an abortion. You'd fit in better with that crowd anyway."

Her words stung the open wounds in my heart and lingered there, like a never-ending bee sting. I hated porn stars even more. My eyes narrowed so much I could barely see their faces, but I looked anyway, making sure they saw my disgust. Not only with the porn, but the absolute insolence to mention abortion around other pregnant women.

Blondie, the little pregnant porn star, fidgeted with the frays of her jean skirt while Angelina rolled her eyes and slumped back in her chair. The cute blonde nurse Jessie admired called a name. Blondie stood, walked away, and disappeared. I thought porn stars lived in California, not here. So close to home, to Jessie—it scared me.

The bee sting pricked me, over and over, in places I didn't know existed. Meanwhile, Angelina rocked back and forth in her chair, rummaged through her purse repeatedly, and repositioned her boobs about fifteen times, pushing them up for the world to see.

Laughable, yes, but with every strange motion from her direction I wanted to ask her why she would want to ruin marriages and be a sexual object to so many men.

Dodging relentless thoughts in my mind, I sat there with a pigeon-toed brain, too wobbly to evade the arrows coming at me from every direction.

Another nurse—thank heavens it wasn't a blonde-haired girl—called my name.

I walked toward her smile. She ushered me in the hallway, took my weight as I wondered what Blondie weighed, and led me to my room.

A door clicked open. I followed the nurse and turned my head to the left. Blondie stood there, wide-eyed and rosy-cheeked. I furrowed my brow, shook my head, and kept walking.

But no matter how far I walked from her pretty little self—or should I say, pretty tall self—a hole in the shape of her body tore through my mind, its serrated contour reminding me of my ragged marriage.

Lisa told me I was almost ten weeks along as she slid the heartbeat monitor over my belly. The baby's heartbeat thudded through the room. Forget horse feet, this child's heart raced much faster than any horse I ever heard.

"Still going strong," Lisa said. "Will you be finding out the sex of the baby?"

"Yes, we will. When will that be?"

She slid the monitor off my skin and wiped my belly with a paper towel. "About twenty weeks. Ten weeks from now." She tossed the paper towel in a trashcan under the sink. "I don't know how true some of those pregnancy myths are, but based off the heartbeat, they'd say it's a boy."

"Well, I don't know how true those are either, but I'm happy as long as it's a healthy baby." I sat up. "Having so much trouble with infertility, I'm so afraid of a miscarriage."

"The good news is miscarriages are most common in the first twelve weeks, and you only have two more to go."

Perhaps she intended to ease my concern, but knowing I still had two weeks to go stressed me out even more. Knowing me, I'd think about it every second, counting down the days, imagining pangs in my abdomen.

Please, Lord. Let this be it. Let this baby make it these next two weeks.

WHEN I ARRIVED HOME, I WALKED INTO THE KITCHEN TO get a glass of water and some crackers to munch on. If I didn't eat (literally all day long) my nausea would worsen and worsen to the point of vomiting. So I always snacked on something, and still felt hungry.

As I poured a glass of distilled water, I noticed a note on the counter by the entrance to the dining room. The closer I got the more I noticed Jessie's handwriting.

Cracker crumbs landed on the note as I read it.

Go to the place we met and find your next assignment. —Your Stupid Husband-

I chuckled inside at his signature. But I didn't want an assignment. Another attempt at romance wasn't something I'd receive well. Not now. Not after the porn star encounter. I exhaled.

I finished my crackers and water, then grabbed my keys, got in my car, and headed to 95 South toward Barnes & Noble in White Marsh. Didn't think much about it. Just went and figured I'd get through it, even if I didn't want to.

As the dotted lines of the highway disappeared behind me, memories of Jessie managed to rinse thoughts of porn, at least for now.

WHEN I MET JESSIE, BARNES & NOBLE IN WHITE MARSH WAS home to me. Hot chocolate, caramel frappaccinos suffocated by whipped cream, extra creamy macchiatos, and books, books, and more books. Call it a bookstore if you will, I called it my corner of heaven.

Sure enough, my table was open. After exchanging five George Washington's for one iced caramel latte with extra caramel, I tucked myself in the corner of the room and watched people.

A young girl—probably seventeen—and her boyfriend sat down behind me as she rambled about how Shane thought she was so hot, but how she didn't care. I would have loved to see the look on her boyfriend's face.

He responded, "So, why've you been talking about it for ten minutes?"

Man, I wanted to jump up and high-five him right there.

But someone caught my attention.

He walked through the door and stood in line at the cafe. My heart stopped. I know that sounds cliché, but honestly, I think it did.

Sometimes life stops and nothing else matters but the moment you're stuck in. You want to pause it so bad, but at the same time fast-forward to see what happens.

That's the best way I can describe the moment I first saw Jessie Graham.

Two weeks passed and I spent every day at Barnes & Noble. Didn't see him for fourteen days. When hope turned sour, the sky turned to raspberry and in he walked, book under his arm, lips slightly upturned, and man oh man, I loved him.

Okay, so maybe love wasn't the right word but you know what I mean.

Pretending to read *The Four Loves* by C.S. Lewis, I turned a page and looked up. He sat down by the window across the room. I looked down, smiled inside, maintained my horrible acting by flipping pages faster than Lewis himself could've read them, and looked up again.

Jessie looked away. I caught him staring at me.

My fingers whipped another five pages while, like any twenty-two-year-old girl would have done, I silently whispered, "Wow," until my brain told me to shut up.

I glanced up again. He stood and walked away. Afraid to lose him again, I stood and followed. He stopped in the Religion section. A Christian? I approached him and tried something Verity did to strangers. "Describe your soul in three words."

He didn't smile. "My soul?"

"I shouldn't have done that," I said to the books.

"My soul," he said. "Well, exploratory, flawed, and idealistic."

I ran my index finger down the spines of a few books. I'd been with Verity a few times when she asked random strangers that question, but I never heard an answer like his?so honest and serious.

"What about you?"

I knew he'd ask. I picked up a book, hoping he wouldn't ask again.

"Well, you can't ask someone that and not expect to answer it yourself."

"Well," I said to the book. "I don't know."

He pointed to *The Four Loves* still in my other hand. His fingers brushed mine. My stomach danced.

"C.S. Lewis, huh?" he said.

"Yeah. I'm studying Psychology at Towson University."

"Oh yeah? What are your plans?"

"I'd like to be a marriage counselor."

"A marriage counselor? Pretty specific."

"I've seen love turn into something evil too many times. I want to help people stay in love."

He looked down at my hands, analyzed *The Four Loves* with an expression I'd later discover the meaning behind, and smiled. Phew. I breathed again.

"You ever been in love?" he said.

"Not yet."

"Well, how do you know you'll be able to help people stay in love?"

"Because," my lips began without my heart's permission, "I've spent my entire life waiting for love, so I can be faithful to the one man I'm waiting to give my heart to. Love is important to me. Marriage is important to me."

"But you're not married yet."

I smiled. "I will be."

"Ah, an idealist."

"Realist," I said.

And he laughed.

I SMILED, INSIDE AND OUTSIDE. THE SPARKLE IN JESSIE'S eyes—and I'm sure my own eyes as well—the day we met, well, I've never seen a light in his eyes like that since. It was a light created for the day our eyes finally found each other's.

I veered off the highway toward White Marsh, listening to my own naïve voice in my head. I want to help people stay in love. Love is important to me. Marriage is important to me. But I didn't know. I didn't know what love and marriage entailed. I didn't understand how deep pain could run.

I stopped at a red light in the left lane.

Less than five minutes from Jessie and I wanted to turn around.

There's nothing to fix, I thought. I need to either deal with it or not deal with it. I can't fix him.

I accelerated, turned, and thought about that first night again.

THE SUN DISAPPEARED BEHIND BARNES & NOBLE AS JESSIE and I sat in the café talking until someone tapped me on the shoulder and kindly asked us to leave. They closed fifteen minutes ago. We had no idea.

Falling in love does that to you.

"Let's go," Jessie said as he tossed a backpack over his shoulder and stood.

I didn't want to.

He smiled, walked over to me and waited to pull out my chair. I stood. He slid the chair from under me. I slipped my purse over my forearm and grinned. Modest, considering I wanted to beam from ear to ear. Didn't want to scare the guy away.

His fingers linked with mine as he led me to the door, opened it for me without letting go of my hand, and smiled again. A trace of cologne brushed by my nose. I inhaled and smiled.

Mom always said, "Wait for the butterflies." She said I'd know when I found the person I was meant to marry because every time I'd see or think about him, I'd get butterflies in my stomach. Well, I was off to a good start. Although I wonder if I should've taken advice from her in the first place.

Either way, my stomach could have been mistaken for a sack of four hundred tiny butterflies. That couldn't have been a bad sign.

We walked down The Avenue and admired the closed shops.

"Hard to believe this was all grass and trees sometime in the past." Jessie smiled, swaying our hands in the April breeze.

"Yeah," I said, followed by the sound of slapping tongues as a young couple made out in front of the movie theatre. Jessie didn't notice them. His eyes were on me. How I longed for that again. For his eyes to be so fixated on me that he didn't see anyone else.

He led me to a bench in front of a woman's clothing store and waved his free hand. "Sit, my lady."

"Ah, thank you fine sir." I laughed and hid my teeth behind a smile.

He kneeled in front of me, looked down, then back up at me. I folded my hands in my lap. Our eyes locked. My stomach waltzed again with a confused excitement.

He held my hand. "Allyson, will you marry me?"

I bit my bottom lip, laughed inside, and looked at the moon.

There's no way he's serious, I thought.

His left hand shook as it loosely held mine. I looked down into his expecting eyes, bright as the moon. Crickets chirped—not in that harmonious, beautiful way—more like blasting horns in the middle of a love song. Disconcerted and just plain odd. But at least something filled the awkward silence.

I didn't know what to say. Or think. I didn't know whether I was still falling in love or if he creeped me out. Without moving my head, my eyes shot up toward the moon then traced Orion. I tried to think of an excuse to leave.

A fit of laugher burst from Jessie's lips. He stood in front of me, clapped his hands, and laughed so hard he ended up on one knee again, stooped over with one hand on his chest and the other on the cement.

I don't know what my face looked like for those few minutes, but when he finally stopped laughing my eyes were dry from not blinking.

"That was awesome. I really got you." He fought to breathe.

"Uh, yeah, that's an understatement." I looked at his hands. "But your hands were shaking. How'd you do that?"

He held out his hand, stiff as the bench I sat on, then it started to vibrate. "You can thank Tisch School of the Arts at NYU."

"Well, thanks Tisch." My ability to get him back wasn't questioned. But he'd find out soon enough. "You're an actor, then?"

"If you want to call it that. But not really. I took a few classes for fun, but went to school for marketing."

"You're finished college?"

"Yeah." He paused. "So, did I freak you out or what?"

I put my hands on the bench and leaned forward. "I didn't know what to think."

"So, you don't want to marry me then?"

"After something like that, well, no."

The unhindered beam on his face told me he knew I was joking.

"Well, you better get home. Maybe I can win you over on our second date."

Little did I know, it wouldn't take a second date.

I PULLED INTO THE PARKING LOT BEHIND BARNES & NOBLE and saw rose petals all over the place. I'm not exaggerating. There were so many rose petals all over the gravel that it looked like a pink blizzard swept through the area. Well, at least part of the area, as they only covered about four car spaces and the grass where we first kissed.

I smiled.

I didn't try to feel the romance and I didn't shove it away when it came. But it came, fluttering about my stomach like the butterflies from the past.

I still loved him. That gentle smile of his, still the same. Those adventurous eyes, still the same. The love between us, although creased and crumpled, still had value. It still lived.

I love him, I thought. He's still my Jessie.

Chapter 52 *Taylor*

A ndy kept his promise. He always did.

I filmed a few more movies with him, hoping Zayta would come and whisk me away, but she dropped off the face of Jupiter, as Gianna would say.

I stopped caring about much of anything, except the baby. No matter how depressed I got, I would not get an abortion.

Andy refused to talk about the baby. I went to my second prenatal appointment with his permission, but not his enthusiasm. I even had an ultrasound that told me I was about thirteen weeks pregnant. Already out of the first trimester. And only three weeks left to legally have an abortion. I don't know why I reminded myself that, but I did.

I returned to Andy's house after that appointment, realizing I had three weeks to choose an abortion or choose to find out what the sex of the baby was. When I told him I made it passed the first trimester he shoved me into a humiliating photo shoot. Details aren't necessary, just know that I was humiliated and I knew his purpose behind it. He wanted me to feel ugly and degraded, even more so than I already did, so that I'd get rid of the baby before my stomach started to grow.

I did the photos and started to walk upstairs, but Andy grabbed my arm and pulled me toward him.

"I don't want you living here anymore," he said.

My back and arms stiffened. I'd been waiting for those words for a long time, but they didn't give me the relief I had hoped for. No, they made me anxious. I didn't know the world outside of Andy. I hadn't for months and I didn't want to. Especially without money and a job, not to mention my soon-to-be pregnant stomach.

"I'll do whatever you need me to do," I said. "Don't make me leave."

"What am I going to do with you?" He stepped back. For the first time since I met him I saw something real in his eyes—something resembling apprehension rolling behind his half-closed eyelids. "I can't work with a pregnant girl. This wasn't supposed to happen."

Arms crossed over my ribs, I waited for him to keep talking. Something was happening to him. The harshness that generally controlled his tongue wasn't there. Instead, he spoke with a sullen whisper.

He shifted his weight from one leg to other, never taking his eyes off his navy Puma's. I unfolded my arms and clasped my hands in front of me. The air waited for one of us to inhale and breathe out words, but I didn't, and he didn't.

Tugging on his sleeves and pulling his t-shirt down, Andy continued to rock his weight from one leg to another, and again, and again until I finally decided to say something.

"You okay?"

He leaned against the wall.

"Look," I said. "If you want me to go, I will."

"I don't know what I want anymore." A whisper so faint I could barely hear it left his lips. He then propelled himself away from the wall with his hands and walked out the door.

"What just happened?" I said to myself as I looked out the window. Andy's car backed out of the garage, down the driveway, and out of view. No tires burning up the asphalt, no music loud enough to stir the neighbors, nothing but the quiet sound of his car swishing by.

I opened the door and sat on the front step. The leaves, still green but ready to turn colors, sailed on a cool breeze. I tucked my knees to my chest and folded my arms around them.

Andy's whispers sauntered around my head as I watched the sky turn colors and fade to night.

When the stars showed their faces, Andy drove up the driveway, parked inside the garage, and then came out and met me on the step.

He stood in front of me. "You can stay here. But not for long. You need to figure something out."

"Like what? What are you going to do?"

"Don't ask questions. Just listen to me. If you want to make it in this world, figure something out and do it. I'm not going to be here much longer."

"But where are you going?"

"I'm leaving, okay?"

"But, what am I su?"

"You're supposed to be a big girl and figure things out for yourself. I'm not your daddy."

"Well, you've sure seemed like it for the passed few months."

Andy stood in the doorway, looking down at me with tenderness in his droopy eyes. "I'm sorry."

I raised my eyebrows. My heart rate followed, galloping like the baby's. I stood and touched Andy's forearm. Maybe this was my chance to love him like he needed. Maybe he was finally ready to change.

He slid my hand off his arm. "You don't know me."

"Let me know you."

He shook his head and walked inside. I followed, closed the door, and trailed his footsteps to the living room.

"Let me know you, Andy. I want to know you."

He sat on the couch. I stood in front of him, feeling like Julia Roberts in front of Hugh Grant in *Notting Hill*, wanting to say, "I'm just a girl, standing in front of a boy, asking him to love her."

Andy leaned forward and held my hands, kissed both of them, and let them go.

A rush of life zigzagged through my body, from my hands to feet, giving me chills and flushing my body with warmth at the same time.

My hands dangled at my sides, lonely, needing his touch, his lips on my skin again.

He pulled my hand, gently, and urged me to sit beside him on the couch. Following my body, I sat down and waited for him to open his heart to me, let me in the room I've been dying to enter.

A clock ticked in the background, along with the buzzing of the refrigerator from the kitchen. I looked down and back up to Andy's troubled eyes. And before the second hand made another tick, he leaned toward me and pressed his lips against mine.

More than my desires to love and change him, I needed him. His kiss, his love, his breath mixed with mine. I needed him to want me, to show me my worth, my value, and my security. Andy was the only one who could give me that.

And with each smooth kiss from his lips, I needed more.

But with one last, lingering kiss, he stood and covered his face. I straightened my posture and reached for his hand. He walked away, his kiss still damp on my lips, his breath still on my tongue.

I waited for him to come back, but he didn't.

Just before the front door closed the door to his heart, he whimpered. And my own tears returned, full force, like the Atlantic Ocean blocked behind an enormous wall and finally set free.

Chapter 53 *Ally*

I parked my car near the petals and scanned the area for Jessie or some sort of clue for the next place to go, but I couldn't see anything. So I got out of the car and walked around, kicking the petals into the air as I walked.

The beauty of grass and gravel laden with what had to be thousands of rose petals is something I will never forget. And the scent. Mmm . . . inhaling the unmistakable sweetness of roses and being surrounded by a blanket of petals. It was ethereal.

My favorite part was the grass. Blades of green poked through the pink petals, and those are my favorite colors together. So soft and bright, feminine and refreshing.

A pink rose with a note, taped to the stones where we first kissed, caught my eye. My next clue.

I peeled the tape back, smelled the rose, and turned in a circle, scanning the parking lot for Jess.

Nowhere in sight, at least not in my sight.

I unfolded the note and read: *My love, just remember in the Fall, beneath the bitter snow, lies the seed that with the sun's love, in the spring, becomes a rose. Come sail away, come sail away, come sail away with me, lad. —Your Dense Husband—*

I laughed. He stole lyrics from two of my favorite songs that he labeled "cheese," and I knew exactly what the clue meant.

I scooped a bunch of rose petals into my arms and got into the car, tossing the petals all over, then I drove off toward Loch Raven Reservoir with more memories in my head.

ONE WEEK FROM THE DAY I MET JESSIE, ON A SATURDAY, WE drove around country roads listening to CDs we made titled "Soundtrack of My Life."

We drove around Harford County and back, down Harford Road's twist and turns, and made our way to Loch Raven while unfolding my life in music. We heard everything from The Rolling Stones to the Backstreet Boys before it was Jessie's turn and oh boy was I in for the ride of my life, or should I say his life.

We drove over a bridge that took us over Loch Raven Reservoir. To the left the blue sky faded to pastel pinks and purples. God's signature on our first date. The water ripples reflected God's masterpiece, only adding to the beauty around us. I could smell wood burning, a fall scent that somehow fit the April moment.

D'yer Mak'er by Led Zeppelin shook the speakers in the car as Jessie added to the car's racing heartbeat by pounding on the steering wheel. In between his efforts to beat out John Bonham in an air drum contest, he explained the history of Loch Raven Dam. Boring information that I could've cared less about, like how it was originally constructed in 1912, to a height of 188 feet. Ten years later, they (whoever they were, I'm not sure) built it to the current height of 240 feet. I pretended to care, but truth is I was more enthralled with the man drumming on the steering wheel and singing his heart out than how the Dam was built.

I'm sure any girl would say the same.

"Now this is music," Jessie said when the next song started. "B.B. King knows his stuff."

"His stuff?"

"Just listen to that. Man. . . ."

Now, air guitar. I swear I thought we were about to drive into a tree. I wanted to watch Jessie, hair falling in his face, fingers sliding up and down an invisible guitar. But how could I when he was using his knee to drive with ten thousand trees on the side of the road waiting for a nice hug from his Del Sol?

"Um," I interrupted.

Jessie turned, his knee still steering our lives toward the nearest tree.

I couldn't do it. I couldn't tell him to put his hands on the wheel. Too

soon to be so, I don't know, annoying. "So, tell me more about the Dam."
A wonderful divergence for a man who loves to talk about random things
no one else knows.

Jessie turned the volume down. B.B. King said *goodbye* as The Beatles
said *hello, hello, you say goodbye and I say hello.*

"Well," he whispered, half-smiling. "On October 26, 1958 two men
claim they saw an egg-shaped UFO a hundred feet or so above the
bridge."

"Yeah, right."

"Dead serious. Although I don't know how serious they were."

"Why do you know this stuff?"

"Magic eight-ball."

Phew, finally his hands fell to the wheel.

Jessie parked his car and looked at me.

I recognized the song playing and looked down, trying to think of
where I heard it before. "Is this—"

"Yes, it's the *Forrest Gump* theme song, but after Milli Vanilli and backstreet's back alright, you have no room to talk."

I shook my head, wondering if I'd lose a few pounds from all the
laughing. Not that I needed to. At that age, I was thin enough to fit into my
coat closet, which was very, very small. And yes, I tried.

"You're beautiful." Jessie interrupted my thoughts.

I blushed. "So, when do you go back to New York?"

"Oh, I just moved back home last week. Finally."

"Are you staying here?"

"I promise."

I smiled. "Is that a threat?"

"No. I promise. And I don't break promises."

Something about his sincerity pacified me. Or maybe it was the way his
serious eyes loved me from across the car.

The sunset faded behind the trees. We talked. We laughed. We kissed.
And I wondered why God chose me. For years I thought I was doomed
to singleness, and now this man with gentleness and adventure looked me
in the eyes and said, "This song is the last on the c.d. It's for this moment,
right now. The beginning of my life."

Soft piano notes broke through the silence, distending and leveling out. At first I didn't recognize the man's voice, or the woman's. Then the chorus swelled and I almost laughed, picturing Kevin Bacon in my mind, but Jessie wasn't laughing. He loved me. I don't know how. People thought we were crazy. Puppy love that would never last, but it wasn't puppy love. It wasn't infatuation. Somehow we knew.

I don't know, maybe it was infatuation, but I knew. He knew. And that's all that matters.

He stared at me. I stared back. The chorus to *Almost Paradise* played again.

I could see forever in his eyes.

Oh, the cheesiness. But I really, really could.

I DROVE OVER THE BRIDGE WHERE TWO MEN SUPPOSEDLY saw UFO's, picturing Jessie's smirk as he told me that, picturing his grin now as he imagined me touring the state with his face in my mind.

Again, I spotted grass covered by rose petals, this time surrounding a tree. When I got closer, I slowed my car and parked. The tree had our initials painted on it and a note below the heart that enclosed them.

I didn't waste any time. Forgetting about porn stars, I lunged head first into my marriage and allowed myself to be loved and to love. Fun. For the first time in too long, I allowed myself to have fun.

The note said:

My teddy bear, remember when I held you that day in September? The air was kind of like it is now, really crisp. You were upset about the meal you burned when we were having our first guests over since we got married. The smoke alarm. The tears. My arms around you. Let me hold you again. —Your Pathetic Husband—

Chapter 54 *Taylor*

A ndy returned, drunk and stumbling over his feet, a few hours after he left his house crying. I never left the living room.

When I heard the door open I hurried to meet him.

He grabbed my shoulder. "Let's make a movie."

I raised my eyebrows and stepped back.

"Come on, girl. Make a movie with me. Just once." The distinct juniper and licorice scent of Gin rose from Andy's tongue.

"You don't know what you're doing. Just a few hours ago you wer—"

He forced me against the stairwell banister. "Didn't I tell you not to talk to me like that?"

The banister cradled my head, but my heart sunk to my knees and fell to the ground.

Andy yanked me up by my shirt. My arms, limp at my sides, had no desire to fight back. So I closed my eyes as Andy gripped my wrist and forced me to follow him up the steps.

For the bazillionth time in my life, a man raped me and used me for my body and my looks to satisfy his perverted appetite. And the entire time I could only think of one word. Baby. Over and over again. I remembered the heartbeat, imagined the first cry, and wondered how she would be different from me. No part of me wanted her to be like me.

I WOKE UP ALONE AND TURNED TO THE CLOCK. 2:59AM CUT through the blackness with its neon green glow.

Andy's voice, muffled but loud, buzzed in my ear. I rubbed my eyes to make sure I wasn't dreaming, then rolled over to try and figure out his words.

More buzzing.

I rolled out of bed and tiptoed to the bedroom door, creaked it open, and listened to his slurred words.

"Divorce is fine with me. I'm not the one that started this." His words tripped over each other.

Hand to mouth, I continued to listen.

"If you would've stopped sleeping around maybe I wouldn't doing this, you know? You act like I'm the one that left. I'm just getting back at you. This is your fault, you hear me?" I pictured his red eyes and spit flying from his lips. "No. I don't want to hear your excuses. You played around, now I am." He paused. "I don't think so. I like this life. The money. The girls. I'm done."

I tiptoed back into the room, closed the door, and crawled into bed. For the next two hours I listened to Andy's voice fluctuate from screams that shook the walls to buzzing sounds I could barely hear.

And no matter how many times I tried to believe it, I couldn't.

Andy Cross had a wife.

BIRDS CHIRPED FROM THE TREE OUTSIDE THE BEDROOM window. The sun flickered in the room, drawing specks of shadows on the wall, and I stayed in bed. 10:48am. I didn't want to move.

Nightmares upon nightmares dressed up in the form of Andy's wife and messed with me all night. I couldn't stop thinking about her. And him.

The door clicked.

I turned my head.

Andy walked in the room, carrying a tray with wobbling eggs, bacon, and toast on top. The smoky smell of bacon made my stomach spin. And the thought of slimy eggs floating inside my body with pieces of pig took away any appetite I might've had, which was weird since I loved eggs and bacon.

"I'm not hungry."

Andy placed the tray on the bed and shrugged his shoulders. "More for me then."

He crunched and swallowed, crunched and swallowed, swishing orange juice between bites.

I cleared my throat. "Are you leaving because of your wife?"

"I don't have a wife."

"I heard you, Andy."

"You didn't hear what you think you heard." He slapped another piece of bacon on his tongue.

"Are you staying in the porn business then?"

"We'll see."

"What about me?"

"What about you?"

"Are you making me leave?"

Andy crunched the last of his bacon and swallowed it, then walked out of the room.

Birds continued to chirp outside the window. The clock turned to 11:00am. And I slumped back into bed, hoping I'd sleep the day away and wake up to normal Andy. Sadly, I missed the bruises. At least I knew he cared about me enough to get mad at me. Now . . . now his behavior confused me to no end.

I felt like another crystal of sugar in his tea, not enough to make a difference, not enough to notice, but still there anyway.

Chapter 55 *Ally*

Mom called on my way to my next clue, which was the apartment Jessie and I lived in when we first married. I ignored her call, but oddly enough, Dad called five minutes later.

I picked up the phone, hoping he'd talk to me until I got to Abingdon, which was a good thirty-five minutes or so from Loch Raven Reservoir.

"Hey, Ally. I've got some bad news and good news. Which do you want to hear first?" Dad said.

"Bad news."

"Are you sitting down?"

"You could say that, although if I were standing I probably wouldn't sit."

"Yes." He chuckled. "You're my daughter. Stubbornness can be a good thing. Sometimes."

"Yes, like the way you are with Mom."

"Yes, like your mother." His breath gushed into the phone. "That's what I need to tell you."

My foot eased on the gas and I veered onto 695 east.

"She's got cancer." He sniffed. "I don't know the details. She wouldn't tell me. And she got off the phone with me real quick. First time I heard her voice, live at least, since you were a kid. She didn't want to leave it on your answering machine and she didn't think you'd call back."

Perhaps my heart should have skipped a beat. Or my vision should have blurred. Or my foot should have burned the gas pedal. But nothing happened.

No sweaty hands. No heart scaling my throat. Nothing.

"Are you okay?" Dad said.

I cleared my throat.

"You should call her, talk to her."

"I'm not calling her." I paused. "I mean, I will, but not tonight. I've been thinking about it for awhile, just didn't know what to say."

I hung up with Dad and focused on the brake lights of the car in front of me.

The car in front of me turned on to I-95 north and I followed, feeling guilty about not wanting to feel guilty. Must've been Mom's plague on my life.

WHEN I PULLED INTO THE PARKING LOT OF OUR OLD apartment building I saw dozens, phew, I mean dozens and dozens of red and silver heart balloons taped to the side of the apartment building.

"How in the world did he pull this off?" I said to myself.

I'm not sure if it was my conversation with Dad or what, but the smile that came so naturally in the beginning of my treasure hunt wasn't coming so naturally anymore.

Mom's words trickled into my day and wouldn't leave.

The truth will set you free.

If that's really true, Lord, I said inside, then why do I feel trapped by the truth?

I am the way, the truth, and the life. I saw the verse in my head. John 14:something. Right page. Top left. Highlighted pink.

The truth, somehow, had become as wondrous as brushing my teeth. I knew it so well I couldn't feel it anymore.

I parked near the huddled balloons and rubbed my eyes. For Jessie's sake, I needed to smile. I needed to love him.

The balloons swayed and tangled with each other, taunting me with their glittering hearts. Holding my breath, I got out of the car, hoping I'd see Jess and smile. I walked to the apartment building and stood under the balloons. The grass beneath my feet looked like a Van Gogh-style ocean of red, white, and pink rose petals.

More than Words sang to me from the balcony above me. Took me a second to realize it was Jessie singing and not the radio. Cute, I thought as

I forced a smile.

Once my cheeks loosened and my lips parted, the smile grew into a genuine light on my face. The balloons parted and Jessie smiled down at me.

He climbed over the rail and hung from the balcony, then let go and landed on the ground in front of me. I stepped toward him and he fell over, holding his left foot.

"Ow." He squeezed his ankle.

Swelling inside, a laugh hid behind my pursed lips.

He looked at me and laughed. "Not so John Wayne, huh?"

My laughter broke the tightness of my lips and meddled with Jessie's growing laughter. A quick image of another woman sprinted through our moment. He told me our neighbor from this very apartment building was more beautiful than me.

Jessie lay on his side, head supported by his left hand. My smile loosened. He wrapped his fingers around my wrist and pulled me to petal heaven. Sitting with my legs tucked under me, I looked at Jessie's nervous eyes. A young girl's voice caught my attention. I turned to see what she looked like as she walked up the apartment steps, smiling at us, but Jessie turned my chin toward him and kissed me.

As his lips touched mine I thanked God the girl looked more like Marilyn Manson than a porn star. Then I battled distracting thoughts as we kissed under the fading blue sky. Some moments of the kiss were genuine, others, well, I almost forgot I was kissing him for a few seconds.

Jessie kissed the corner of my mouth and looked at me. "It's not going to feel like it did the day we met, Ally."

I looked to my left.

"It's different now, but we're still us. I'm still me." He moved a piece of hair from my eyes. "Don't you think it's still exciting?"

"This isn't easy for me," I said. "Trust me, I want to get over this." I picked up a petal. "I mean, do you think I like seeing these women in my head every day, all day, and comparing everything about them to me?"

"Don't do that." Pieces of white fell from his hand. "Stop comparing yourself, Ally. You are my wife. I want you. Those women are nothing more than a fantasy. They aren't real to me. You are."

"Don't talk about it like that."

"Like what?"

"I don't want to hear words like fantasy, okay? The idea of you needing a fantasy kills me, Jess. You don't understand what this feels like. You wouldn't unless I cheated on you."

"You almost did."

I stood and wiped the petals from my jeans. "That was nothing. And I didn't spend our entire relationship sneaking around thinking about other men in a way I'm only supposed to think about you."

"Have you thought about him?"

"Who?"

"Have you thought about Sean?"

"What are you talking about? In what way?"

"Point proven."

"You haven't proven anything." My voice broke. "Is this your idea of romance? Is this your idea of excitement?"

Jessie stood. "Look"—his eyes squinted as his voice raised—"I am trying everything I can. I am trying. Do you know that? I love you. I don't want to lose you, okay? Especially to Sean. He's a jerk, Ally. Can't you see that?"

Marilyn-Manson-girl walked back out of the apartment building and grinned at us. I looked back to Jess. "He never, ever treated me as bad as you have. And I don't think he ever would."

"Oh, right. That's why he'd have no problem helping you have an affair. There's a reason he goes through so many girlfriends and never gets married. Are you blind?"

"How can you talk to me like that?"

"How can you talk about him like that?" Jessie closed his eyes and exhaled loudly. "I'm sorry. I just don't like the guy. He's not someone you should trust."

"You don't even know him." I looked down, realizing how much I defended Sean but not my own marriage. "How did you find out anyway?"

"So, it is true." He shook his head.

Chapter 56 *Taylor*

Turned out I couldn't find out the sex of the baby until 20 weeks. I had an ultrasound around thirteen weeks and Lisa told me my due date. April sixth. Yeah, I never had an abortion, but let me tell you, I really, really wanted to sometimes. Especially with Andy constantly badgering me. No, he didn't leave porn. And yeah, he made me continue filming while pregnant, but I wasn't showing too much, so he didn't have to sacrifice his reputation for me.

Anyway, on November twentieth, I made it to twenty weeks and two days and found out the sex of the baby.

Lisa, so sweet, smiled her way through the ultrasound and made me guess the sex by pointing to the baby's pelvis area.

I pointed to the screen and said, "That looks like a boy to me. I see a bump."

Lisa perched her glasses on the tip of her nose. "No, sweetie. You're looking at a baby girl."

My body relaxed on the table. Staring at the ceiling, instead of the swimming glob on the ultrasound screen, I imagined her face. I wondered what her name would be. And I freaked out, imaging crazy scenarios like Andy stealing her or the hospital finding out who I am and not letting me take her home.

I looked back at the screen. The baby poked into my hipbone. Lisa took measurements of the head and other things while I daydreamed about marriage. No one would marry me, so my daydreams would stay that, just dreams. I imagined a husband sitting next to me as I discovered the sex of my first child, playfully arguing with me over names.

"You've got an active one," Lisa said. "I can barely keep up with her."

I half-smiled. Then it hit me. Layla. The baby's name would be Layla. I hadn't thought about before. And I didn't think about it much then. But I knew Layla was her name. Layla Renee.

"Are you planning on having a natural birth?" Lisa said.

"Um, I haven't thought about it much, but I probably won't." I pressed my hand into my stomach, trying to find Layla. "Won't it hurt too much?"

She put her hand on my arm. "It hurts bad, but it's bearable. Depends on what you want though. Think through everything and write a birth plan."

"A birth plan?"

She laughed, not in a way that made me feel young and stupid, but in an I'll-take-care-of-you kind of way. And she did care for me. She set up an appointment with me to go through everything a few days later.

During the next visit she explained episiotomies, anesthesiologists, transition phases, cervical dilation, oh man, she explained it all. I didn't retain all of it, but it helped me understand labor and pregnancy better. With only five months to go I feared the day. Not just the pain, but I didn't know how to go about adoption and I wasn't sure I wanted to.

I went home to Andy after my Lisa-explains-it-all visit and saw a note stuck to the door with electrical tape.

I changed the locks. I won't be back for a few months. Don't look for me until I get back.

The clock in my heart stopped ticking. Time, for me, didn't exist. Four months pregnant with a job history of porn, I had nowhere to go. I thought of Gianna, but she disappeared during my third month of pregnancy and soon after her phone number stopped working.

I sat on the top step of Andy's house—the same house that stained my life with blood and semen and fluffy powders—and I considered my options.

A job outside of porn that offered me as much money as porn, that would've been a nice option, save the fact that no one would hire me.

A sharp breeze swirled through my hair. I tucked my hands inside my sleeves and hugged myself.

Memories. So many memories here. The first time Andy tempted me with his smile and shoved his camera in my face. The first time I got so drunk I threw up. The first time I smoked weed and snorted cocaine. So many firsts in such little time. Then there's the one I'll never forget.

I looked at the ground.

My body. Torn and stolen, just like that.

I should've left that day. For good. But I didn't. And I knew why and hated the reason.

I needed him then as much as I do now.

"God, if you exist," I said to the bush, "I hate you."

Another breeze touched my hair.

Thankfully, the bush didn't talk back. And neither did God. Which proved His non-existence to me even more.

I shoved Andy's note into my purse and pulled out my car keys. One last look at his house. I stared at the shutters, the windows to the rooms I cried myself to sleep in, and the garage where Andy busted my lip for the first time. Then I turned and walked to my car.

"Alright, Layla." I touched my stomach. "It's you and me now."

THE BITTERNESS OF DECEMBER CAME AS SLOW AS IT POSSIBLY could. I made it to five months pregnant by sleeping in my car and stealing food from Super Fresh or Weis Markets. Sometimes I'd go in and eat olives and fruit right out of the salad bar. Other times I'd slip something up the sleeve of my shirt or plop it in my purse and walk out. I didn't know what else to do.

I applied at McDonald's and Chick-Fil-A, but by the time my interview came—on January sixteenth—my stomach stretched my clothes and Layla made sure the world knew she existed. Even McDonald's didn't want me, a pregnant girl with no job history, at least no job history worth printing on an application.

My cell phone stopped working because it was in Andy's name since I didn't have enough credit, but I tried to call Gianna a few times from a payphone. Nothing.

I showed up at Naomi's apartment, but a young married couple answered the door. So, I checked Rite-Aid and they said she stopped working there and moved out of state.

Zayta. I even called Zayta, but she told me to come back in two years after I matured a little. Not sure what that meant, but I wasn't thrilled about going back to porn anyway, so I didn't argue.

I had one option left.

I KNOCKED ON MOM'S DOOR ON JANUARY EIGHTEENTH JUST after the sun settled behind the trees. Light flakes of snow disappeared on my hand as I knocked a second time.

Something rumbled on the other side of the door. I stepped back and looked at the windows. The curtains fluttered. A figure backed away.

Breathing deep with my head tilted back, I fought with myself.

Knock. Don't knock.

Do it. Don't do it.

You need help. Not from her.

I stepped toward the door, extended my arm, and walked away.

She saw me. I knew she saw me. And she saw my pregnant stomach too. Like everyone else, she didn't want me.

Maybe an abortion would've been an easier road.

Layla kicked my rib. I pressed her foot down with my hand and Lisa's words floated into my path like the snowflakes around me. Remember, the best road is rarely the easiest.

The best road seemed non-existent.

I sat in my car and drove to a nearby side street, put my forehead on the steering wheel, and noticed the empty gas light on the dashboard. I had a full tank months ago and I tried my best to only drive short distances to make it last as long as possible.

I guess three months was as long as possible.

Chapter 57 *Ally*

After we ruined Jessie's romantic scavenger hunt with our argument about Sean and other women, we drove away in separate cars.

I called Mom to distract myself from thinking about Jessie. She picked up after the first ring.

"I didn't think you would call," she said.

Words hung from the tip of my tongue, but none were said.

"You have been talking to your father a lot now?"

"Have you been treated?" Last thing I wanted to talk about was the life of Allyson Graham. "What kind of cancer do you have?"

"I've got breast cancer. It's treatable." She paused. "They say the tumor is small and once it's removed I won't need any other treatment, but who knows."

"Well, I'll be praying for you. When will you have it removed?"

"Next week. But I think this might be it."

"It? What do you mean it?"

"I don't think I'm going to make it, Ally. I think the cancer has spread."

"You'll be okay, Mom." I pressed my lips together to keep from laughing. "Trust the doctors, they deal with cancer all the time. They know what they're doing."

"Not always," she said. "Remember our old neighbor, Mrs. Lindell? She died of breast cancer when they thought they could get rid of it. Doctors don't know everything. It's just like the weather channel. Sometimes it's wrong. They do their best, but sometimes they can't predict everything right."

"Mom, really, calm down. You will be fine."

If she wasn't known for her explosive panic I would've assumed her pity party was bait to jerk me back to her side, but no, she genuinely worried more than anyone I knew.

Finally, I convinced Mom to calm down and we hung up. She never brought up the incident and I didn't care to either. I wasn't ready to forgive or forget, so I played her game of ignorance and hoped I'd forget before I needed to forgive.

Jessie and I didn't talk to each other much of the night. He cleaned the house from the laundry room to every toilet in the house while I wrote to God in our bedroom.

God, I don't understand why everything had to go wrong at once. If you were trying to teach me something, couldn't it have been in pieces? I'm trying the best I can, but the amount of baseballs flying at my face is insane.

Will I ever stop comparing myself to other women? Will you always throw porn stars in my path to make me remember what he did? Why didn't you make her show up the next day when I wasn't there? Why do I have to remember? Why can't I forget everything, all of this, and move on?

What was the point of the porn star girl today? What is the point of Mom's cancer? What's the point of Jessie's struggle? And my thoughts of Sean? What's the point of all this negative, God? Where's the peace? Where's your goodness, faithfulness, and love? I don't see it right now, in anything.

Have you abandoned me?

Jessie walked in the bedroom. I put my pen inside my journal and placed it on the table next to my side of the bed.

He undressed, turned the light off, and sunk into bed beside me. "Let's live in the right now, not the past, not the future, just here, you and me, right now."

I agreed.

FOUR MONTHS AFTER JESSIE TURNED OFF THE LAMP THAT night, I woke up alone, which would've been normal if it wasn't 3:29 in the morning. The date—January tenth—is practically written on the back of my eyelids.

I rolled out of that bed like a snake crawled up my leg and walked to the door as fast and quiet as I could.

My hands shook as I turned the doorknob and lightly pulled the door open.

Jessie's voice trailed up the steps and into my heart.

I can't repeat the words he said. They're the only words I've shut out of my heart and head forever. And I hope they stay that way.

When I realized what he was doing I sprinted down the steps, broke one of the cracked banister bars off on my way down, and stopped on the landing.

Jessie, on the couch, looked over his shoulder with the phone still attached to his ear, the girl's voice on the other end still attached to his sexual gluttony.

Arms at my sides, fists clenched, I walked over to him, took his cell phone from his ear and said, "Can I help you?"

"Yes, you can," the sultry voice said.

"No, I can't and neither can my husband." *Click.*

Jessie stood, looking like a five-year-old kid who stole candy from the grocery store.

"How could you?" I said. "Who is she?"

"She's not real."

"Humorous," I said, without a laugh. "Who is she and why is she better than me?"

"It's just"?he cleared his throat?"uh, I called a 900 number."

Hands in his pockets, he looked down and nodded his head.

"Are you kidding me?"

"You're not mad?"

"Of course I'm mad, but I can't believe you actually bought that."

"I don't think it's real, but I justified it because I thought it wasn't as bad as porn since I wasn't looking at anything."

I climbed over the back of the couch and sat cross-legged on the cushions in front of Jess. "Not as bad as porn? You were physically talking to another woman."

"Yeah, but it wasn't real."

"That's what you always say. It's not real, it's not real, it's all a fantasy. Okay. If it's all fake then what is so alluring about it? Can't you get over it already? Why don't you want to have sex with me?" I looked at my swollen belly. "It's the pregnancy, isn't it?" I smiled. "Look at the bright side, I'm a little bigger now, more curvy like you like."

Jessie closed his eyes. "I like you the way you are."

"Okay." I stood. "Then prove it."

Chapter 58 *Taylor*

The orange-lit gas pump in my dashboard quickly became my enemy. I assumed I had ten miles or so left before the car ran out of gas. So I decided to do two things.

First, I drove to the nearest church, a St. Something Epiosiotical church—at least that's what I called it—and walked up to the front of the building. It wasn't a Sunday so I figured not many people would be around, but I hoped someone would be.

The front doors, wood painted red with black trim, were locked, so I walked around the side to find another door. A sign pointed to a rectory or something. I followed its arrow.

The doorknob clicked and opened as I twisted.

A strong powdery smell, like the perfume of an old woman, filled my nose. I sneezed and walked in, shutting the door behind me. When I looked up I saw an older lady with orange hair high on her head.

She put a tissue on the edge of her desk and pointed to it. "You didn't cover your nose when you sneezed."

"Um, I'm sorry, I was wondering if, um."

She pushed the tissue toward me. "Yes?"

"I kind of need help."

"Kind of? What sort of help are you inquiring about?"

"I need money."

She stared at my body. I could see her gaze stop at the length of my skirt and look back up to my stomach.

Layla kicked my hipbone. I jumped.

"I'm sorry," the lady said. "You will need to come back later. There's nothing of the sort we can do at this time."

The phone rang. She answered it, pushed the tissue toward me again, and shooed me out the door like an unwanted critter.

CHURCH SEEMED ABSOLUTELY HOPELESS TO ME, SO I TRIED my alternative. Please don't judge me, I really had no other options.

Hungry, six months pregnant, and tired, I needed something to pay for gas and food and some sort of shelter.

I drove into Baltimore City the I-83 way, knowing I-95 would cost a toll I didn't have, and went down one-way street after one-way street until I found what I needed. The Block on Baltimore Street. I knew enough about it to know I could get what I needed, hopefully. If porn used pregnant women, I figured prostitution would too.

I parked my car in a safe parking zone where I didn't have to parallel park—I still didn't know how—and turned off the ignition so I wouldn't waste any more gas than I needed to. The sun hadn't fully disappeared for the day, but the street felt so dark and cold that it seemed like the sun never shined its face there, but at the same time, it didn't look as bad as I imagined.

The buildings, beautiful and historic, watched as cars drove by, lots of cars, so many I had to make sure I was on the right street. The neon lights, curved into the names of strip clubs and bars, reassured me. I came to the right place.

Layla twisted her body. I placed my hand on the top of my stomach and pushed her foot from my rib.

The glow of The Block waited for me. I didn't think any of the clubs would want a pregnant girl, but maybe I could stand on a corner, make enough money to get through the last three months of my pregnancy, and go from there.

Prostitution had to be better than porn, I told myself. Nothing could be as bad as porn.

I looked at the dimmed gas pump on my dashboard and sighed.

Alone.

Chapter 59 *Ally*

The clock chimed. Four o'clock in the morning. Jessie didn't move, didn't speak.

"Did you hear me?" I said.

"How do you want me to prove that I love you? You know I do."

I walked behind the couch, toward the step landing. "You'll figure it out."

I went upstairs. Despite my pride for not firing angry bullets at his heart, my shoulders still pulled me down. I ran my hand along the railing, remembering the many counseling sessions I spent wondering why the woman across from me couldn't handle her husband's struggle with lust. It's his problem, not yours, I'd say in my head, listening to her sobs.

But I didn't feel the same now.

I went into the bedroom and reclined in bed.

I am the crazy woman, I thought. Losing my mind, comparing myself to women every day of my life, never measuring up, and being paranoid about everything Jessie does.

Staring at the ceiling, my mind carried me down a stream of smiles and tears from childhood until now.

I clicked on the light and picked up my journal, which never left my side, and started to write.

Dad left. Mom got married and her husband did a good job at keeping out of my life, even still. I didn't seek attention from boys in school, like so many fatherless girls. I never questioned my value. Then I turned my face to Jesus and placed my life at His feet.

Now, here I am.

This doesn't make sense, I thought. My life was never like the typical fatherless girl who seeks her value in the opinions of men and then flies off the track, gets married to the first guy who asks, and ends up in trouble.

I touched pen to paper again.

Did I really place my life at your feet, Jesus? Is that the problem? Do I seek affirmation from other things, maybe even myself, but not You?

Please, just help me fix myself and my marriage and everything.

I WOKE UP THE NEXT DAY TO AN EMPTY BED AND A TINY person moving inside of me. Jessie and I chose not to find out the gender of the baby, but part of me wanted to know the baby's name, bond with it in a deeper way, you know, maybe stop saying it. Sounded too Stephen King. I wanted a name.

Well, I thought as I rolled out of bed, he better prove himself today and continue to for a long, long time.

Down the stairs I went, hoping to find a thousand rose petals on the floor. I'm not saying it would have made any butterflies return, but at least it would have been a start.

The house, empty and cool, didn't conceive hope. Quiet and still, everything remained untouched since last night.

Craving a tangy glass or three of orange juice, I went to the kitchen and reached in the fridge for the Tropicana carton.

Jessie's handwriting caught my eye.

A note, taped to the orange juice box.

Don't worry. I'm working on proving it. —Jess P.S. I knew you'd go for the OJ.

I poured a glass with the note still on the carton and wondered what he'd do to prove his love. Then I called my midwife and told her I'd like to schedule an ultrasound for this afternoon's visit.

"Sure thing," she said. "I'll see you two later."

We hung up and I called Verity.

"Can I come visit before my prenatal appointment today?" I said.

And of course she didn't deny.

VERITY'S HOUSE SMELLED LIKE ROTTEN APPLES.

I kicked my shoes off and lounged on her sofa. "What is that horrid smell?"

"What smell?" She sat down across from me and tucked her feet underneath mine.

"How can you not smell that?"

She shrugged. "So, what's new with you? How's staying at home going?"

I nodded.

"Nice, isn't it?" She smiled.

"When are you getting a job?"

"Probably when Timmy boy settles in and we know for sure we're staying in Maryland." She leaned forward and touched my stomach. "It's a boy."

"Oh yeah? Well, I'm finding out today. Going to surprise Jess."

"How is Jessie? Ah!" She jumped back. "The baby poked his hand out. I saw it."

I shook my head and smirked. Verity placed her hand on my stomach again and we laughed.

"So, really, what are you gonna do about this whole porn shebang?" She pressed her lips together. "Um, no pun intended."

"I'm trying. Honestly, I don't know what to do. How do you not compare yourself to other women?" I rubbed my face. "Doesn't it bother you if Tim thinks someone is prettier than you?"

"Eh, nah. I don't think about it like that. That's all fantasyland. If he needs that, whatever. I'm not gonna stop him, it's just what men do. All of them."

"You sound like Jessie. With the fantasy part, I mean."

"Well, it's true, Ally. Why do you care so much about what you look like anyway? Those models are all airbrushed to appeal to men in that fake way. It's not real."

"No, porn stars are different. They are real. And besides, he flat out told me tall blondes are more beautiful. Not to mention, it's not right what you do. You know you don't like it, but you give in because you can't get him to stop. That's not going to help the intimacy in your marriage. It's going to deteriorate it. Maybe a slow death, but a death nonetheless."

"Honestly, I don't get anything out of it, but still. It's not that big of a deal compared to what he could be doing."

"Except that it could easily lead to worse things. Fantasyland can go wherever your fantasies take you. What if he decides one day that he wants to have another woman come into the bedroom?"

"He's not like that. Look, you are beautiful. You've got beautiful hair, eyes, lips—what's the big deal? Stop freaking out about those other women and just be yourself. He married you, not them."

My hands moved from one side of my stomach to the other, keeping track of the baby's position. "I just want to be the most beautiful woman to him. Not in the world, just to him. And I don't want to be competing with these sexual fantasies."

"So don't."

Hopeless. Somehow I thought she'd provide me with insight, you know, something wise, maybe a way to fix my stupid insecurities and stop thinking about other women so much. But of course she's Verity. She doesn't live based off feelings, and sometimes I wonder if she has any at all.

Our conversation, thanks to me, veered into another direction, a rather pointless direction. We talked about everything from moon bounces to orange popsicles, killing time until my next prenatal appointment.

Chapter 60 *Taylor*

Nope. No other option, I convinced myself. If I wanted to care for my baby and survive the next few months until my due date, I needed to make money.

I mentally listed the places I applied to work for. Maybe the fact that I didn't have a working phone number added to my bad luck. I did use a payphone to call a few managers and they said they weren't hiring, even though they still had "Now Hiring" signs on their doors.

Oh well. I pulled down the visor of my car and checked my reflection.

Scraggly hair, no makeup, circles under my eyes I never knew existed—obviously my bathing sessions at the sink in Walgreens hadn't done much for me in the looks department. So much that I wondered if anyone would even want to have sex with me right now.

I looked at my stomach. Something needed to be done. In order to buy makeup and clothes to make more money, I needed to make some now.

I stepped out of my car, crossed the street, and positioned myself on the edge of the curb near one of the strip clubs. A few times I considered sticking my thumb out, but thought I'd do it wrong.

The sun made its way to the other side of the world as the neon glow peeked between buildings and highlighted my skin. The lighting kind of made me look better, so I was thankful.

I pulled my skirt up a little, pushed my swollen breast implants up, and waited for someone to drive up to me. The December air gave me goose bumps. I needed a warm car, quick.

Cars passed. Men looked me up and down. But their taillights disappeared down the street and they'd pick up another woman. Every time a woman got into a car, another one took her place. I thought for sure they planned it and I wondered if I was standing in the wrong place. Or maybe no one wanted a pregnant woman.

I sat on the curb, feeling Layla's hands or feet, and imagined her heartbeat. Hopefully she wouldn't feel what was about to happen to us.

A glossy black SUV slowed a few feet in front of me. I stood. The car inched closer. My reflection, painted on the door with neon lights in the background, gave me chills.

The window hummed its way down, revealing a man with short gray hair and a business suit. I saw the glimmer of a wedding band on his left hand. He nodded for me to get in.

I did, shivering from my fingers to my knees.

"Wow, you have a nice pregnant glow, don't you?" He smiled at me. Not through me. Right at me like he knew me for years.

I tried to smile, but noticed my shaking foot and couldn't focus on anything but the growing nausea in my stomach.

"How much do you want up front?"

The only price I could think of was enough to provide gas to get through a few more weeks.

"Twenty-five dollars." My words blew through the air in puffs of frosted steam.

The man licked his lips and nodded. "I think you're worth a little more than that." He pulled over in front of dingy motel not far from The Block. While looking at me he fished through his wallet and handed me five twenties. "I think this is better, what do you think?"

Nodding, I put the money in the front pocket of my jean skirt, right under Layla. I saw the strange man staring at my belly and I realized the top button of my skirt was unbuttoned. Since my stomach grew I couldn't button it anymore.

I fidgeted with the frays on my skirt and tried so hard to calm my foot.

The stranger touched my face. I shivered.

"How old are you?" he asked.

"Twenty-one." I lied.

He nodded to the motel and smirked, then got out of the car and walked around the SUV to my side of the car. Everything I saw in him?the way his shoulders swung forward, the way he kept another side of himself hidden under a suit and tie, the way he wore an almost constant wicked smile—reminded me of The Joker.

And I was about to give my body to him.

But it would be worth it to take care of Layla.

The Joker opened the door for me and offered his hand. The same hand that sparkled with a wedding band. I ignored his help and slid out of his SUV.

Again, he tried to take my hand. Overlooking it, I walked in front of him toward the motel. The January wind whipped its arms around me, holding me in the cold where my heart wanted to stay, but my body kept walking toward the motel.

The Joker's pressed pants swished by me as he rushed to open the door for me. His sloppy grin grew larger. I refused to look into his eyes, but I wondered what was behind them and if he was hurting like me.

But I didn't need to look into his eyes to know the answer. His actions told me he was hurting. And in some sick corner of my brain I thought maybe I could help him. Maybe he'd want to talk instead of having sex. Apparently, I had a savior complex.

He checked in and led me to a room. The two was falling off the door and looked more like a five. He clicked the door open and walked inside. After all the films I made, my heart still thumped so fast it made me nauseous. That craving, that deep in the mind craving to get high lingered inside of me. Cola, my old friend. Too dangerous for a baby, but I still missed him. I still wanted him in times like this almost as much as I wished I could go back to the day Daddy died and tell him not to leave.

The Joker sat on the bed and patted the area beside him. I walked over and sat with him, hoping he'd talk to me, but he touched my face and said, "Can I see that belly of yours?"

I tried to swallow but my mouth was too dry. I know, I know, I did so many porn films, had sex with so many strangers, this should have been cake to me. But it was too intimate, too scary. The absence of cameras made me feel more exposed.

Joker tugged my shirt. "You are beautiful," he said. "Show me."
Beautiful.
I hated beautiful.

Chapter 61 *Ally*

Two things to be thankful for as I walked out of my prenatal appointment. One, I didn't see Blondie. And two, the baby's heartbeat was strong and she was a girl. A little girl. Jessie wanted a girl for years. I wanted a boy first, but mainly because I longed for an older brother as I grew up.

I couldn't wait to tell Jessie.

As I drove back home I planned his favorite dinner in my head. Steak, medium well, mashed potatoes with chives, sweet corn on the cob, and sparkling white grape and peach juice.

The baby—our baby girl—kicked. She must've liked the idea of dinner. I held my belly as I drove home, hoping Jessie wouldn't be there so I could surprise him.

JESSIE'S CAR, PARKED IN THE GARAGE, DISAPPOINTED ME, BUT I still couldn't wait to tell him about his little girl.

I walked inside and saw him sitting on the living floor surrounded by pillows and Chinese food. My favorite.

I smiled and sighed. He's trying to prove it, I thought.

Soft music hummed in the background. Candlelight flickered on the walls and everything they surrounded. Jessie watched me walk to him. I knew he loved me, I could see it in his weak smile, but I wanted him to love me enough to let go of the other women.

I sat next to him on the floor.

His fingers ran down my arm and stopped at my hand.

"You are the only woman I want."

I wanted to believe him.

"And I love you."

I smiled and looked at the cartons of Chinese food, remembering our first meal as a married couple on the floor of our empty apartment.

"I'm really trying, Jess. It's hard for me to understand why you can't stop. If you really love me and this baby, why can't you stop?"

"I am getting better. You might not believe me, and that's fine, I understand why you don't, but I really am getting better. It's such a bad habit, formed over decades. That alone should help you realize that it's not about you."

"But if it's not about me, then why did you choose to come downstairs and call a 900 number instead of waking me up?"

"It's not like that. When I woke up that night I had a ton of anxiety from this job and the emotional distance between us. I felt like a failure so I came downstairs to get something to drink since I couldn't sleep. Then one thought lead to another and I fell again."

"Why didn't you come to me when the temptation started?"

"Honestly?"

I nodded, although the question mark on the end of honestly made me wonder if I really wanted to hear the rest.

"Once it gets to that point and I'm alone . . . it's hard to turn back."

"But why do you even put yourself in th?" I stopped myself, breathed, then started again, "Let's not talk about this right now. Let's eat."

"I want to pray before we eat."

I looked down.

Jessie closed his eyes. I watched his lips move as he thanked God for our marriage, the food, our baby, and asked Him for provision and grace.

When he opened his eyes I reached for a container filled with fried rice. Jessie went for the egg rolls and duck sauce.

"I have news," I said between forkfuls.

With practically an entire egg roll in his mouth, Jessie raised his eyebrows and urged me to go on.

"Can you guess?"

"What are you up to?"

"Nothing, but I was wondering if maybe you would want to talk about names for our baby."

His face lit up. "But I thought you wanted to wait until the third trimester?"

"I am in the third trimester." I laughed. "Only three more months to go and we'll get to meet her."

"Wow." He ate a mouthful of house lo mien. "I can't believe she will be here in three?" His fork fell to the container below it. "Wait. Did you say her?"

My smile grew.

"A baby girl?" Jessie laughed. "It's a girl? This isn't a prank, is it?"

"No. It's really a girl."

For the next thirty minutes we finished our Chinese food, laughed about random memories, and named our child. Jessie'd stop every few minutes to laugh and say, "Are you kidding me? A baby girl?"

AVELINA JOY GRAHAM. WE BOTH KNEW WE WANTED HER NAME to have meaning. Joy immediately crossed our minds since we waited so long to finally get pregnant. And Avelina, which means life, just happened upon us when we did a random baby name search online. Life and joy couldn't describe her more.

I couldn't wait to meet her. So badly I wanted her life, the combination of Jessie and myself, to heal our marriage and take my mind off those other women. I knew one day I'd get over it, and I wanted Avelina to help me get there.

So for the next few weeks I occupied myself with thoughts of her. Jessie and I painted the nursery lavender. I shopped for her all the time, even if I didn't buy things I still meandered through the baby clothes for hours, feeling her feet in my side. Anything I could do to keep my mind off of Jessie's fantasyland and be happy.

AND BEFORE I KNEW IT, JESSIE AND I VISITED LISA.

She gave me a big smile and said, "You're full-term. Avelina is healthy and able to come out when she's ready. Now you just have to wait."

Jessie smiled at me. Avelina twisted inside of me, so I rolled slightly to my left to push her foot from my rib. I loved feeling her feet, imagining her little toes, all wrinkled and pink. Avelina means life and there's no denying it. That girl always kicked inside of me.

"If you want we can do a pelvic exam just to see if you're dilated at all, but we don't have to do that." Lisa flipped through my folder.

Jessie and I looked at each other.

"I think we'll wait," I said. "She'll come when she's ready."

Lisa smiled.

"Are you sure I'll know when I go into labor? Will I be able to get to the hospital before she comes out?"

"Oh, dear one." Lisa loved people through her smile. "You'll be fine. Most likely you will be in labor for at least ten hours or so with your first baby. I'm not saying it doesn't happen quick sometimes, but most likely you'll be at home walking out contractions before you even come here." She stood and patted my knee, then helped me sit up. "Avelina will be here before you know it."

Her words lingered in my mind the rest of the day.

Chapter 62 *Taylor*

Prostitution worked. It never got easier for me, especially as Layla began to fill out my stomach. I could actually feel her head in my pelvis and it scared me every time a strange man led me to a musty hotel room. But I sold my body a total of ten times and made a little over a thousand dollars. And it was enough. I saved it all for food and gas (minus the two maternity outfits I bought at Goodwill) and I made it to full-term.

When I went to Lisa's office for my thirty-eight week check up I saw the same woman who stared at me like I was a dirty animal. I sat across from her and pretended to read a magazine as I waited for my name to be called. I don't think she recognized me though. The maternity clothes I picked out were oversized and frumpy and I think they hid my former self pretty well.

The woman flipped through a baby magazine with one hand pressed into the top of her stomach. I looked down at Layla. My hand was in the same spot.

I moved my hand to my lower stomach and watched the delicate features on the woman's face. Her hair, now brown, curled and flowed around her face. She seemed brighter now, happier.

"Allyson Graham," a nurse called from the hallway. "You can come back now."

Allyson stood and looked at me. No, wait, she looked through me. Her eyes seemed delicate as they read the words printed on those magazine pages, but when she looked at me I saw no gracefulness.

I watched her wedding ring disappear through the doorway to the hallway. I don't know why she didn't like me, maybe it was Gianna's abortion statement, but either way, I wanted to trade places with her. I wanted that natural beauty she had, the wild hair and defined face. But more than all that, I wanted a husband to take care of me. Someone to love me.

LISA PULLED HER PLASTIC GLOVES OFF AND PLOPPED THEM into the trashcan. "Looks like you're three centimeters and maybe 70% effaced. I think you might go early, but you never know."

I couldn't look at her. All the times people touched me sexually I still didn't like people touching me down there.

"Do you have plans for the birth yet?" She seemed like a mother, a mother unlike my own. One that really cared. "Will someone be bringing you to the hospital?"

"My boyfriend." I lied. "I've been staying with him these last few weeks and he will be taking me when the contractions start. I will know what they feel like when they come, right?"

"Yes." She smiled. "It will feel like period cramps, but they get worse and worse. Sort of like a big mountain. Imagine the contraction pulling around your back or lower abdomen and getting more and more intense, then it will hit a peak and go back down the hill, and repeat until they get closer together and last longer on those peaks." She helped me up and looked into my heart. "You will be fine. I'll take good care of you and Layla."

I believed her. Besides Daddy and that girl who took me to church, Lisa was the only person to really care about me. Everyone else had a selfish reason, but some people just loved. I didn't know how they did it, but I liked that about them.

Lisa opened the door and looked back at me. "God has blessed you, Taylor. He has really, really blessed you."

She left the room. But her words didn't.

God.

Funny.

If he's blessed me, I thought, then I don't want to know what hell is like.

Chapter 63 *Ally*

My thirty-eight week appointment was nice, except for the fact that I saw Blondie. She didn't look like a porn star anymore. She aged and looked like she hadn't slept since she was five. I tried not to look at her too much. Her face reminded me of things I didn't want to think about. And her blonde hair irritated me beyond belief. Especially since I dyed mine back.

Lisa told me I was 4cm dilated and 80% effaced. My heart rate picked up and stayed there until I got in the car and called Jessie with the news.

"That's so good to hear," he said. "So does that mean you'll be in labor soon?"

"Well, technically I already am, it's just the early phase. It's not labor labor yet. But I'm dilated so technically I am in labor."

"That doesn't make sense."

"Well, take comfort my dear, it doesn't need to make sense to you. Just know that she could come into the world any time now."

"Wow. So, what do we do next?"

"We eat lots of spicy food, drink tons of castor oil, and do lots of walking."

"Castor oil?"

"Yeah, or pineapples."

"Sounds nasty."

I held back a laugh. "Lisa did mention Primrose Oil though. She said it helps soften the cervix. But I don't know, for some reason I don't want to rush Avelina's birthday. I figure God has planned her life and given her to us, we mine as well let Him choose her birthday."

"Agreed."

ANOTHER WEEK PASSED AND NOTHING PROGRESSED. EVERY little stomach cramp or twinge that I got would send me to the computer to find out if I'd go into labor early. But the end of my thirty-ninth week approached before I showed any true signs.

Then, right before my pregnancy reached forty weeks, I lost my mucous plug. I'm not sure how that goes for others, but for me it wasn't too bad. People call it a "bloody show" sometimes, but for me it wasn't bloody at all.

I went to the kitchen and called Lisa after I finished up in the bathroom.

"Are you sure it was your mucous plug?" she said.

"Absolutely. What should I do now?"

"You are so close to seeing your little girl, Ally. Relax, watch a movie, let those contractions start and time them, when they are coming frequently and consistently give me a call. You'll know when it's time to come in."

She said that many times, but for some reason I thought I'd end up popping the baby out on my living room floor.

Jessie walked in the front door and hung his coat on the rack by the door.

"I lost my mucous plug." There's no way I could have hid the excitement in my voice.

Jessie attempted a smile.

"You okay?"

He nodded.

"What happened?"

Every time I asked him that question my chest hurt and it seemed impossible to breathe enough air. His bad mood could've had nothing to do with me, it just as easily could have been a tough client who didn't like his work. But every time he walked through the door with that look on his face I prepared myself to hear about the other woman.

I didn't know this time—of all times—it would be true.

Chapter 64 *Taylor*

I know it sounds crazy, but I was proud of myself for surviving months in a car with no help from anyone. Well, I shouldn't say that, Lisa helped me a lot. She even gave me free prenatal vitamins at every visit, but other than that, I took care of myself. For the first time in my life, I didn't need someone else to help me live.

I'm not exactly sure how far along I was when I got my first contraction, but it was April ninth and beautiful outside. Flowers and trees budding in every direction. The sun shined in a cloudless sky. And the air had that fresh, moist scent of spring.

At 3:46 in the afternoon on that April day, a mild period-like cramp squeezed my insides. I was in the drive-thru at McDonald's. Yeah, yeah, I know, but it was cheap and I craved salt. As soon as that contraction happened I got out of the drive-thru line and sped toward the hospital, hoping I'd get there in time.

But on Route 1, right near Ruby Tuesday's, my car ran out of gas.

I drove on *E* for a few days, but I didn't drive too much so I didn't think it mattered, and I wanted to save my money so I could check in to a hotel after Layla was born. The last thing I wanted was to drag her into my house on wheels.

I managed to drift to the side of the road. Another contraction tightened my stomach, like two arms reaching around my back and squeezing.

Not too bad, I thought. It doesn't hurt much at all actually.

Or maybe all the pain from having my, um, area ripped so many times dulled the pain.

I got out of the car and walked to the curb. Car after car after car passed me and didn't stop. I couldn't help but notice one of those fake metal fish things on the back of a car with a bumper sticker next to it that said, *No Jesus, No Peace. Know Jesus, Know Peace.*

Laughable. Except I didn't laugh.

I watched the bumper sticker until I could no longer see it. People and their Jesuses, I thought. They all have a different Jesus. How do they know their peace isn't just their peace? Whatever they feel comfortable doing is peaceful, forget doing something uncomfortable.

I inhaled and puffed the air back through my nose. I don't know why but Christians annoyed me more than any other group of religious people. Well, Naomi was nice, but still. Most of them only followed Jesus when they wanted to, and apparently they never wanted to when they saw me.

Another fish drove by.

Maybe Jesus would drive by me too.

Know Jesus. Know Peace.

Another contraction, still no worse than a period cramp.

Jesus, I said inside. I don't know if you're God and I'm gonna guess you aren't real. But if you are and you can magically hear me right now, help me. Peace would be nice, too.

The idea of talking inside my head to a so-called man who once lived and was God's son born of a virgin lady, um, let's just say I thought it was nuts, but it was my last resort.

Finally, I decided to go into Ruby Tuesday's to find help since the Jesus fish people weren't doing much for me. But before I turned to walk away a cop car pulled up with his lights on.

Phew.

I hadn't had another contraction for over fifteen minutes, but my stomach whirled with nausea with each minute that passed. I needed to get to Lisa.

The cop walked around the front of his car. "Are you okay, miss?"

One look at him and my face flushed. My abdomen tightened. Andy's friend, the convenient cop, recognized me, but he pretended like he never met me before.

I didn't want his help.

Chapter 65 *Ally*

The bright April day I went into labor just had to be the day Jessie confessed every last secret he kept over the years.

"If I don't tell you this now I'm afraid it will haunt us in the future and I don't want it to. I thought it was over, but I realized today that it wasn't."

I sat at the kitchen table. He followed.

"Jess, I'm going to have a baby very, very soon. Did you have to bring this stuff up today?"

He licked his lips and breathed hard. "That's why I need to tell you. When Avelina comes into this world I need everything to be right. I need you to know everything."

"I'm glad you're doing this because you need something. What about me? How come you never think about how this makes me feel?"

"Believe me, I do. Which is why I haven't told you everything you should know. I didn't want to hurt you."

I shut my emotions behind a wall of stone. Again. The wall was getting high. "You're making me think the worst possible thing happened."

"I've struggled with porn for a long time, Ally. It's almost like it's built into me, but I know it's not. I always thought it was healthy to be so, I don't know, sexual. But I realize now I need to change something."

I fidgeted in my chair, wondering when I'd feel a contraction, wondering when Jessie would get to the point.

"Before we met . . . I slept with someone."

My wall of stone cracked and crumbled. I never thought it would. Not so easily. Tears glazed my eyes and blurred Jessie's face. I didn't expect that one. Not in a million years. All that time I thought we were both virgins when we married.

"It wasn't a romantic relationship or anything like that. I've just had this problem my whole life. I love you, Ally. I don't think of you like I think of other women. They are like drugs to me, but I love you." He tapped the table. "So, this woman came back around a couple years into our marriage."

I hoped my tears would climb back into my eyes. "Please. Stop. I don't want to know this time. I don't need details."

"I didn't sleep with her again. But I came close to kissing her. And a few times when you've gotten angry with me over this stuff I've wanted to go back to her. Not for a relationship, just for sex."

"I said I didn't want to know." I wiped my face.

"Please, please forgive me. I needed to tell you all of this because if you don't know the temptations will eat away at me."

"I don't know what to think anymore. This has been going on for too long. You're too wishy-washy with it all."

"Do you forgive me?"

"I guess so. I mean, I can forgive you and all, but how am I going to forget? How am I going to trust you when you still have issues with this stuff?" My stomach tightened. "I think I'm having a contraction."

Jessie's chair screeched as he stood up. "What? How do I do this?"

"It's okay. We can stay here until the contractions are regular. That was my first one."

"Didn't it hurt?"

"Not too bad."

I stood.

Jessie reached for me, but pulled away.

"Lisa mentioned walking around. Maybe we should go for a walk."

JESSIE AND I FINISHED OUR WALK, BUT THE CONTRACTIONS still weren't regular. So we put a movie in the DVD player and hoped we wouldn't be able to finish it. I just needed a distraction. I didn't want to talk about Jessie or his other women. So, we pretended to watch Frodo and Sam. Every now and then I'd pay attention, but only to the directing. It amazed me that they made Gandolf look so much bigger than Frodo with camera angles. It looked so real.

The movie ended and my contractions seemed regular, but they still didn't hurt bad enough for me to think they were real.

"How often are you having them?" Jessie asked.

"About every five or six minutes."

"Shouldn't we at least call Lisa?"

He handed me the phone and I speed dialed Lisa.

"Lisa, it's Allyson Graham. My contractions are every five minutes or so, should we come in now?"

Before she could even finish saying yes I smiled at Jessie and held back more tears. My baby. Finally. After so many years of trying, it was finally time to hold her.

Jessie grabbed our hospital bags, the keys, and his jacket. We walked to the door and I turned to the living room where a yellow soothing vibrations chair sat near the couch. A pink blanket with Avelina's name on it draped over the arm of the couch. And right beside that sat a bundle of diapers and wipes.

"Just think." I turned to Jess. "When we come back we will have Avelina with us."

He glanced around the room then back to me. "Let's go get her."

Chapter 66 *Taylor*

E very time Andy's cop friend spoke, I imagined him pleasuring himself as he watched my videos. The thought disgusted me. I never said a word to him. I guess he knew why. He figured out my problem on his own and called for someone to bring gas.

"You're not in labor, are you?" he said without looking at me. I could tell he was embarrassed. Probably wondered if it was Andy's baby.

I ignored him as another contraction pulled my back into my stomach.

He got into his car and left seconds after an orange van pulled up.

"You the one that ran out of gas?" a man said through missing teeth.

I nodded and looked away, toward the passing cars, the passing Jesuses. He popped the gas tank lid, screwed the cap off, and poured some gasoline into my car's thirsty tank. I hoped he'd fill it all the way up.

Another contraction. They were closer together now. And lasting longer.

"Thanks." I walked right past him and got into my car.

He helped me start it and I drove off eager to see Lisa's face. Then it hit me.

Layla.

My baby would soon be in the world. Alive. And I had no apartment, no family, no job, just a car without a car seat.

Daddy, oh Daddy, please, please, help me. Heeeeeelp me.

WHEN I CHECKED IN AT THE FRONT DESK IN THE LABOR AND delivery section of the hospital (thankfully Lisa gave me a tour earlier) the girl looked me up and down and said, "You don't look like you are in labor."

"Can I talk to Lisa?"

She ignored me and answered the phone, but I heard Lisa's sweet voice around the corner. I walked into an empty waiting room with televisions and a bathroom.

"Excuse me," the front desk girl said with the phone pressed into her neck. "You didn't finish checking in."

I ignored her and sat down in the waiting room. Soap operas flickered on the TV screen while the sun brightened the room through the cracks in the blinds. Another contraction clenched my insides. Not that bad, I thought. Still no big deal.

Lisa's voice got closer, so I walked out of the waiting room. She saw me and rushed over, her arms reaching out toward me. I smiled when her palms rested against my cheeks.

"Oh, dear one," she said. "Is it time?"

I loved her.

"Yes," I said. "Well, I think so."

"Let's get you a room so we can see what's going on."

She waved at the front desk and led me through double doors and into a small room. For some reason I think she may had done something wrong, just by the way the girl at the desk rolled her eyes and another waiting pregnant lady gave me a dirty look. But I didn't care. I liked being special for once, even it was at the cost of someone else.

Lisa helped me onto the table.

"On a scale from 1-10 what would you say the pain is like?"

"Um, I don't know, maybe a four?"

She leaned me backward, checked my cervix, and said, "You're six centimeters. Looks like it really is time. Do you have a high tolerance for pain?"

I shrugged and watched the contraction monitor rise with my next contraction. "I mean, it's just not that bad yet."

"Well if you do this naturally, you're going to be clinging to the hospital bed in a few hours, so enjoy this while it lasts."

Somehow I didn't believe her. It didn't hurt so far, there's no way it could get that bad.

"Isn't six centimeters close?" I said.

"Yes. But you could still be in labor for another day. It depends on the woman and the labor. You could give birth in two hours or twenty." She picked up a folder and held it to her chest. "I'm going to make sure we get a delivery room set up for you. Stay right here." She winked and left the room.

Another contraction. The line on the monitor peaked a little longer than last time. To my left, a cup of ice chips sat untouched. Lisa brought them in earlier, but I forgot about them. I sat up a little straighter and crunched until the ice smoothed down my throat.

The room, blank and sterile, didn't make me feel hopeful. Instead, I felt as blank as the walls and sheets around me. As synthetic as the smell of plastic filling my nostrils. I wanted color. I wanted life. I wanted this baby. But none of those things seemed attainable or maintainable really.

More than anything—I crunched another ice chip—I wanted a Daddy or a man, someone who truly loved me, to be here while I gave birth to my first child.

Chapter 67 *Ally*

I analyzed passing trees and timed my contractions, while Jessie probably wondered what I was thinking about. Then I saw a couple zoom by on a motorcycle. The woman's arms were wrapped around the man. So confident in his ability to keep her safe, she rested her chin on his shoulder. She trusted him with her life. She lived. Carefree.

I looked at Jess.

"Hey," I said. "I want to get through this. I don't know how, but I want to make this work. I want freedom."

"Me too." His eyes glazed over. "Thanks for that."

The drive was short, thankfully. I feared I'd give birth to Avelina in the car.

We walked into the hospital, checked in, and waited in the waiting room while soap operas annoyed me from the television mounted on the wall in the corner of the room. Pretty faces and half-naked bodies made me want to spit, or turn off the TV, but I didn't want Jessie to sense my insecurity. The fact that they even let women in underwear prance around on daytime television baffled me. I would not want my kids seeing that.

A nurse, finally, called my name. Jessie's eyes were closed, his head down as though in prayer. I poked his shoulder. He looked up, glanced around the room then back to my eyes.

"You coming with me or what?" I said to him and looked back at the nurse.

Jessie stood and we followed the tall, manly female nurse through double doors, down a hallway, and into a room big enough to hold the examination table, a monitor, a sink, and perhaps a total of three people.

"This is where I give birth?" I looked at the nurse and back to the room. "This doesn't look like the delivery rooms I saw."

A contraction, this time deeper inside of me, felt like it ripped apart my insides as it tugged at my muscles. I bent over and leaned on the table to breathe through it.

"Did you get a tour?" the nurse asked, her voice as manly as her looks.

"No."

She rolled her eyes and walked out of the room without saying another word. Guess it wasn't her best day of the week. Jessie opened the door after the nurse closed it and peeked around the corner.

"Want me to go get someone?" he said.

"I'm sure a doctor will be here soon."

Three contractions later, Lisa walked in the room. I was so happy to see her I nearly jumped into her arms, but a contraction hit me as she smiled and greeted us, so I breathed through it then looked back to her.

"Getting stronger contractions now, aren't we?" She put on rubber gloves and snapped them at her wrists.

I nodded.

"Go ahead and lay back on this table here. I'm going to check your cervix then we'll put these monitors on to keep an eye on the baby's heartbeat and your contractions."

I leaned back and let her do her thing.

"You are seven centimeters. Getting into the nitty gritty now. This transitional phase is going to be tough, but you'll make it if you've gotten this far."

I smiled. She made me feel like natural childbirth was possible. Painful, but possible.

She wrapped two straps around my stomach, but seemed to have trouble with the second one.

"Your baby always has been a tough one to get a good heartbeat from. Always moving around." She moved the strap over so the monitor was a little higher on my stomach.

Jessie looked at me.

I looked away and watched Lisa's lips, waiting for them to smile, but they pursed more and more as time went on. She moved the strap up, down, left, right, but never felt satisfied enough to leave it.

The white room closed in on me, making the walls feel black.

"I think this strap might be broken." She tried to smile, but I heard seriousness in her tone. Unusual for her. And I didn't like it. "I'm going to get a new one and try that."

"What's wrong?" Jessie asked.

I shrugged. "She's always had trouble getting the heartbeat from Avelina. Either she moves too much or she's just in a weird position. I'm sure it'll be fine."

I tried to believe my own words, but underneath them my heart raced so loud and fast that it hurt me and distracted me from the contractions that should've pained me worse.

Jessie asked me a bunch of questions, but I didn't listen.

Lisa came back in the room with a new strap and an ultrasound monitor.

"I'm going to get a quick ultrasound." Lisa wheeled the machine over to me. "Just want to see where that kid is so I can get this strap on right."

Jessie paced the room and finally settled, arms crossed, in a chair across from the ultrasound screen.

Lisa gelled my stomach and rolled the cold device over it. She rolled and rolled and rolled, then looked at me and said. "I think your baby might be in a really funky position. I'm going to get another nurse in here to see if I'm just going nuts."

She left the room and Jessie's scrunched brow taunted me.

Everything's okay, I thought. Everything's fine.

Chapter 68 *Taylor*

oy, was Lisa right. The contractions got way worse within a few hours of being in my delivery room. I'll tell you what annoyed me the most. I had Group B Strep, so they attached a wheeling antibiotic bag to my arm via a tube and needle, and they never, ever let me get unhooked from the thing.

When a super painful contraction lurched me forward I imagined the needle ripping from my arm. And don't even get me started on all the monitors they hooked up to me. I felt like a prisoner and ached for an epidural so I could lay still.

But I had to do this. I had to do something on my own with no help. Something good, something meaningful.

I rocked back and forth on a large ball as the contractions split apart my insides. The only thing that helped was when I focused on the room. I took in every detail from the flower patterns in the brown curtains, to the way the streetlight lit the room, which I asked to have dimly lit. And I made sure to soak in everything I could so I could tell Layla everything. I wanted her to feel special, like she mattered.

Unlike me.

Lisa came back in to check on me. "You're almost there."

She pressed her hand into my lower back. The pain hurt so much I didn't mind her hands on me. And it seemed to help.

I wanted her to stay the entire time and make the nurses go away. Only one of the nurses was nice, but her shift ended. The other ones didn't seem to care about me or anything about birth. They just checked the monitors and went on their merry way. I wanted to scream at them and beg Lisa to stay every time she left the room, but she had to keep checking on another patient.

A strong, splitting contraction gashed my mental complaints. I leaned forward onto the bed and pulled the sheets into my fists.

"I can't do this anymore." Before I could finish my words another contraction began its upward climb to the peak of torment. I squeezed the sheets again and held my breath.

"Relax and breathe." Lisa came in the room and knelt beside me. "You're almost there. You can do it."

I inhaled and exhaled, doing my best to relax amidst the worse pain of my life. But another one started, grabbed my insides, and squeezed as tight as possible.

I looked up at the ceiling. "Daddy." My voice, high and loud, rose beyond the ceiling.

A tear soaked into the sheet as another contraction peaked.

"Pressure," I said. "Lots of pressure down there."

"I think it's time to push." Lisa stood and helped me onto the bed. Sit back, and pull your legs up so your knees are as high as you can get them. I want to see where the head is and then we'll start pushing."

"I can't," I cried.

"Yes, you can." She looked at the ceiling. "Your Daddy is up there." She pointed. "And He's here for you. Lean on Him for strength. He'll get you through."

I sat back, pictured Daddy's face just before he died, and then reached under my thighs and pulled my knees toward me as much as I could.

"The head is right here, Taylor. You're going to see your baby soon."

Chapter 69 *Ally*

When the other nurse confirmed what I didn't want to know, Lisa looked at me with tears in her eyes and said, "I'm sorry."

"What are you sorry for?" I asked as another contraction messed with my brain. "I'm in labor. My baby is coming. What are you sorry for?"

"Allyson, we can't find a heartbeat."

"There's a mistake." I ripped one of the straps from my stomach. "I'm having contractions. I'm in labor. This doesn't make sense."

"Allyson, I'm sorry." Lisa's gentle tone scratched my wound. "We can see on the ultrasound that your baby's heart is not beating. This is the worst thing I could ever tell you, but the fetal heart rate is a flat line."

My gaze fell on Jessie, curled up in the chair across the room with his face covered.

"Get me a c-section," I yelled. "Get her out so you can save her."

Lisa looked at Jessie and back to me. "It's too late. I'm so sorry. I'm going to give you a few minutes. I have another baby to deliver. I'll have another midwife take care of you and explain your options until I'm finished. But don't worry, I'll check on you every chance I get."

OPTIONS. SHE SAID WE'D TALK ABOUT THE OPTIONS. BUT TO me there were no options. My baby died. The only baby we managed to keep alive until full-term, and she died. She died at the very last minute. I know this because I felt her kicking just before we came to the hospital. If only I would've come sooner, I kept telling myself.

When the new midwife, Pamela, wheeled me into the delivery room on the second floor the sun had almost parted for the day, leaving the fluorescent lights of the hospital to do their job. Jessie walked beside me and I felt like the chair wheeled over my heart every time Pamela took a step. Every contraction reminded me of the dead life inside of me. The life whose name meant "lively and pleasant."

I feared giving birth to her. I wanted a c-section so they could take her away without me seeing her little fingers and toes. There, in our bag hung on Jessie's shoulder, a pile of baby clothes and diapers sat tucked away, waiting to be filled with life. And the blanket at home, the one with her name on it. And her crib. And her lavender room.

"The best thing for you is to deliver your baby vaginally," Pamela said, trying to coat her words with as much sympathy as possible. "However, you can have an epidural if you want. I know that wasn't your original plan, but it might ease the pain."

Nothing could ease the black cloud settling on my soul. But I didn't question the epidural. Sure, I didn't like the idea of that thing sticking in my spine before, but things changed. This labor would be the most difficult thing in the world for me and I needed drugs to get me through it.

Sorry, but I did.

Pamela settled us in the room, then left to notify an anesthesiologist. When he came in to do his thing, I already felt numb. The contractions still hurt—yes, no denying that—but the pain hid behind my agony. And agony didn't do the feeling justice.

It felt as though someone twisted my heart and flung it outside of my body. I watched it float away down the flat line of my baby's heartbeat, and nothing mattered anymore. My Avelina. My dear, Avelina. Please, wake up when I push you out, I told her in the silence of my brain as my heart drifted even further away.

Jessie, there in the corner of the bright delivery room, sulked in fetal position. I wanted to grab his legs and force him into another position, but I couldn't move.

Why would you do this to me, God? Why me? Why Avelina?

I closed my eyes and hummed songs in my head, trying not to focus on the pressure. Soon, I'd be forced to push my dead child out of my body. Dead. The word still made no sense to me. Somehow I hoped they were wrong, that my Avelina would come out screaming and breathing in the hospital air.

Pamela came back in the room after what seemed like hours of silence between Jess, the occasional nurse, and me. No one seemed to care about me anymore. There were no monitors wrapped around my waist. No Group B Strep antibiotics draining into my body, even though I had GBS. I wanted to tell them to hook it up just in case she came out alive, but my mouth couldn't find words.

"I want to check and see where the head is." Pamela sat at the edge of the bed and checked. "The head is right here. Are you ready to push?"

Tears. They stung underneath the pain in my eyes. But they wouldn't come. I shook my head. "I can't do this. Where's Lisa? I want Lisa here."

Jessie walked over to the edge of the bed and held my hand. His eyes said, "I'm here," while his crinkled brow said, "I'm hurting, too."

"I can't do this, Jess."

"Yes, you can, sweetheart. I'm with you."

I squeezed Jessie's hand into my chest.

The quiet in the room seeped into my heart and resided there, stirring thoughts and pictures I didn't want to imagine—pictures of my beautiful baby girl, my first baby, without a breath on her lips or a blink of her eye. This should've been a time of excitement; instead the stillness was as still as Avelina. My hollow chest ached.

"Pull your legs up to your chest." Pamela's faint voice made its way through my messy thoughts.

I didn't feel anyone pull my legs up, but when I looked down I saw Jessie's hands and a nurse's hands wrapped around each of my legs, holding them up so I could push.

I shook my head and flopped my head back on the pillow.

"You can do this," Pamela said to my knees.

Tears burned their way to my cheeks. "It wasn't supposed to happen like this."

Jessie took one hand from my leg and rubbed my cheek. "I'm sorry."

His words, those two words, lingered in my ears. I grabbed his hand and pulled it to my lips. My heart, beating fast, so much faster than Avelina's flat line, made me realize how much I needed my Jessie. Finally, I let the sobs shake my chest and lips.

Through my glazed-over eyes I looked at my husband's wet, creased face.

"I'm sorry, Jess. I'm sorry for not being able to keep the baby alive. I'm sorry for pushing you away. I'm sorry for thinking only of my needs and not seeing your problem." My words flew out without acknowledging anyone in the room but my husband. And my tears poured. "I'm sorry."

Jessie broke down beside my bed and nuzzled his head into my swollen belly, my Avelina. When he peered up at me with tears covering his face, I wiped his face, then my own, and looked at Pamela. She nodded. And I nodded.

It was time.

Chapter 70 *Taylor*

After an hour of pushing, Layla's head pressed through. It stung. Bad. Worse than losing my virginity. Way worse. But more than anything, the pressure is what made me feel like I would die before I got her out.

Lisa pulled my hand down to feel Layla's head. Her hair, so much of it, gave me the strength to keep going.

"Push again." Lisa smiled. "Good. Nice and hard. Breathe."

With all my might, I pushed and squealed at the pain. My shaky hands made their way down to Layla's head. For some reason it made me feel better to keep my hands down there.

"That's it," Lisa said. "I've got one shoulder. One more push and your baby will be here."

The world stopped. The room spun. The idea of Layla being in my arms scared me as much as I wanted to see her. I feared failing her. I feared her longing for a daddy, just like me. And I wanted to keep her safe, inside of me, where she'd never feel pain.

"One more push," Lisa said. "Take a breath. You can do it."

The pressure hurt, like a ton of bricks crushing my body from the inside out. But Layla needed me to push. I inhaled. Exhaled.

Lisa's eyes met mine. "Almost there. One more push."

I pressed my eyes shut and pushed. The other shoulder came out and Layla's little body squirmed out of me. Lisa smiled, the nurse smiled. When I saw my baby, all blue with her eyes rolling around, I freaked out and reached for her. "Is she okay?"

Lisa placed Layla on my chest. "She's fine. Her color will change in a few minutes. She's perfect."

Her little cheek pressed into my chest. Her dimpled hands curled into fists. I slipped my index finger into her left hand and pulled it to my lips. Her dark eyes peered up at me. She looked like Daddy and me.

I held her as long as I could, then one of the nurses took her to the table beside me to clean her up and dress her. Meanwhile, I never took my eyes off of her. Lisa helped me deliver the placenta, which hurt more than I thought it would. Maybe it's just me, but it burned and I didn't like the feeling of that thing oozing out of me.

Layla never cried. When the nurse finally handed her back to me, her pink color settled in. She looked perfect.

"Do you want to try to nurse her?' Lisa asked.

"Nurse her?"

"Breastfeed." She smiled.

"Oh, um, I don't know about that. I don't think I know how." Not to mention the implants, they probably ruined my chance of that.

"Doesn't hurt to try."

I nodded. "How do?"

Lisa's hand gently held the back of Layla's head while she touched my breast. All the times people touched me in the past few months didn't make me feel any more comfortable with the situation, but thankfully it went by fast. She pressed Layla's mouth onto my flesh. Like a pro, Layla suckled.

Nothing in the world could compare to the feeling I experienced in that moment. Love. Pure love.

"Okay," Lisa said. "Looks like you are both quick learners. I've never seen a mom and baby catch on so fast." She turned to the nurse and whispered something about a stillbirth, then gave me a weak smile. "I need to go deliver another baby. I'll be back to check on you soon."

Chapter 71 *Ally*

The epidural helped, I'm sure. I don't know how I would've been able to push my Avelina out without that. Lisa came back, finally. But with Jessie by my side, with his hand in mine, I didn't need her anymore.

It only took five pushes until we saw her face at 4am on that bittersweet April day. Lisa pulled Avelina out and I immediately saw the reason behind her death. The chord was wrapped around my little angel's neck twice and under her arms once.

"Oh, Avelina." Tears rained and rained and rained.

Jessie fell into my chest and wept. I'd never seen him weep like that before, even through our hard times. Lisa placed Avelina on my chest. I pulled her into my neck and wet her head with my tears. Jessie caressed her bruised face with his trembling fingers. I did, too.

Never in my life had I felt closer to my husband than I did when Avelina brought us together, right then.

When my eyes finally dried up, Lisa took Avelina from me to clean her up. Then Jessie and I dressed her in one of our outfits for her. Even though she wasn't alive, I still dressed her with delicacy. She looked so cute—her face like a porcelain doll, minus the bruises and scrapes on her because of the chord. I tried not to focus on those marks though. They made me wonder about the pain she went through as the chord strangled her in my womb. And I didn't want to think about that right now, I wanted to savor every moment of her before they took her away.

I cuddled her in my arms, held her lifeless, cold hands, and kissed her neatly closed eyes. "I love you, sweet girl." Tears came again. "I never want to forget your face."

Jessie never asked to hold her, but I could tell he wanted to. I held her up and nodded for him to take her, but honestly, I didn't want to give her up. As I watched his long fingers smooth over Avelina's eyes, nose, and lips, I fell in love with Jessie all over again. And for the first time in a long time, I looked up, through the ceiling over my heart, and said to God in the quiet of my soul, "I know I can't fix everything. I'm not you."

When Jessie handed Avelina back to me, I talked to her closed eyelids, cuddled her, and longed to see her smile. I imagined what she would've been like. I pictured her wobbly first step and her first tooth poking through. And when it was time to finally let her go, the sun was up again and my heart was setting on the other side of my world.

But I let her go.

And instead of letting my heart leave with her, I gave my heart to my husband. In the quiet of the room, alone together for the first time in twenty-three excruciating hours, I placed my hand on Jessie's chin and pulled his face to mine. On the bed, with the sound of birds singing in the background, I kissed my husband, my sweet, sweet husband, and silently thanked God for him.

Chapter 72 *Taylor*

I stayed in the hospital for one day after I gave birth. And Layla never, ever left my side. Not even for any of her tests. She even slept on my chest, all cuddled with me in bed. One of the nighttime nurses came in to check on something, looked at us and said, "You're not supposed to do that."

I swallowed.

"But I won't tell anyone." She smiled and walked away.

After Lisa came in for the final checkup and talked over some things with me, she told me Layla and I could finally leave.

I dreaded that moment.

My knees were so weak I could barely stand, so I didn't. I sat on the bed and distracted myself by changing Layla's diaper, which I just changed a few minutes prior. I must say, I became quite the expert for never doing it before in my life. Mothering was the only grownup thing that came sort of natural to me.

"Is someone here to pick you up?" Lisa said.

"Yes." I lied. "My mother will be here in a few minutes."

"Okay." She believed me. "I'll have one of the nurses wheel you out to wait for her."

My stomach twisted, almost like a contraction. Guess it's a one of those uterus-going-back-down things, I thought.

"Everything okay? Bleeding normal?" she asked.

I nodded.

"Can I hold Layla before you go?"

I handed her over and feared what the next few minutes would bring.

ONE OF THE NURSES WHEELED ME OUTSIDE OF THE hospital, where I saw another lady sitting in a wheelchair waiting to be picked up. My hands were full with Layla in my lap, but the other woman didn't have a car seat or a baby anywhere around her. I wondered why she was in the labor and delivery part of the hospital.

She looked over and I noticed her eyes. The same woman from the prenatal check up. The one who eyed me up and down and made me feel like a piece of trash. She looked even prettier. I wished I could look like that, like a woman, instead of a little girl. Again, she eyed me up and down, but this time I saw no judgment.

"My mom will be here soon," I said to the nurse behind me.

She nodded and walked away, which is what I wanted even though I thought she'd stay. I couldn't believe she wheeled me out without calling my "ride." But I needed her to not care about me so I could figure out what to do next.

I looked around and saw no one. No one except the empty-handed woman who kept staring at me.

Cradling Layla in my arms, I looked up to the sky.

I know I've pleaded with you a thousand times before, but God—or something—if you are up there, I need you now. Please don't drive by me again.

Chapter 73 *Ally*

fter one long day, Jessie and I were ready to leave the hospital. We could have left earlier, but I asked to stay an extra day. I don't know why. Maybe I didn't want to forget the smell of the hospital or the taste of the stale air. Maybe I didn't want to lose my only memories of my first child, my daughter.

Jessie and I, hands locked, signed papers. A birth certificate and death certificate in the same minute. Odd, to say the least. And heartbreaking to fill out the death certificate. The final stamp on the reality of my dead baby. And I didn't want the stamp to exist, or the reality beneath the stamp.

But it did. And I stamped it. Then we called a funeral home and made arrangements and notified our parents.

The hospital staff gave us a little box with a footprint charm, a white rose, and pamphlets on what to do next and how to get through the grieving process. So tired of processes and rules and do-this-or-that's, I threw those pamphlets away and kept the ones about making funeral arrangements. I had no idea how to go about that.

We said our goodbyes to the staff, who seemed as cold as Avelina when I held her in my arms. Not Lisa though. She didn't smile, but she beamed with hope. I think she saw the reconnection between Jess and me.

After a ten-minute goodbye, Lisa gave me her personal cell phone number. Then she wheeled me outside. As Jessie walked away to get the car, Lisa gave me a hug, kissed my cheek and said, "You have a beautiful heart. Look ahead, not behind. And always remember her."

I thought of Jess. And pictured Avelina's limp fingers. I could still feel her feet in my ribs. What I would have done to hold her one more time. Her cheek, I could still feel it against my hand. And her eyes. I wished I could've seen them open. Just once.

"Don't look back." Lisa smiled and walked away. "Oh." She turned around. "Call me anytime."

She walked through the doors and disappeared behind darkened glass. Out of the corner of my eye I saw another woman in a wheelchair, caressing her baby girl's face. My eyes filled up with tears again. I couldn't wait for Jessie to get back with the car so I could get away from the happy mom and baby.

I looked closer.

I longed to hold my baby again, to see her toes wiggle to life. The young mom looked up. I recognized her gorgeous eyes. Blondie, the porn star. Envy in all shapes and sizes coursed my mind and heart. Especially the fact that she looked so skinny already.

Looking at my pouch of a belly, I held back tears. I knew I'd think of my loss every time I changed a pad or felt my uterus contract as it went back down to its normal size. How difficult it would be to go through the healing process without a baby to hold.

Jessie parked the car in front of me. Thankfully.

He spotted Blondie and sighed, then looked at me. I looked down and tried not to cry. Last person I wanted to see me cry was Blondie.

Jessie helped me out of the chair and into the car. When he walked away, I caught one last look at Blondie. She looked around, back to her baby, and back into the parking lot. Her eyes never stopped moving. Neither did her head. It moved up and down, back and forth, looking for something.

Jessie reached for my hand. "You okay?"

I turned to him, then looked over my shoulder at the pink car seat in the back. "Our baby should be in that seat."

Jessie choked up. I squeezed his hand.

You have a beautiful heart. Look ahead, not behind.

I looked at Blondie again.

And we know that in all things God works for the good of those who love him, who have been called according to his purpose.

Left page, halfway down, highlighted orange with a star next to it. I looked out the window and ignored the verse.

"Huh?" Jessie said.

"Did I say something?"

"I couldn't tell." Jessie accelerated.

Blondie and her baby shrunk in the side mirror of our car. The verse sunk into my brain again. This time I let it go to my heart and there His purpose revealed a hope I hadn't seen before. His purpose is greater than mine. But His purpose didn't feel good. And I didn't want His purpose. I wanted Avelina in her car seat. Where she belonged.

Chapter 74 *Taylor*

The woman got into her car to leave. I caught her staring at me through the window, then her mirror. She must've really hated me for the comments Gianna made.

I thought of Gianna, Naomi, Andy, Mom—who would help me?

The woman and her husband drove away. I couldn't help but notice the Jesus fish on the back of their car. Obviously God wanted to drive by again, which proved to me one thing: He didn't exist. At least not in my life.

The car stopped and backed up.

My eyes darted back and forth.

The woman got out and walked over to me. I pretended not to notice and held Layla tighter, thinking the crazy lady would steal my baby. But she didn't. She stood there for a second with tears in her eyes.

"Are you okay?" she said.

"Yes, I'm fine."

She turned around, but didn't walk away. A few awkward seconds passed until she turned back around.

"Do you have somewhere to stay?" she asked.

"Yes. Why?"

"You seem lost, like someone forgot to pick you up."

"Nope. I'm fine."

"You sure?" Another tear ran down her face.

Butterflies danced in my stomach. Layla's eyes soaked in the bright April day. Her first day outside. I looked up at the sky, then to the woman in front of me. With her hand over her mouth, she stared at Layla.

"Do you need a ride?" she asked, still watching Layla.

"No." I glanced at the Jesus fish, then back to the woman. "I'm waiting for my mom."

Chapter 75 *Ally*

It was the hardest thing I ever did—more difficult than forgiving Jessie, more difficult than getting my bachelors degree, more difficult than giving birth to my strangled Avelina. When I stood there convincing a porn star to get into my car and put her baby in the seat meant for my daughter, my knees where shaking, but my heart came back. It came back because I knew that without my empty seat, I wouldn't have been able to help this girl.

But I did it.

And she refused. She looked me right in the eyes and said, "No, I'm waiting for my mom," but I knew she lied. And I couldn't handle a lie. So, I left the girl and her beautiful baby girl. Jessie welcomed me back into the car. His eyebrows pointed toward his nose. But I didn't have the energy to explain.

"Let's go. I'm so tired."

We drove off. Jessie held my hand. And the pink car seat in the back sat alone. Empty. I wanted to throw it out of the car. God, this isn't fair, I screamed inside.

"Are you okay?" Jessie said.

I shook my head and tasted my tears.

Jessie parked. "It's the worst pain I've ever experienced."

I couldn't speak. Couldn't look at him. I wanted to turn around and find Avelina's body. Her skin, her hair—I needed to touch her one more time.

The bible verse rang in my heart again, like an unsolicited salesperson. I didn't want to hear it. Not now.

"How will I ever get over this?" I said.

"You won't. You don't need to." He brushed my tear-soaked hair behind my ear. "You'll always miss her. We just need to live for her."

Blondie's face flashed in my mind. Her baby, so alive, squeezed my heart. I left them. Just like that.

I dried my face. "Maybe we should give that girl a ride."

"Who is she?"

"A porn star."

Jessie backed away. He looked out the window, then back to me. "A porn star?" The word didn't hurt me, like it did before. Porn. Something about it seemed different. I just didn't know what.

"Yes," I said. "I saw her with a friend. They were at a prenatal appointment. Her friend told her to get an abortion. Mentioned something about the porn stuff. I can't remember."

He shook his head. If he shook enough times, maybe he'd realize he wasn't dreaming. Maybe I would, too. Peering between us, Jessie saw the car seat. I didn't want him to say anything. I should've kept my mouth shut.

"It's up to you. If you want to go back, we will."

"WE CAN AT LEAST GIVE YOU A RIDE TO YOUR MOM," I SAID, looking at the girl's baby, hoping the porn star would say no. She ignored me. I analyzed her features. She seemed so young. Like a kid playing house. "You can't just sit here. What if your mom doesn't come?"

"My mom doesn't talk to me."

"Well, who is picking you up?"

"Why should I tell you? Why do you care about me?"

"Honestly, I don't know." I swallowed. "This isn't easy for me."

"Why are you doing it?"

"I don't know. It's not about me right now. It's about you. And we need to get you and your baby"—my voice shook—"somewhere safe and warm."

"I am warm. And I have nowhere to go." The girl looked down. "I have no one but Layla."

"What's your name?"

She looked at my eyes. "Why?"

"I'm trying to help you. I just want to know your name."

"Jane."

"Well, Jane. It's nice to meet you. I'm Allyson, but you can call me Ally."

She nodded.

"Will you come with us? We can figure something out at our place. And I'll give you some money if you need it."

Jane kissed her little girl's forehead and stood. "I don't know about this."

She hesitated, but I assured her with my eyes. She inched toward me, then followed me toward the car. I helped her into the back seat and watched her buckle her baby into the car seat. Before she got to the second buckle, I walked around the car. My Avelina should've been in her seat. But I saw the purpose of everything. The good amidst the pain. Without my tragedy, Jane wouldn't have had anywhere to go. My empty seat gave her another chance.

It still hurt. Wounds and cuts and blisters always hurt, but somehow when you see the purpose behind it you can get through it, sort of like a healthy childbirth, although I didn't know from experience.

When we all settled into the car and drove off, I turned around to look at the girls in the backseat. Not at all what I imagined the day to look like. I should have been in the backseat mesmerized with my own daughter.

Jessie wiped his face and sniffed.

"This is my husband, Jessie," I said.

"Why do you have a car seat in here, but no baby?" Jane said.

"We lost our baby. She had the chord wrapped around her neck and died before she was born." I didn't look behind me. Didn't want to see her face as I told her the truth. "But without our pain, yours would've been worse."

"Oh, please don't say that, I don't want to be the cause of your pain."

"No, no," I said. "You're not."

Chapter 76 *Taylor*

Allyson told me that her baby died before birth. I almost jumped out of the car. The thought of her loss being a door for me to be helped freaked me out. I didn't want someone to suffer for my sake.

But she said, "No, no. You're not."

I got it. God didn't drive by. Ally came back. She practically begged me to come with her. And when she offered money, I couldn't say no. Not now. Not when I needed to care for Layla.

My body weakened. Dizziness spun my brain in circles. Kind of like the way it felt to crave Cola. I thought of Naomi to get my mind off the nausea. Then I thought of the moment I had at the beach. And it all made sense. The times I reached out to Daddy and asked for help. The dream I had about touching the feet at the end of a blazing white robe. It all clicked. After all the questioning, anger, hate, and horrible things I did—God chose to stop. He didn't give up on porn stars. He gave me Ally and Jessie. Maybe if I realized sooner their baby wouldn't have died.

Layla used my pinky finger as a pacifier. I watched Jessie and Ally. They held hands, wiped their eyes, sniffed. A cramp tightened my stomach again. A gush of liquid soaked my pants. I looked down. Nothing. I took my finger from Layla's mouth and felt my thighs. Then I saw blood.

Ally looked back at me. "Are you okay?" She unbuckled her seatbelt and turned toward me. "You look pale."

Layla's face and Ally's face blended together.

"Something's wrong," I tried to say, pointing toward the blood on the seat.

Then the world blurred. Ally's words muffled. Jessie turned around.

Another cramp. Another rush of something down my legs.

"I'm sorry . . . sorry . . . for messing up the car," I said.

"The seat is nothing," Ally said. "We're going back to the hospital. Hang in there." She leaned over the car seat. Her hand warmed mine. "I'm here."

I closed my eyes and let her words find a home in my heart.

Chapter 77 *Ally*

I looked at Jessie. "I think she's hemorrhaging."

"Will she be okay?"

"If we get her back in time."

The speedometer zoomed from fifty to eighty-five within a matter of seconds. Only a few seconds after that, red and blue lights flashed behind us. I looked at Jane. Her eyes rolled around her head. She didn't have much time. It looked like a gallon of blood spread onto the seat, but I prayed it looked worse than it was.

"God," I prayed aloud, holding Jessie's hand. "Help."

Jessie squeezed my hand and stopped at a red light. The cop got out of his car and jogged to our car, looked in the backseat, and knocked on Jessie's window with his knuckle. Jessie pressed a button. The window opened.

"Officer, I know we're speeding. We have an emergency." Jessie pointed over his shoulder. "She just had a baby. Losing a lot of blood."

"I know her," the cop said. His words sounded more like a stoic apology. "I'll get in front of you. You can follow me back."

He jogged back to his car and pulled in front of us. He stuck his hand out the window and motioned for us to follow him. We sped behind him through every red light on Route 24 until we reached Upper Chesapeake. Jane's eyelids lifted, she looked at Layla then back to me. "Please, take care of her if something happens."

"You'll be fine. We're here now."

"Promise me you'll take care of her."

I looked at Jessie, then Layla, then Taylor. "I'll try."

"Promise."

"I will make sure she's taken care of. I promise."

We hurried out of the car. Jessie ran inside to get a nurse or someone, anyone. I opened Jane's door, stroked her hair, and told her over and over again she'd be okay. She seemed like such a child to me. I couldn't believe how jealous and mean I had been toward her. "We'll all get through this and be home soon." But there was a lot of blood. Her blood.

Lisa ran out of the hospital, face flushed, glasses falling off her face. She yelled for a nurse to come quick. It felt like the lights on the cop car climbed inside of my head. Hectic, tense—her reaction worried me.

"You are Taylor's sister?" Lisa asked.

"Taylor?" I said and moved out of the way.

"Come on, girl." Lisa helped Jane into the wheelchair.

The nurse pushed her away. Fast.

Lisa looked at Layla. "Are you family?"

"No, but. . . ."

"I'm going to have to take Layla and keep her here. If something happens to Taylor." She paused. "If something happens to her she will be in the State's hands." She looked at the hospital doors Taylor passed through. "I don't know what relationship you two have or had, but she lost a lot of blood. This is serious."

Lisa took the car seat with Layla in it. I wanted to stop her, to tell her it was Avelina's car seat and I wanted it back. Jessie walked out of the hospital doors and over to us.

"Her name is Taylor?" I asked Lisa.

She nodded.

"Can I stay to make sure she's okay?"

She nodded again. "I told you."

"You told me?"

She smiled. "Let's go."

"I'll park the car," Jessie said.

I followed Lisa inside. No one seemed phased by the bloody girl who came back through those doors. No one except Lisa and me. Maybe women hemorrhaged a lot.

Lisa nodded to a row of chairs along the wall. "I'll be back soon. Hopefully, with good news." She walked away.

I sat down. The smell reminded me of Avelina. I wondered where they took her tiny body. Maybe she didn't leave the hospital yet. Jessie walked through the door, his hair windblown and in his face. What a ride, I thought.

"I just want to make sure she's okay," I said. "I miss Avelina."

He wrapped his arm around my shoulder. "Me too."

"She was a porn star."

Jessie hugged me again, pulled back to look at my face, then hugged me again. It all made sense, as much as I didn't want it to. I wanted to accept God's plan, but I still missed my baby. And I missed my marriage before porn.

We sat down and waited. An eternity passed. The sunlight disappeared and the moon revealed its face. After the stars stared at us for almost an hour, Lisa came back.

"She asked for you." She shook her head. "We don't normally want people in there, but she's got no one and I don't think she should be alone. Seems like she's had enough of that. And I can tell she's really scared."

Half unwilling, I nodded to Jessie and followed Lisa to a hospital room where people crowded around the bed.

I walked over to Jane, or Taylor, and held her hand. "I'm here."

She looked up, barely, and whispered something I couldn't understand through the oxygen mask. I leaned closer.

She tried again, "Whores . . . believe . . . sorry."

Lisa touched my shoulder. "She may not make a lot of sense right now. Just talk to her like she does."

But when I started to say something to her I noticed her chest stopped rising and falling. The flat line I saw on Avelina's monitor came back. I squeezed Taylor's hand and put my other hand over my mouth. Tears tripped over my nose and landed on my fingers. And when I looked down at the girl I once hated, I didn't see a porn star. I saw a girl who seemed to have spent most of her life in the shadows and then died holding a strangers hand.

I sniffed and fell to my knees. Someone shoved me out of the way. Voices yelled. People scrambled. I ended up in the hallway, next to Lisa. My tears fell, hard, and I couldn't stop shaking. Every few minutes, when I stopped crying enough to think, I prayed that God would bring her back to life. That the doctor would save her. Over and over I wanted to ask Him why. But I knew I didn't need to know why.

I stood, cupped my face with my hands, and closed my eyes. Someone tapped my shoulder. I turned. Lisa's face, wet like mine, reflected the lights from above us.

"You know what she said to me when I came in here?" Lisa took her glasses off and cleaned them on her shirt.

I shook my head. ·

"She said, 'God kept trying to get me. When they stopped to help I knew He finally used someone to make me understand. I'm sorry. I don't deserve God, but I want Him.'"

My hand fell to my mouth again. Lisa held out her arms. I fell into them, crying harder than I had in my life, even through all the pain I just went through. If I would had come to the hospital sooner, if Avelina would've made it, if we didn't back up the car—if, if, if. . . .

I cried harder, finally understanding the weakness of if and the power of faith. After Lisa confirmed Taylor's death, I walked back to Jessie. He held out his arms. I collapsed in them. And we cried together. A few minutes later, he led me out of the hospital. In the parking lot, next to our car, he pointed up.

"What?" I said, looking at the stars.

He pulled my chin to his. Our lips touched. And Orion watched as our salty lips kissed under another April sky.

As much as I wished I could've changed things—maybe have gotten induced early and made sure Avelina lived—the pain of her lifeless body entering this world brought me back to my love. Both of my loves. My God and my husband. The torture her death knifed into my heart held a purpose in the blade. The cut went deeper than the wounds Jessie gave me and showed me that no matter how hard I'd try, I'd never be able to fix things and make them the way I wanted them. I couldn't bring Avelina back to life. I couldn't change Jessie's mistakes.

But I could change my reactions.

And Avelina made me do just that—on April 10—when she entered the world without a breath of our air ever meeting her lungs.

Avelina and Taylor gave me something I lacked for so long. Hope. I'd seen enough death the last few days to know that life was valuable. And I was prepared to make the most of it. To take the pain, the bruises, and the broken dreams and let God mold them into something well worth the pain.

Something beautiful.

Epilogue *Ally*

Five years later, Jessie and I brought our little boy home for the first time. We had a quick, healthy, natural delivery. Mom greeted us as we walked through the door on an early February morning.

"Oh, look at him," she said, touching his cheek. "He's perfect."

I looked around. "Where's—"

"Sleeping," Mom said. "Took me forever to get her to go to sleep. So excited to see her baby brother." She touched the baby's hair. "Your father called. He said he'll come by tomorrow."

The steps creaked. Her blonde hair glistened in the morning rays. My eyes lit up, so did my heart. I walked to her as fast as I could. She ran down the steps and into my arms.

"Is Kyle here, Mommy?" She peeked through the railing. "He's here! He's here!"

Layla ran to her baby brother. I turned to Jessie. He sniffed and smiled.

"Oh, Daddy," Layla said, "He's so tiny, so cute. Can I hold him?"

"Sure can, princess. Hop on the couch and I'll bring him to you."

Seeing Layla hold her little brother gave me butterflies. I thought of Taylor. I promised her. It wasn't easy to adopt Layla. She ended up with foster parents. They wanted to adopt her, but then they got pregnant and decided they didn't want her anymore. Sad, but it happens. I didn't think we'd get her. But I'll never forget the day we saw her again for the first time since her mommy died. She climbed on to Jessie's lap, pointed to the trees on his shirt, and said, "Is a twees sheet." A few tiring months later, Layla came home.

Every day after, I tucked Layla into bed and told her I loved her. And every time, I saw Taylor's face and the brokenness behind her eyes as she took her last breath. I hoped Layla would meet her real mommy one day. Some nights I wondered how life changed so much. A porn star's baby became my little girl. My Layla. And every night, from under her pink sheets, she called me Mommy.

Whenever I wondered how or why, I remembered Dad's words.

Not everything in life has an instruction sheet. Sometimes God leads you where He wants you without telling you exactly how to get there.

And I guess, more than anything, Layla's face, every day, reminded me that I was exactly where God wanted me to be. Her smile gave me hope. And every time I got up in the middle of the night to comfort her, I knew I didn't need an instruction sheet. Faith meant following without asking so many questions. Believing that purpose lived in every blade. When I held Layla, faith wrapped around my heart and married a hope that could never die.

No matter how deep the wound.

Acknowledgments

MARY DEMUTH
Without you, I'd still be swimming in adverbs and adjectives. Without you, I would consult a grammar book much more often. Without you, I probably wouldn't have as much bread on my table. (How did you hear about Tekeme Studios? Oh, you know, Mary DeMuth.) Mary, you are a blessing in my life. *Exposed* was a finalist in the Genesis last year because of your input. You knife my words with such grace. You encourage me when I want to give up. I'm so thankful for you. Not just because you're my human grammar book, but because you are a beautiful soul, a soul I am blessed to know. I love you, Mary! Thanks for being a walking example of Jesus Christ! You shine with Him. Love that about you!

JENNI BURKE
You are the best agent in the world. So personable, so professional, so loving, so real. You shine with the light of Jesus, even in your work relationships. If I ever decide to keep writing you better be around. I'll be knocking on your door!

GINA HOLMES
Ms. Picky Pants, thanks for giving *Exposed* a chance. Thanks for your honesty, your love, your beauty. Although we haven't met face-to-face as I'm writing this, I absolutely adore you. I am blessed to have your endorsement, you best-selling author you.

JIM RUBART
You. Jim. James. Jimbo. Expert of all things related to rooms. You are a

hugely encouraging person. I remember that first conversation we had with you. Your kind words have been in the back of my mind all throughout the writing of *Exposed*. And the little moments at ACFW last year where you pushed me forward with your love. You are awesome. Love ya. And I forgive you for leaving us in the dust when you visited for your book tour. Just watch out. You never know what's in the ROOM. :)

CHIP MACGREGOR
Thee hunter of all Jerry's. Thank you for answering my 3,848,108 emails over the last three years. I found your blog when I began this journey and it has shaped me so much. But I have some advice for you . . . stop pretending like you know it all and get a real job! :) Thanks for everything MacGreg.

SANDRA BISHOP
Thank you for giving me your time, even without signing me on as your author. Thank you for being real and signing authors who speak with authenticity. Thanks for believing in the heart of *Exposed*. You are so genuine and beautiful. I know every writer under your wing is truly blessed.

SHELLEY LUBBEN
Your presence in my life means more than you know. When I first discovered George's porn addiction I was crushed to pieces. I thought I'd never heal. Almost three years later, I sat down for lunch with a beautiful, intelligent, passionate ex-porn star. I know, I know, the labels. :) But it's true. And here we are. On this road together. I love you, Shelley. You have helped me with this book in ways no one else could have. But you are also a significant reminder in my life of God's amazing goodness and faithfulness. My reminder that there is so much beauty after rain.

SUSAN MEISSNER
Pegasooz, thank you for slicing my words with honesty and care. Thank you for threatening to slap my character if she didn't get in line. :) Your honesty has taught me so much. I am so thankful that you were able to look through *Exposed* and help shape my newbie-ness with love.

SUSIE SHELLENBERGER

Oh, Susie. What a blessing you are. From the good 'ole *Brio* days until *Susie Mag* galore. You have believed in my writing since way before the birth of *Exposed*. And you have believed in *Exposed* since day one. Thanks for allowing me to write for your lovely magazine, and thanks for being such a great friend and encouragement to me. I love you!

ALLEN ARNOLD

What a genuine soul. Thanks for taking the time to hear my heart last year and for talking with me about *Exposed*. Thanks for giving light to *More than Desire*. Without you, that blog wouldn't be here. So many women write to me about how much they love the blog and I want to forward you all of their letters, because without your help and guidance the idea may have never come to life. You are a blessing. A real blessing. Not only to me, but to so many lives affected by porn. Thanks for being so compassionate. You are such an awesome person to be the VP of TN. So sweet. Thanks for everything!

DONNY PAULING

I wrote all of the scenes about porn and thought of you often. I thought of how much you aren't like Andy. And I thought of how far you've come from producing porn to loving others through the love God has poured into you. I pray for you often. And I pray for all of the hearts that will be touched by your life and your story. You are a beautiful example of God's love and grace. Thank you for being you.

D'ANN MATEER

I just love you. I so enjoyed our time at ACFW. And I'm so thankful for your encouraging emails, not only about writing, but life and kids and crazy stuff. You are a great friend. I wouldn't trust many people with my heart, but you are one of them. You are so careful and kind. I love that about you. So beautiful. I am so, so honored to be your friend. And I am ecstatic about your book deals! I can't wait to hold those puppies in my hands. Thanks for everything, D'Ann. You have blessed our family more than you'll ever know.

VICKY BOHLMAN
You shaped my writing before I even took writing seriously. You adored my journal entries and gave me hope. You bought my book before any of my friends or family. You are family to me. Thank you for believing in me and *Exposed*. Thank you for being another mom in my life. Your wisdom, prayers, and love are so needed in my life. Thank you. I love you!

VIOLA K. HOY
You have been gone from this world for five years now, but I think of you every day. I never forget how much you believed in everything I did from coloring pictures to singing songs on your answering machine. You wrote me letters and sent me stamps to write you back, but I selfishly used them for my friends. I selfishly did a lot of things during those years, but you selflessly loved me the entire time. You never stopped loving me. You never stopped believing in me. And you never once had to mention the name Jesus to me—you lived Him in my life. Thank you, Grandma Hoy . . . I miss you and love you more every day.

BARBARA RAYMOND
You always told me I'd write a book one day. It hasn't been easy, but with the help of all the people in this section I have been able to accomplish it. Thank you for believing in me and calling me a "writer" long before I ever called myself by that label. And thanks for encouraging me to keep writing since my early years! I love you!

MY HUSBAND
Lover of my heart, you complete me. There isn't a day that passes where I don't thank God for you. What we went through wasn't pretty, but where we are now is more beautiful than I ever thought our marriage could be. Waking up to you every morning is a blessing. Thank you for fighting for me. I am yours forever. And thank you for allowing me to "expose" our hearts by writing this book. You have shaped this book in so many ways, from the story to the name to the execution. Thank you. You . . . I love you Geebs.

MY JESUS

Jesus, there are no words, none, that give you the honor and credit you deserve. This book . . . it is only here because of you. Thank you for healing my marriage, for healing my heart, and for using me to bring hope to other women suffering through the same fire of lust and betrayal. You have taken brokenness and used it for good. You've shown me how to live, how to love, and how to accept the fact that I will so often fail at both. Your grace, your purpose, your dying heart on the cross—all of it lives on forever. You live on forever. My heart is yours. I love you. Everything about you. Truly, I am nothing with you. My words are empty without you. Thank you, Jesus . . . for everything.

And I can't forget to thank the following people for their beautiful encouragement in my writing life and the life of *Exposed*: Kristyn Magness, Julie Briggs, Michelle Sutton, Don Pape, Chris Ferebee, Jonathan Clements, Christina Berry, Jenna Blanford, Heather Oroyan, Bill Hendrix, Sherrie Ashcraft, Julia Boyd, Ronie Kendig, Katie Ganshert, David Graves, Greg and Stacey Oliver, Luke Gilkerson, Kennisha Hill, Elaine Olsen, Dawn Opitz, Stephanie Taylor, Melanie Doner, and Heidi Bylsma. If I forgot someone . . . so, so sorry! I blame my mommy brain.

Ally's Blog

Dear readers,

My story doesn't end on the last page of this book. I've decided to keep an online journal to "expose" my heart and the heart of our marriage. If you want to read more about our lives, our restoration process, Jessie's recovery, the healing of my heart and insecurities, and our marriage, please email your proof of purchase to ally@morethandesire.com and we'll send you the username, password, and blog address.

Thank you so much for reading my story!
Allyson Graham

{ *More than Desire*
hope for women in the shadows of pornography

....

I've never met a woman who hasn't been burned by the desire to be good enough. And I've met many, many women who struggle to believe they are beautiful because their husbands or boyfriends nursed a pornography addiction. After I discovered my husband's pornography addiction, I blogged about the healing process. Since then I've been overwhelmed by emails from women who struggle to find their worth after porn knocks on the door of their marriages.

According to Internet Filter Review, 40 million US Adults regularly view porn online. The porn industry is a billion dollar industry. It's everywhere. And it's affecting marriages across the globe. I thought I would've found help in the midst of my healing, but most resources said the same things over and over. "Don't look to men for validation; look to God." I knew that, but I wanted something deeper. I'm hoping this blog can be the something deeper for you that I needed when I went through this myself.

Know that you are loved. And you are not alone. It may feel like you are, but there are so many women out there who find this very blog (just like you) because they are looking for hope in the shadows porn brings to their hearts.

www.morethandesire.com

....

CovenantEyes®
THE STANDARD OF INTERNET INTEGRITY

What Is Covenant Eyes?

The Covenant Eyes Accountability program was developed to change people's lives. They have a strong desire to make available to everyone the ability to foster self-control, self-discipline, integrity, and personal accountability when using the Internet. Job 31:1 states, "I have made a covenant with my eyes." They provide a tool enabling Internet users to maintain that covenant, regardless of whether their temptation is pornography, gambling, or simply time spent on the Internet.

Covenant Eyes Hardship Program

Simply put, if a household family or individual needs our services but cannot afford them because of financial hardship, Covenant Eyes will provide our services free based on a family's ongoing financial need. This program is funded by Covenant Eyes and by gracious partners, such as *Exposed* author Ashley Weis. For more information, please send your contact information to hardship@covenanteyes.com.

When You Buy *Exposed* Receive A Discount To Sign Up For Covenant Eyes

Use the code EXPOSED when signing up for Covenant Eyes and they'll donate 15% of their monthly fee to the hardship program for the entire life of your membership with them. Also, use the EXPOSED code and get the first 30 days free to try it out.

WHEN YOU BUY *EXPOSED*, A PORTION OF THE
PROCEEDS SUPPORT THIS MINISTRY.

www.covenanteyes.com | Promo Code: exposed

What Is XXX Church?

XXX church is designed to bring awareness, openness, and accountability to every heart affected by pornography. XXX Church is an online community that tours the world speaking at colleges, churches, and community centers. The website exists to help those who feel swallowed by pornography—both consumers and those in the industry.

Craig Gross is the founder and leader of XXXchurch.com. Working alongside Craig is an amazing group of people. XXX hurch is a non-profit 501(c)(3) organization sitting under the umbrella of Fireproof Ministries with a board of directors overseeing the ministry. It is a provocative ministry that is memorable, as it combines the seedy and the sacred. XXX church is here to make you think, react, and to decide where you stand on the issues of porn. They do not exist to sling mud or throw rocks, but to shove the envelope, draw lines in the sand, and try to do some good. It's fresh, honest, fun, and designed for people just like you.

If you sent a bottle of vodka to every home in America every week for a year, you would no doubt have a whole wave of alcoholics. The Internet has created a wave of pornography addicts with its pervasive porn delivery-mechanism. XXX Church is there to help. Check out the site if you need help or want to reach out and help XXX Church help others.

WHEN YOU BUY *EXPOSED*, A PORTION OF THE
PROCEEDS SUPPORT THIS MINISTRY.

www.xxxchurch.com

What Is The Pink Cross Foundation?

Pink Cross Foundation is a faith-based IRS approved 501(c)(3) public charity dedicated to reaching out to adult industry workers offering emotional, financial and transitional support. We largely focus on reaching out to the adult film industry offering support to women and men. Pink Cross Foundation also reaches out to those struggling with pornography offering education and resources to recover.

Pink Cross Foundation, a humanitarian outreach and international movement will respond to needs of people who are victims of pornography. Their mission is to share the good news of Jesus Christ and to meet human needs in His name without discrimination. They also combat community deterioration due to pornography and prostitution through attempts to educate legislation in order to enforce health and safety laws within the pornography industry, to protect adult industry workers from sexually transmitted diseases and other job-related abuses, to ameliorate the secondary negative effects of pornography on the general public and to toughen laws to protect children from accessing online pornography. This ministry is motivated by the amazing love of God.

WHEN YOU BUY *EXPOSED*, A PORTION OF THE
PROCEEDS SUPPORT THIS MINISTRY.

www.thepinkcross.org